Eden Valley

Also by Tom Milton

The Silver Locket
Orphans of War
Invisible Wounds
Leave of Absence
Outside the Gate
The Golden Door
Sara's Laughter
A Shower of Roses
Infamy
All the Flowers
The Admiral's Daughter
No Way to Peace

Eden Valley

Tom Milton

NEPPERHAN PRESS, LLC
YONKERS, NY

Published by Nepperhan Press, LLC
P.O. Box 1448, Yonkers, NY 10702
nepperhan@optonline.net
nepperhan.com

PUBLISHER'S NOTE
This is a work of fiction. Names, characters, places, and incidents
are the product of the author's imagination or are used fictitiously,
and any resemblance to actual persons, living or dead, events, or
locales is entirely coincidental.

Printed in the United States of America

Library of Congress Control Number: 2017950543

ISBN 978-0-9899571-9-9

Cover art was licensed from iStock by Getty Images

For Marie

Once we start to think about the kind of world we are leaving to future generations, we look at things differently; we realize that the world is a gift which we have freely received and must share with others. Since the world has been given to us, we can no longer view reality in a purely utilitarian way, in which efficiency and productivity are entirely geared to our individual benefit. Intergenerational solidarity is not optional, but rather a question of justice, since the world we have received also belongs to those who will follow us.

Pope Francis, encyclical letter *Laudato Si'*

Eden Valley, 2017

ONE

EVEN BEFORE SHE saw the dog lying on its side in the middle of her driveway, Lena had a premonition, which must have come from the virulent hostility of her opponents at the town meeting. A man she had never seen before threatened her, saying that if she didn't change her position on the issue that divided their community, she would be sorry. That was less than an hour ago, and now in her driveway, illumined by the headlights of her car, it looked like he had carried out his threat.

She stopped the car and got out slowly and moved toward the body, knowing it was Grady, the English shepherd that she and Devon bought as a puppy from a kennel in another valley not long before Devon was diagnosed with lung cancer. With tears in her eyes, she knelt and touched the soft white fur on Grady's chest— he was still warm, so it must have happened after the meeting. There was a wound in his shoulder and another in the back of his head, suggesting that he was brought down and then executed. She imagined Grady, who served not only as a herd dog but also as a watch dog, confronting the car of his assassin as it came up the driveway, barking loudly, charging at the hand that held the revolver through an open window, and taking a hit. She leaned over and pressed her face against him, smelling the time before she lost Devon, and she started sobbing, feeling as if she had lost him again.

After a while she sat up, resolving to call the sheriff and report this crime. Since there was no cell phone service in the valley, she would have to go into her house and use her landline. She was about to move Grady out of the driveway in order to take her car up to the garage when she realized that it would be better not to disturb the crime scene, so she left the dog and the car where they were, and she walked up to her house. It was on a hillside that eventually led up to a ridge, where the land became suitable for corn and soybeans. In the valley there were only pastures and wooded areas, with strips of land suitable for hay.

She approached the house, and with a tremor in her hand she unlocked the front door. It led into the lower floor of the house, which in front had an office, a guestroom, and a bathroom, and in back a basement and a storeroom. Opening the door, she was greeted by Katiuska, who mewed as if she knew what had happened to Grady. She paused to give a stroke of comfort, and then after switching on a light she climbed the stairs with the cat attached to her right leg.

The upper floor had a living room, a dining area, a spacious kitchen, two bedrooms, and a bathroom. It was where she lived, except for periodic bouts of work in the office. With her husband gone and her two daughters living elsewhere, she had the whole house to herself, with only her two cats for company.

As she headed for the phone, which was in the kitchen, she was intercepted by Kazimierz, her male cat, who acted as if he had only one thing on his mind.

"Yah, yah," she told him. "I'll get your dinner. But I have to do something else first."

She picked up the phone and punched the cell phone number of the sheriff, which she knew by heart.

He answered after one ring, saying: "Lundquist here."

"Hi, Earl. It's Lena. I hate to bother you at this hour—"

"It's all right," Earl told her. "I'm always here for you. What's happening?"

"Well, I called to report a crime."

"What sort of crime?"

"A murder."

"What?"

"They killed my dog," she said before he got too excited.

He sighed in relief. "You mean Grady?"

"Yah. They executed him."

"Oh, jeez," he said as if she was his teenage daughter who had gotten herself into a jam. "I'll come right over."

She figured it would take him at least ten minutes to get there, which gave her time to feed the cats before she went out to meet him in the driveway. Watching the cats at their food bowls, she noticed that Kazimierz ate with his normal appetite but that Katiuska only picked at her food, from time to time making a low sound of mourning.

She left the cats and went back downstairs. Before going out, she switched on the spotlight above the door of the garage, which would help Earl see what had happened, and then she walked down to her car. At the sight of Grady lying on his side she started crying again, and her face was still wet with tears when Earl arrived.

He got out of his cruiser slowly. He was a big man, with enough of a belly to make him not intimidating, at least to Lena. He and Devon had been good friends, and after Devon died the sheriff assumed the role of her protector as if he was keeping a promise. He had been the sheriff for many years, and every time he approached the end of a term he talked about retiring, but since no one else seemed to want the job, he kept being re-elected.

He was a good-looking man, with a full head of white hair and lively blue eyes. On his nose was a scar where he had been slashed with a broken bottle by a crazy drunk at the Legion bar, where he had been called to deal with a brawl. For a reason that Lena couldn't explain, the scar actually made him more attractive.

"Thanks for coming," Lena told him.

"What the hell happened?"

"Look. You'll see." She led him around her car to the body.

"Oh, jeez," Earl said with sympathy. He liked animals, and whenever he came into her house he always stroked at least one of the cats. He squatted to examine the body. "It looks like they shot him in the shoulder and then they shot him in the back of the head."

"Yah, that's what it looks like," she agreed.

"I assume the dog had no enemies, so they didn't do it to hurt him. They did it to hurt you."

"That's what I think. They knew what this dog meant to me."

"If they did, then either they're members of this community, or they have good sources of information about you."

"I'd hate to think that members of this community would do such a thing."

He gazed at the dog in silence, and then after gently stroking its back he stood up, saying: "Whoever they are, they want you to change your position on the sand mining. And this is just a warning. If you don't change your position, they'll escalate."

"They won't if you catch them."

"I only got one deputy, and I can't have him stand guard here day and night."

"I hope you're not advising me to change my position."

"No, I'm not. I never advise people to do things I know they won't do. It's a waste of energy." He looked back at the dog and asked: "Do you have any idea who did this?"

"Well, there was a man at the town meeting who threatened me, saying that if I didn't change my position, I'd be sorry."

"Do you know him?"

"No. But if I ever saw him again, I'd recognize him."

"Maybe he's one of those speculators who bought land here because of the frac sand."

"Maybe. Can I help you find him?"

"I don't think so. But there's a way you *can* help me." He paused as if to make sure he had her full attention. "You can hire an armed guard to protect you."

"How would that help you?"

"It would make my job easier."

Rejecting the idea, she said: "I'm not going to hire an armed guard. For one thing, it's against my principles, and for another thing, I couldn't afford to pay for one."

"All right. Then there's another way you can help me. You can install cameras around your property so if the guys who did this come back to hurt you, I'll have a video of them."

"So if they kill me you'll have a video of them."

"They won't kill you," Earl said as if he understood their mode of operation. "But if you don't change your position, they'll do something else to hurt you."

"You mean they'll kill one of my goats?"

"Yah, maybe more than one of them."

If they killed her goats, which provided income that she needed since she couldn't live on what she received from Devon's social security, they could squeeze her economically. "How much would it cost me to install cameras?"

"I don't know, but it would cost less than an armed guard, and it wouldn't be against your principles, would it?"

"No, it wouldn't," she agreed.

"Then I'll call you and give you the name of a security guy who won't rip you off."

"Okay, thanks. Now, what do you want me to do with Grady?"

"With your permission, I'm going to take his body and give it to Vern, who can do a medical examination." Vern was the local veterinarian, whose main practice was treating large animals, dairy cows in particular, but he also treated Lena's goats. "He might find a bullet, which could be helpful."

"You can take the body, but I want it back. I want to give him a proper burial."

"Don't worry. You'll get it back."

She watched while Earl lifted the body and respectfully carried it to his cruiser, cradling it in one arm while he popped his trunk. He laid it gently on a bed of newspapers. When he closed the trunk she was reminded of the coffin closing on Devon.

Earl paused and asked: "Will you be all right?"

"Yah. I won't have my watch dog, but I'll still have my cats."

"With all the shit that's happening, I worry about you being alone here. Maybe you should get a tenant."

"I tried that. Remember?" She rented the guestroom to a girl who had dropped out of college. She soon learned that the girl had a serious drinking problem, which led her to commit acts of violence, and she needed Earl's assistance to evict her.

"Oh, yah. Well, girls aren't all like that, so maybe you could find a good one."

"Maybe I could. I'll think about it. Right now, I gotta go and check on my goats."

"Do you want me to stay while you do that?"

"No, I can handle it. I do it every night."

With a hint of tenderness in his eyes the sheriff expressed his concern for her, and then he opened the door of his cruiser, saying: "Take care."

She stood in place while he headed out the long driveway, waiting until his tail-lights turned onto the gravel road that served the valley before she went into the house. She got the lantern from a shelf in the hallway, and she went back out, having noted that the cats were nowhere in sight, probably sleeping off their dinner.

She followed the path that led from the house to the compound where the goats spent the night. There were actually two separate areas, a large one for the does and a small one for the bucks, with a proportionate shed in each area. Inside the gate was a doghouse that had provided shelter for Grady. It made her think about the difficult task of finding a replacement for him. The advantage of a puppy was that she could train it to do what she wanted, but it would have no experience. The advantage of a grown dog was that it would have experience, but it wouldn't necessarily do what she wanted.

She latched the gate behind her and headed for the shed where the does spent the night. There were fifty-six of them, ranging in age from three months to eleven years. About forty-eight of them produced milk, which she made into cheeses and sold through a distributor to specialty food stores and high-end restaurants in the Twin Cities. This operation had been going for more than ten years since the summer when they sold their house in Winona and moved to the valley. It had started with a pair of baby goats that she saw at the county fair and fell in love with. Devon was initially against going further, pointing out that there was an enormous difference between keeping a pair of goats as pets and maintaining a herd of them as a business, but she prevailed and he went along with her, eventually getting involved in the process of breeding and raising animals, producing milk, and making cheeses. He had loved every step of the process, but he especially loved making cheeses since it drew on his creative faculties.

The shed had a roof that sheltered the goats from rain and snow, and it had three walls, with an open front that could be closed at times of extreme winter weather. Now, at the beginning of summer, the front was open, and the goats were more loosely gathered together than they were in the winter, though they were still concentrated near the back wall of the shed as if they wanted to be as far removed as possible from danger. The mothers and kids were nestled together, and the lone does were scattered like islands. It wasn't practical to count them at this hour, but there wasn't any sign of foul play, so Lena left them and headed to the shed where the bucks spent the night. There were only three of them, including one that had just been weaned. Except at breeding time, the bucks were separated by fences from the does, and they reveled in their masculinity like the guys at the Legion bar. They slept apart, though the young one was only about two feet from the oldest one, whose name was Rex.

Her giving names to the goats had been an issue between her and Devon, who thought it was sentimental, but she prevailed, and she gave names to all of them except for the male kids that they culled after weaning. She gave the goats Roman names, for which Devon had a long list from his studies in the classics, and she gave the cats Polish names.

There seemed to be no problem with the bucks, so Lena left them and headed toward the house. Inside, she was greeted by Katiuska and Kazimierz, who had slept off their dinner and were looking forward to a full night of sleep with her. They never left the house since in the valley there were a lot of predators for which they were no match, including coyotes, foxes, and owls. In fact, the owls were the most dangerous since they could sweep down out of the sky without warning and their prey would never know what hit them.

It was now after the time when Lena normally went to bed, and she had to get up for the morning milking, so she made sure the doors were locked, she brushed her teeth, she changed into a cotton nightgown, and she set a glass of water next to the bed. It was a queen-size bed, which had served her and Devon for the thirty-five years of their marriage. After ten years of being without him she still slept on the side of the bed where she had always slept with him, though occasionally a leg drifted across the middle line. The cats now occupied his side of the bed, and she believed he wouldn't mind this.

She turned off the light next to her side, and she lay on her back, thinking.

The issue arose several years ago with the discovery in their region of a mineral that, if not as valuable as gold per ounce, was worth a lot to the oil fracking industry, which by then had achieved strategic importance in the global energy war. The mineral was a fine sand, called frac sand, that wasn't found in such abundance anywhere else in the nation. Since this type of sand was essential for fracking, its price soared, and a farmer who lived only at subsistence level could now sell his land for a million dollars to a company that would bring machinery to mine the sand. The process of mining stripped off the soil and dug out the sand and left the land ugly and useless, not to mention the wear on the roads, the dust in the air, and the pollutants in the water.

Lena hadn't known about frac-sand mining until a young man who had moved down from Minneapolis to establish an organic dairy farm in another valley alerted her to the problem. His name was Jordan, and he was committed to working and living in ways that didn't harm the planet. He spotted her at a town meeting and offered to drive her to a valley near the Mississippi where the sand had already been mined. And she was appalled by the destruction: what had once been a fertile, green valley was reduced to something worse than a desert because natural deserts at least had some life in them. But this valley was devoid of life, as dead as the surface of the moon.

Imagining what would happen to the whole region if the mining wasn't stopped, she joined Jordan in running for the county board, and they were both elected, which gave them two of the five seats on the board. Of the people who held the other seats, two were in favor of sand mining as a way to develop the local economy and create jobs, though they couldn't offer satisfactory explanations of how the county would benefit from the money paid to farmers who retired to Florida and spent it there, or how jobs would be created after the mining company departed, leaving the land unfit for farming. The fifth person on the board was a lawyer who so far believed that it was in his financial interest to stop the mining.

Last summer the mining company targeted the county since it was very rich in sand deposits, and it made offers for several farms that ranged from one to two million dollars. These were dairy farms in the valleys, where it was hard to make a living, unlike the farms on the ridges that were mainly owned by corporations, growing corn for ethanol and soybeans for export. She and Jordan convinced the lawyer on the board that it was in his long-term interest to stop the mining company, and by a vote of three to two they passed a law that temporarily prevented land from being sold for the purpose of mining. That made enemies of the farmers who had hoped to sell their land, get rich, and retire to Florida, but more importantly it made an enemy of the mining company, which was part of a global energy conglomerate that had a lot of money to spend for influencing politicians. It bought enough politicians at the state level to pass a law that seemed to override the law passed by the county board, and there were lawsuits on both sides, working their way through the court system. With the help of a lawyer from St. Paul, the county board proposed a law that was in compliance with the state law but would stop all mining in the county, pending review by higher courts. It was at the town meeting to discuss this law that the unknown man had threatened her, and his snarling face was the last thing she remembered before going to sleep.

The next morning Lena got up at five as usual, fed the cats, and made a mug of green tea, which provided some caffeine but didn't upset her stomach as coffee did. She took the mug to her office, turned on her computer, and waited for access to her browser. Since there was no cable service in the valley, she connected with the internet through her phone line, and it was slow.

When she finally got into her email, she found only the usual spam. There were no messages from her daughter in St. Paul, her daughter in Yonkers, her friend in New York, or her brother in Buenos Aires, and those were the only messages she liked to read since the others came from her bank, her insurance company, or her phone company. She then perused the *New York Times*, which she subscribed to online, but there was nothing much in the news.

She was in the kitchen, taking a last sip of tea when Heather arrived to help her with the milking. Heather had grown up in another valley where she still lived with her parents, though she was now thirty. At the age of eighteen she went to the university in Minneapolis but "fell in with the wrong people," as her mother put it, and became addicted to opioids. She spent some time in an institution and then came home, drug free. Between her milking shifts with Lena at six-thirty in the morning and six-thirty in the evening, she worked at a co-op that received organic produce from farmers and distributed it to the Twin Cities.

Heather was dressed for work in baggy faded jeans and a loose blue tee shirt with white letters on the front that said: "Arendal Eagles." Her lush brown hair was tied back in a ponytail to keep it out of the way for milking. When she let her hair down and wore tighter clothes, as she occasionally did in the evening, she was stunningly attractive, but her main goal in life now was to stay out of trouble.

As she approached the dining area, Heather said: "I'm sorry about Grady."

"How did you hear about it?" Lena asked, surprised that the news had already reached another valley.

"My mother was on the phone last night talking with Mrs. Lundquist when the sheriff came home and told her about it."

"Oh, yah." She remembered that Heather's mother and the sheriff's wife had been friends since high school.

"Do you have any idea who did it?"

10

"I have no idea. I can only guess who they are."

"Do you think the sheriff will catch them?"

"I hope so. He took the body so the vet can examine it and maybe find a bullet."

"Well, it's awful when people kill for money," Heather said with a tragic look in her sheer blue eyes.

"It is," she agreed, getting up from the table. "I'll be right with you. I gotta make a pit stop before we go to work."

A few minutes later they left the house and headed toward the compound. They walked in silence, but they didn't need words to communicate. They had done the milking together for almost three years, and each of them knew her role in the daily routine. Heather would go with Grady to the doe shed and bring the goats to the dairy barn, and Lena would go into the milking room and get the equipment ready. Today, without Grady, there was only Heather to bring the goats, but the goats knew the routine so there shouldn't be a problem.

The milking room had doors at each end, with ramps leading up to them. Inside, there were twelve stations where the does stood with their heads through openings that gave them access to buckets of alfalfa pellets, which they could munch while they were being milked. Since the lines had been left in good order yesterday evening, it took Lena only about ten minutes to get them ready, and then she opened the entrance door.

Heather was out there, and she allowed twelve does to walk up the ramp, with Juno first and eleven other does behind her. They each took a station in order, and after sanitizing them Lena hooked them up to the machine, which pumped their milk through clear plastic tubes into a stainless steel vat in the next room, where it would be pasteurized and made into cheese. The swollen udders of the does were gradually deflated as the milk flowed out of them and was finally reduced to a trickle.

When the first batch was done, Lena opened the exit door, and the goats filed out and down the ramp, making room for the next batch. It took about five minutes to milk twelve goats, but milking all of them took about an hour, including time for getting the does to their stations, sanitizing them, hooking them up, unhooking them, and sending them out.

With the next batch Lena had to deal with Tulia, who always insisted on being milked at the fourth station no matter where she was in line, so if she was ahead of fourth in line she blocked the others from their stations, and if she was behind fourth in line she made whoever was already at the fourth station relinquish her place. After many attempts to get Tulia to accept whatever station she came to, Lena was resigned to her behavior, though in her mind she repeated what her grandmother said when as a child she behaved like Tulia: *"Jesteś uparta dziewczynka."*

After the last batch was done Lena went into the adjoining room and checked the vat. Since each goat could produce about three quarts of milk per day, there were about eighteen gallons in the vat from the first milking. The vat was new, a combination pasterurizer and cheese maker, which greatly simplified the process. She pasteurized the milk every day, and she made cheese every other day. Since she had made cheese yesterday, she only had to pasteurize the milk today.

She went to the control panel and set the dial to heat the milk to a temperature of seventy-two degrees Centigrade. While she was waiting for it to reach that level, Heather came in, having done her job of resettling the does.

Joining Lena at the vat, she said: "They're acting lost without Grady."

"I know," Lena said. "I feel kind of lost without him. But the milking only took a bit longer, thanks to Tulia."

"In a way, she's my favorite. I mean, I can identify with her."

"I understand," Lena said, patting her shoulder.

When the thermometer registered seventy-two degrees she set the panel to stir the milk while it simmered for about a minute, and then she set it to cool the milk down to four degrees Centigrade. In the early days she had placed pots of milk in an ice bath to cool them down, but this was quicker and easier. Finally, when the milk was cool enough she started the pump that sent it to a refrigerated tank, where it would be stored until tomorrow.

With that done, they spent the next half hour cleaning the milking equipment, flushing out the plastic hoses, and sterilizing the silicone liners that attached to the teats. And then they did the other daily chores, which included replenishing the hay feeders, filling the water tanks, and freshening the floors of the sheds.

As they made their rounds Heather asked: "Will you get another English shepherd?"

"Oh, yah. I'll go to the kennel where we got Grady. I mean, if they're still in business. It was more than ten years ago."

"If you want, I'll go there with you."

"Thanks. You can help me pick out a good one."

"I can also help you train him."

She put an arm around Heather's shoulder as they headed for the gate.

Since Heather had to leave for her other job, Lena went into the house alone. Upstairs, she noticed that the light on the phone was flashing, which indicated that there was a message. It was after nine, so the sheriff might have learned something from the vet.

The message said: "Hi, it's Earl. I left the body with Vern at the crack of dawn, and I just heard from him. He found a bullet, the one that hit your dog in the shoulder. My deputy will take it up to Rochester for tests, and maybe we can trace it."

The phone rang only a few seconds after she put it back on its base, and seeing from the caller ID that it was the sheriff, she answered, saying: "Eden Valley Farm."

"Did you get my message?" Earl asked.

"Yah, I did," Lena said.

"Well, at least we have a lead." He paused. "I also wanted to give you the name of the security guy. Have you got something to write with?"

"Yah." A pad and a pen were on the table where she kept the phone.

He gave her a name and a phone number, and then he said: "If you tell him I referred you to him, he'll give you a fair deal."

"Okay. Thanks."

After putting down the phone she reached for the worn spiral-bound book in which she had accumulated phone numbers over the years. She had bought the book at a stationary store in Winona shortly after her wedding with the intention of organizing her life as a married woman. She was only twenty-one at the time, a girl who knew almost nothing except what she had learned in school and college. But within a few months her learning accelerated with the discovery that she was pregnant.

For some reason she couldn't remember the name of the kennel where they bought Grady, which bothered her since she had always been good with names. It was a name from more than ten years ago, so it should have been in her long-term memory, and wasn't that the type of memory that still worked as you got older? Or was it the short-term memory? She couldn't remember.

On a hunch she flipped to the pages for "K" and she found the name under "Kennel," which she must have placed there anticipating that years later it would be easier to find there. The name of the owner was Mike Conroy, whom she could now picture—a genial man with a freckled face and a shock of sandy hair, who had left a marketing job at 3M in St. Paul and moved down here to raise English shepherds. He was probably in his early fifties when they bought Grady from him, so he would be in his early sixties now. At that age he should still be in business. After all, *she* was still in business, and she was sixty-six.

Without wasting any more time, she punched his number into the phone. She waited patiently while the phone rang at his end. After eight rings she was about to end the call when a man answered, saying: "Conroy Kennel."

"Hi. This is Lena McLean. Are you Mike Conroy?"

"Yes," he said, drawing out the word.

"I'm sure you don't remember me, but my husband and I bought a puppy from you more than ten years ago."

"Where do you live?"

"Eden Valley."

"Yes, I remember. You needed a dog for your goats, right?"

"Right," she said, impressed by his memory.

"Well, I hope he worked out."

"He worked out fine. But last night someone killed him."

"Someone killed him?"

She realized that she should have said the dog died of old age since Mike might wonder if her farm was a safe place for his dogs. "He was hit by a car."

"Oh, I'm sorry. The way people drive today, it's not safe anywhere."

"I lost my husband, but I still have goats, so I need another dog. Are you still breeding English shepherds?"

"I still am. I lost my wife, but I still have dogs."

There was a pause as there usually was when Lena and a man discovered that they had both lost spouses. Of course she already had a boyfriend, and she didn't need another one, but she didn't interrupt the pause.

"I have some puppies available now," Mike said, moving ahead with the conversation. "So why don't you come over and look at them."

"Could I come over this afternoon around four?"

"Yes, that would be fine." He gave her directions, which she wrote down on the pad.

She then called Heather, who would be at work now. She had made the appointment at four since she knew that Heather was off at three, so she would be able to go with her and help her pick out a dog. In a short conversation she arranged with Heather to come to her place by three thirty, so they could go in one car.

Then she called the security guy that Earl had recommended. His name was Bill Linzer, which sounded German. About a third of the people in the county were of German descent, and about a third were of Norwegian descent, with the remaining third of various descents, including Polish. The Germans were Catholic, having mostly come from Bavaria, and the Norwegians were Lutheran. Those were the two dominant religions, though there were also some other religions in the county.

A woman answered and told her that Bill would call her back

in about ten minutes, which gave her time to go to the bathroom before getting on the phone again. She arranged with Bill to come to her place around eleven, and she spent the time until then doing chores around the house, which included replacing the contents of the litter box.

Bill arrived in a van with his name on its side, and she met him in the driveway. He was a tall lean man who looked about forty, with receding hair and silver-rimmed glasses. She could feel the bones in his hand when she shook it.

She had told him on the phone that Earl recommended him, which might have explained why he was able to see her that day. For an introduction to her problem she led him to the spot in the driveway where she had found the body of her dog. There were bloodstains on the gravel, which eventually the rain would wash away.

"It looked like he was brought down by a shot in his shoulder," Lena explained, "and then he was executed by a shot in the back of his head."

"When did it happen?" Bill asked.

"Last night. They must have come here right after the town meeting."

"You think it was more than one person?"

"It must have been. I mean, someone was driving, and someone had a gun."

"A pistol or a rifle?"

"I don't know. But Earl has a bullet, so he can determine what it was."

"Whatever it was, the shooter had to get out of the car to shoot your dog in the back of the head, and if you'd had a camera here, you'd have a video of him."

"So I should put a camera here?"

"You should put cameras in several places, starting at the gate. I assume it's the only entrance to your property."

"It's the only entrance for a car. But they could come on foot through the woods."

Bill gazed across the pasture toward the woods. "They could, but then they'd have to climb over that fence. How high is it?"

"It's five feet. It's to keep the goats in."

"Well, whoever these guys are, I doubt if they'll climb over that fence. They're more likely to cut through it."

"Then the fence won't stop them."

"It won't stop them, but it will give us opportunity to get them on video."

"You mean while they're cutting through it."

"Right. So you need cameras that are aimed along your fences. You need them at the gates. You need one to cover the entrance of your driveway. And you need one to cover the entrance to your house."

"That's a lot of cameras."

Bill paused, studying her through his glasses. "Do you expect them to come back here?"

"I do. Unless I change my position on the mining."

"My wife heard you speak at the meeting last night. She said you were great."

"Thank you. But there were people at that meeting who didn't think I was great. In fact, a man threatened me."

"Do you think he killed your dog?"

"I think he might have. Your wife might not have mentioned it, but there was a lot of hate at that meeting."

"She said it got ugly."

"The sheriff said that killing my dog was a warning, and if I don't change my position, they'll escalate."

"Are you going to change your position?"

"No." She shook her head emphatically. "I'm never going to change it."

"Then you need cameras," Bill told her. "You need to cover your entire property."

TWO

LENA AND DEVON discovered the valley on a trip they took on a Saturday in late June to regain their sanity after an especially difficult time with their teenage girls, who over the past few years had been transformed from angels into devils. Patty, who was sixteen, had come home one night with the smell of whisky on her breath, and Brenda, who was thirteen, had returned from a sleepover with her hair dyed blue. As far as Lena knew, they weren't having sex yet, but they were doing everything else, and they both had the attitude that they knew everything and their parents knew nothing. The only bright spot was that unlike other siblings she had heard about they got along with each other, they did things with each other, and they watched out for each other, to the point where they routinely lied to cover up for each other.

They were spending the weekend with their grandparents, who still lived in the house that Lena's great-grandfather had built during the 1890s when Winona was booming. It was an elegant Victorian house with a wrap-around porch and ornamental woodwork that testified to the carpentry skills of its builder. Lena had grown up in that house, which still held a lot of mostly happy memories for her. And for some reason the girls behaved there, whether it was the ambience of the house or the patience of their grandparents.

Lena and Devon left their own house around ten in the morning, and they headed south on Highway 61, which ran along the Mississippi. They had no particular destination, and when they came to the junction where they had a choice of heading east across a bridge to La Crosse, continuing south toward Iowa, or heading west toward the endless prairie, they decided to head west, and they soon found themselves in a country that even though it was less than an hour from Winona, they had never seen before or imagined. As Lena later learned, the southeastern corner of the state was an area that hadn't been flattened by glaciers, so it had kept its ancient hills, ridges, and valleys, and it was said by travel brochures to resemble the Basque country. Devon agreed, saying it reminded him of the Pyrenees.

They traveled for about a half hour on a paved road that followed a winding river, which had carved a path through the wooded hills. There were fields and pastures on both sides of the road, except where the path through the hills narrowed, and then there was only the road and river. At times the hills seemed to approach the height of mountains, so Lena didn't know what to call them, but whatever they were, they were amazing.

After one of the bends in the river they saw a sign at the edge of the road that said "Gihon River," giving them a name for the river. At the time the name meant nothing to Lena, but later she understood its significance.

They slowed and turned onto a gravel road, just to see where it might lead them, and they followed it into a beautiful valley. Like the paved road, the gravel road followed a winding stream, which required a bridge whenever it swung to the other side of the road, and in the back of her mind Lena started counting the bridges.

Meanwhile, she gazed out the car window at the woods and the pastures, where occasionally a herd of black and white cows were grazing. The few houses all looked old, and they all had barns with rustic silos.

"Six," she said as they drove across another bridge.

"Six what?" Devon asked.

"Six bridges."

"Is there a lucky number?"

"Yah. It's seven."

When they had crossed the seventh bridge there was a sign at the edge of the road that said: "Land for sale."

"I think we should buy it," Lena said.

"You're crazy," Devon said with affection. "You don't know how much land it is, or how much they want for it."

"Whatever it is, I feel it was meant to be."

"You're a superstitious Polack."

"You should talk," she laughed, "you superstitious Mick."

"Okay. Enough of the ethnic slurs. Are you serious about buying land here?"

"Well, I've never seen anything as beautiful as this valley. Have you?"

"No. It looks like paradise."

"Then back up, so I can get the phone number."

He carefully backed up through the cloud of dust they had left behind them, and she wrote down the phone number on a pad from the glove compartment.

They continued along the road, which after about a half hour began to rise, and they followed it up to the top of a ridge, where they were in a different world. There were rolling fields of corn and soybeans that stretched as far as they could see. There was a paved road, and there was a new house at the end of a long driveway, as big as the houses the lumber barons had built in Winona. Dismayed, they turned back into the valley and retraced their way along the gravel road. They stopped at the for-sale sign, got out of the car, and looked around. In front of them was a meadow with blue flowers, which she later learned were bluebells.

Pointing across the meadow toward a hillside, she said: "We could build a house there."

"We don't know how to build a house," Devon said.

"We could learn from my father."

"I guess we could."

At that moment a car approached them, slowed down, and stopped. The driver rolled down his window and asked: "Are you in trouble?"

"No, we just stopped to look at the land here," Lena told him.

"Do you know the owner?" Devon asked him.

"Yah, I know him. Are you thinking of buying it?"

"We're interested," Devon said.

"Well, don't pay what he's asking. He's a greedy old son of a gun."

"Do you know how many acres he has?"

"He has about two hundred acres in this parcel, and he has more in other parcels." The man paused. "If you really are interested, I can recommend a lawyer who'll help you deal with the old miser."

Lena went to their car and got the pad and wrote down the name and number of the lawyer as well as the name and number of the driver, who owned a farm at the end of the valley near the paved road and the river.

"Does this valley have a name?" Lena asked the man.

"Yah, it's called Eden Valley."

She exchanged a look with Devon, who had said it looked like paradise.

"That used to be an appropriate name," the man said. "But now I don't know. There're so many outsiders coming to live here. I mean no offense."

"I understand," Lena said. "But I promise we wouldn't spoil it."

Looking at her steadily, the man said: "I don't believe you would. In fact, I believe you'd take good care of what we have here. But there are people who don't give a damn about it."

"You mean people who live in this valley?"

"No, people who live up on the ridge, though they don't really live there. They only build big houses there to show how rich they are."

"Do they harm the valley?"

"Yah, they do. We get the run-off from their fertilizers and pesticides, so gradually they're poisoning us."

She exchanged another look with Devon, who understood that if they bought the land they would have a worthy cause to fight for.

Standing in the driveway, Lena reviewed the proposal for the surveillance cameras. It included ten wireless cameras with night vision, five dummy cameras, and a monitoring system. The ten cameras would be deployed in key positions where they could take videos of anyone entering the property through the driveway or from the woods, cutting through the fences, harming the animals, or breaking into the house. The dummies would be deployed in positions where they would be noticed and thereby function as a deterrent. Their cost per unit was only a fraction of the cost of actual cameras, so in Bill's words they would leverage her investment. Even after a generous discount, the total cost was more than Lena had in the bank, but Bill agreed to let her pay monthly over three years.

They had shaken hands on the deal, and Bill would come back the next day with the paperwork and a team to install the system. Since the project would be done by the end of the day, she only had to worry about being uncovered that night, though getting a dog would help fill the gap. She realized that the people who wanted her to change her position on the mining could always kill another dog, but at least a dog would help protect the goats from predators who might otherwise sneak into their compound. A barking dog would scare them away.

Lena spent the next hour walking around the property, as she had with Bill, remembering the positions for cameras that he had indicated. Of course, the cameras wouldn't necessarily stop people from harming the animals or her, but the only thing that *would* stop them was armed guards around the clock, which she couldn't have afforded and couldn't have accepted. The idea of gun battles in Eden Valley utterly appalled her.

She worked for a while in her office doing the accounts, she made a ham sandwich for lunch, and then she went to check on the goats. She found the does sitting in the shade of the maple trees in the middle of the near pasture, a dozen or so under each tree, chewing their cuds and ruminating, and she found the bucks grazing at the edge of the woods. It worried her that while she and Heather went to the kennel there wouldn't even be a dog to protect the goats, but at least the four-legged predators wouldn't bother them during the day, and if the two-legged variety saw Heather's car in the driveway, they would probably think someone was at home. In any case it would do no good for her to worry.

That was something she had learned from her mother, not to worry since everything was in God's hands. It wasn't fatalism, it was faith—faith that no matter what happened, you were always safely in God's hands. It was the faith that had evolved in Poland over centuries of being attacked by wave after wave of barbarians, who pillaged and looted and raped and killed and left the country in ashes. Again and again the victims of war arose from the ashes, and with every recovery their faith got stronger. It was something she had imparted to her daughters, both of whom at least for a while had gotten lost in the woods of life but finally found their ways, Patty in a hillside neighborhood of Yonkers with a husband and two children of her own, and Brenda in a residential neighborhood of St. Paul with a longtime partner who also was her business partner. Thinking about them made her realize that she was overdue in visiting Brenda, whom she tried to see every few months. Either she drove up to St. Paul, or Brenda and her partner Jane drove down to Eden Valley. When they visited her it gave her someone besides herself to cook for, and both women were hearty eaters. With all that was happening, she couldn't go and visit them now, but maybe this weekend they could come and visit her, so she could bring them up to date on things.

She went back into the house and into her bedroom, where she stood before the image of Our Lady of Częstochowa, which her father had carefully hung on the wall the day they moved into the house. According to tradition, the image was a portrait of Our Lady done by St. John after the Crucifixion of Our Lord, and it remained in the Holy Land until it was taken to Constantinople, where it remained for five hundred years before it was taken to Poland. Eventually finding a permanent home in the town of Częstochowa, it survived many attacks by pagans and heretics, which resulted in two slashes on her cheek and one on her throat. And many miracles were attributed to Our Lady, including the time when the Russians, attacking Warsaw, quickly withdrew after her image appeared in the clouds. Since the pigment on Our Lady's face and hands had darkened over the years, presumably from candle smoke, the image became known as the Black Madonna. In the Polish community where Lena had grown up, every family had a copy of this image somewhere in the house.

She recited the prayer she had learned as a child: "Holy Mother of Częstochowa, Thou art full of grace, goodness, and mercy. I consecrate to Thee all my thoughts, words, and actions—my soul and my body. I beseech Thy blessings and especially prayers for my salvation. Today, I consecrate myself to Thee, Good Mother, totally—with body and soul amid joy and sufferings to obtain for myself and others Thy blessings on this earth and eternal life in heaven." Today she added: "Holy Mother, please protect my family, my friends, and my animals, including the dog I hope to buy this afternoon. Amen."

She made the sign of the cross, and then she got her pocketbook and went out to meet Heather, who arrived within a few minutes.

It took them about a half hour to drive to the kennel, which was in another valley. There was a compact house and extensive out-buildings for the dogs as well as a fenced-in yard where they could run around. For a moment she envied Mike for having animals that didn't have to be milked every day, but then she enumerated the joys of having goats.

Mike came out of the house and greeted them. He looked the same as she remembered, except that he was older and thinner. After the introductory remarks he led them into a building where they could view the puppies.

"They're adorable," she told them. "I wish I could take all of them home."

"You can," Mike said. "I'll give you a volume discount."

Of course he was kidding, and she was glad he hadn't lost that ability as a result of losing his wife. "But they're not old enough to be herd dogs or watch dogs."

"They'll be old enough within six months."

"Do you have any older dogs?"

"As a matter of fact, I have a dog who's six months old. I was training him for someone who changed his mind, so I'm stuck with him since everyone wants puppies."

"Can I see him?"

"Sure. He's out in the yard."

They went out, and Mike pointed to a dog who was playing

with a beat-up stuffed rabbit. With his coloring, he could have been Grady's son or brother.

"How much does he weigh?"

"About thirty-five pounds."

"Then he's almost full grown."

"He has a little more growing to do, but not much."

"Does he have a name?"

"He has a name on his papers, but I don't use it. I only use names for dogs I keep."

"You weren't intending to keep him?"

"No. I was hoping someone would want him. But if no one wants him, I'll keep him and give him a name. He's a good dog."

She walked out into the yard and knelt down, calling the dog, who came to her as if he knew her, wagging his tail. She nuzzled him, asking: "Do you want to come and live with me? I have a herd of goats, which you can help me with."

The dog seemed to respond affirmatively.

She turned to Heather, asking: "What do you think?"

"I think it's love at first sight," Heather told her.

"Then I'll take this guy."

Mike led them into his house and into an office, where he got the dog's papers and the evidence of shots.

"Do I get a discount because he's not a puppy?"

"Yes, you do. But I get a premium for training him."

"Did you train him to herd goats?"

"No. I trained him to do whatever you want."

She laughed. "Fair enough."

He gave her a price, she wrote a check, and the deal was done.

On the way home he sat on the seat between her and Heather with his eyes directed forward as if he had a role in navigation.

"I think I'll call him Brady. What do you think?"

"I like that name. And it's appropriate because he looks like Grady."

"What do *you* think?" she asked the dog.

The dog's head bobbed, whether because he was responding affirmatively or because they had gone over a bump in the road.

When they got home she introduced Brady to the cats, who pulled rank on him but weren't hostile, and then she brought him into the compound, where she put him on a leash attached to the doghouse that had sheltered Grady. She wanted him present while they did the milking, but she didn't want him to get involved. From a safe distance he could view the goats and begin getting familiar with them.

They did the milking at six thirty, they pasteurized the milk, and they pumped it into the storage tank. They now had about thirty-six gallons of milk available for making cheese the next day. By the time they had finished cleaning up it was after eight, and they were both tired, so they said goodnight and Heather left the compound. Lena unleashed Brady and let him sniff around. The does were settled in their shed for the night, and the dog only went as far as the entrance to have a look at them. While he was becoming acclimated, Lena went into the house and returned with a bowl of food for him, hoping he would like the chow that Grady had liked. She set the bowl in front of the doghouse, and he bounded over, sniffed it, and began devouring it. With only a few misgivings, she decided to leave him in the compound for the night, where he could begin learning how to be a watch dog, so after she filled his water bowl, she knelt down and hugged him goodnight.

She fed the cats and then had dinner of goat yoghurt and granola, sitting alone at the dining table where she had sat with Devon and the girls, and then Devon, for so many years. She felt a little better tonight than last night since she had a dog now, but that didn't make up for the absence of Devon or even Grady.

The next morning, after pumping the pasteurized milk into another storage tank, they pumped the milk from the previous day into the vat and added the culture. It would have to stand for about two hours at room temperature, so after doing the usual chores Heather left for her other job and Lena went back to the house, where in the living room she saw the light flashing on the phone. She retrieved the message, which was from Jordan. He wondered if she could come over to his place in the early afternoon to discuss strategy.

She immediately called him, figuring that by now he would be done with milking his cows.

He answered after two rings, saying: "Hey, Lena. How are you doing?"

From the way he asked this, she could tell he must have heard about the murder of Grady. "I'm doing okay."

"I'm so sorry. I know what Grady meant to you."

"Thanks. I got a new dog from the kennel yesterday."

"That's good. Well, I hope the sheriff catches whoever did it."

"He's trying, but he has so many suspects. I mean, all the people who hate us."

"If they don't agree with our position on the mining, they should vote against us in the next election. They shouldn't kill our animals."

"The sheriff believes that killing Grady was only a start. But he didn't advise me to change my position on the mining."

"What did he advise you to do?"

"He advised me to install security cameras, so that's what they're doing today. And I don't know what time they'll be done."

"If they're done by three, we could still meet. Why don't you call me around noon and let me know how they're doing?"

"Okay. I will."

After putting down the phone she looked outside to see if the security team had arrived, but there were no extra vehicles in the driveway, so she sat down and reviewed the list for her weekly shopping, which she did at the co-op in Passau, the county seat. The co-op had almost everything she needed, and it had low prices. But about once a month she went to the supermarket in La Crosse to fill any gaps. They also had a Walmart in that city, but on principle she refused to go there, conscious of all the small stores they had put out of business.

The next time she looked up she saw Bill's van in the driveway, so she went out to greet them. Along with Bill were two young guys with tattoos, which reminded her of the horror she had felt when she saw a tattoo on Brenda's shoulder, but that was many years ago and she had gotten used to it.

Bill introduced the two young guys and explained that they would walk around the property and identify positions for cameras, beginning with the entrance of the driveway and ending with the house.

Relieved to know that Bill would remain to supervise them, Lena only tagged along with them so that she would know where the cameras were. It took about a half hour, and when they were done, Bill had a map that showed the locations of all the cameras, which he would reproduce at his office and give her a copy of.

At that point Lena retreated to the house, where she saw the light flashing on the phone. The message was from Earl, who said: "We know what kind of gun was used to kill your dog. If you call me, I'll give you more details."

She called the sheriff on his cell phone, and he answered right away. It made her wonder if anything else was happening in the county.

"It was a Glock," Earl told her. "Forty-five caliber, a popular model. It has a capacity of thirteen rounds."

"Can you trace a particular gun to its owner?"

"My deputy can run it through a database of vendors who sell ammo for it. We'll go as far afield as Chicago, and we'll get a list of suspects. It'll probably be a long list, but we can narrow it by the addresses of people who bought ammo for it. If we're lucky, we'll find people who live around here."

"Do many people around here own that kind of gun?"

"You'd be surprised. You'd think they only have guns for hunting, but they also have guns for killing people, which they believe will keep them safe. But most of them couldn't hit a barn with that kind of gun."

"What could they hit with it?"

"Family members. In accidents," the sheriff added laconically.

She was encouraged by this report, but she realized that it would take the police a long time to trace the gun if they were even able to, and in the meantime its owner could do a lot of damage.

So she put the matter out of her mind and went down to her office to review her plan for making cheese. She made plain goat cheese, which accounted for about half of her production. It was the type of goat cheese they used in salads and in cooking. She also made cheese in the styles of Brie, Camembert, Gouda, and Tomme. The last had suddenly become popular, but she didn't want to risk having too much inventory of it because tastes changed. In fact, it wasn't long ago that Americans wouldn't think of eating goat cheese, and now it was all the rage.

She kept her records on a laptop computer, which she had begun using for this purpose more than ten years ago. Devon had a phobia for computers, so she had acquired her skills from a girl who was studying accounting at Viterbo University in La Crosse. She kept her accounts, her inventory records, and her production plans on the computer in a simple system that the girl had set up for her. Now, when she got into the system she found her inventory of cheeses, which she studied before deciding to use the current supply of milk to make plain goat cheese plus some in the Camembert style, the inventory of which was low. She then checked her inventory of supplies and found that she needed starter culture and rennet. Those items she bought online, and she used her computer to order them from her supplier.

She figured that while the guys were installing the cameras she would have time to work on the cheese, so she left the house and went to the dairy barn, where she set the dial of the control panel to heat the cultured milk. When the temperature reached thirty degrees Centigrade she added a mixture of liquid rennet and water, and she let the milk rest until curds formed. She set the curd cutters into motion and watched them separate the whey. She removed batches of curds from the vat and placed them on the work table, where she put them into plastic molds and left them to drain.

It was almost noon, so Lena went out to see how the guys were doing. She found Bill at the doe shed, where they had just finished installing a camera at the top of an interior wall. The camera would not only record anyone who came into the shed but it would also record the activity of the does inside the shed.

"So I can monitor them," Lena said.

"Yah, that's a bonus."

"It makes me think I should have a camera in the birthing shed."

"We could do that for you. In fact, we have an extra camera, so we can put it there." He paused. "I won't charge you for it."

"Thanks," she said, touched by this gesture.

She led him to the birthing shed, which was next to the doe shed, and when they had installed a camera there, the only thing left to install was the monitor. With one of the guys, who carried the monitor, Bill followed her into the house and asked her where they should put it. After some debate, she told him to put the monitor in the living area, next to the television, which she rarely watched. There were no signals or cables for television in the valley, so the only way you could get service was with a dish antenna. Believing that a dish wasn't worth the money, she used her television only to watch movies on disks. And now for entertainment she would also have a monitor to watch.

When it was installed, Bill turned on the monitor and showed her how to move from camera to camera, and how to get the views from more than one camera on the screen at the same time. He recommended that she make the view from the camera at the entrance of the driveway the default view. He had written the location of each camera on a sheet, with an identification number, and she could type this information if she wanted to.

Finally, he gave her some papers to sign, including a note for the financing, and they were done. It was only a little after one, so she called Jordan and told him she could be at his place in a half hour.

Jordan lived in a valley that was shorter and wider than Eden Valley but otherwise similar except for a bluff at the western ridge. The land below the bluff was ideal for sand mining, but luckily the owner was a committed environmentalist who would never think of selling it for that purpose. Jordan's land was across the stream from the bluff, and it had fields, pastures, and woods. In the fields corn and hay were growing, in a far pasture his cows were grazing, and on a hillside was an array of solar panels, which provided enough power for the farm and the house. He was hooked up to the grid of the power company, and at times he needed power from them but at times he provided power to them, so over a year it balanced out. His house was on a hillside, like hers. In fact, most houses in the valleys were on hillsides since when there were torrential rains, the streams rose and flooded the lowlands. For the same reason, barns and other shelters for animals were also on hillsides, so even though crops were endangered by floods, the animals were safe.

Approaching the house, Lena noticed the mud oven to the left of the driveway. Jordan was an avid baker, who made bread from scratch. He began with seeds, which he ground into flour, and he leavened the flour with a variety of starters. He baked the bread in that mud oven, twice a week, and he produced more than enough for his family, so he gave it away to neighbors and friends. He had taught Lena how to make sourdough bread, from flour not from scratch, but having only herself to feed she only made it before visits of Brenda and Jane.

She parked her car next to his pickup, and when she got out she was greeted by the mixed terrier who was the children's pet. She paused to scratch its ears, and then she went to the back door and knocked to let them know she had arrived.

"Come in," the voice of Anna said.

She went in and found Anna at the kitchen table with Jenny and Pete. They were nine and seven, safely distant from the teenage turmoil that lay ahead. They were being home-schooled until high school since Anna wanted to instill in them not only the fundamentals of a good education but also the values of her religion before they were exposed to other influences. They were good kids, and Anna deserved a lot of credit for raising them so well.

Lena exchanged greetings with them and responded to the children's inquiries about the goats, whom they had seen right after the last kidding. They had loved the baby goats and had asked their mother if they could have a pair of them. Their mother had told them maybe next year after they joined 4H.

"Is Jordan in his office," Lena asked, not wanting to interrupt them longer.

"Yes, he should be there," Anna said.

She went from the kitchen to the dining room and then to the living room, knowing her way. There was no television, but there was a radio as part of a console that also played music. Against one wall there was also a piano. Anna was trained as a classical musician, and judging from the occasional concerts she gave at the Lutheran church in Passau, she had a lot of talent. In addition to schooling her children she gave them piano lessons.

Jordan was in his office, sitting at his desk and gazing at the screen of a computer.

"Hi," she said, hesitant to break his concentration.

"Oh, hi," he said, snapping out of it. He rose and hugged her the way you would give a member of your family the sign of peace. He had changed out of his work clothes for lunch with his family, and he was wearing khaki shorts and a green tee shirt with yellow letters that said: "Save the Earth." He was in his late thirties, a lean man with sinewy limbs and well-defined facial features. He had the eyes of an apostle.

"Is this a good time?"

"It's a perfect time, especially after what they did to you. Let's go into the living room, where we can sit down."

She followed Jordan to the living room, where they sat down in two easy chairs that were probably occupied by the children when the family got together in the evening to talk or listen to the radio. She knew that as a matter of policy these children didn't have smartphones, so the family gatherings were face to face without those addictive distractions. Based on the behavior of most current children, whom Lena had observed in Passau, La Crosse, and St. Paul, she was glad that her own children had gone through school before there were smartphones, which would have complicated their lives.

"You know," Jordan told her, "I worry about what they might do to you."

"You don't worry about what they might do to *you?*"

"No, I worry about what they might do to Anna or the children."

"Then maybe you should hire an armed guard."

"Maybe I should. It would only be until the next board meeting. If we pass the law, they won't have a reason for hurting us."

"You're assuming they're rational."

"Well, so far they *are* rational. They want to stop us from passing the law so they can get money from mining the sand. But if they couldn't get that money, what would be their motive for hurting us?"

"Revenge," she said.

"You mean they'd want to get back at us for depriving them of that money?"

"Yah. It happens all the time."

He shook his head sadly. "Among other reasons, we left the city to get away from people who only care about money. We didn't expect to find them here."

"They're probably not from here."

"But are they hired by people from here?"

"It's possible, but I don't think so. I think they're hired by the same people who bought the politicians in St. Paul."

"You mean the mining company."

"I mean the global energy conglomerate, which the mining company is only part of."

"Well, they're impersonal. If they lose here, they'll move on to the next opportunity. They won't stay here to get revenge."

"I guess they won't. So when we pass our law," she said with more confidence than she felt, "they won't have any reason for hurting us."

He paused for a moment. "Well, I hope we still have a majority on the board."

"Do you think Neil is wavering?" Neil was the lawyer who so

far believed that it was in his financial interest to stop the mining.

"I have no reason to think he is. But they have a lot of money, and they could always pay him to change his position."

"He must care about something other than money."

"I think he cares about his children."

"Then we should appeal to that," she said. "We should make him realize what kind of world will be left for his children if we let those people destroy our valleys."

Jordan nodded. "We should make him understand that sand mining in our county is only part of a grand strategy to keep us dependent on fossil fuels."

"So should we both talk with him?"

"I think we should. In the meantime, I've been working with Porter to make our law more resistant to an appeal." Porter was the lawyer from St. Paul who had drafted the law in response to the law passed by the state legislature. "The changes won't be material, so we don't need to have a town meeting to discuss them. We only need to review them before we vote."

The county board met on the third Tuesday of every month, so the next meeting was on July 21. Recalling what had happened at the last meeting, Lena said: "I hope we don't have another meeting like the last one. Did you see the guy who threatened me?"

"I saw him," Jordan said, "but I didn't recognize him."

"I didn't either. He must have come from outside."

"Do you think he might have been involved in the murder of your dog?"

"I think he might have. The sheriff has a bullet from Grady's body. If we're lucky, he'll trace it to that guy."

"If he does, we might find out who hired him."

"I think we know who hired him."

"Maybe we do, but we don't have the evidence to prove it."

"Well, I'll pray that the sheriff finds the evidence."

"I'll pray for that too," Jordan told her. "And I'll pray that we can keep Neil on our side."

They agreed that each of them would talk with Neil and report back to the other, and then they ended the meeting since Jordan had to milk his cows and she had to milk her goats. She passed through the kitchen, where she said goodbye to Anna and the children, and then she got into her car, which she noticed was getting low on gas, so she took the long way home and stopped in Arendal to fill her tank. The gas station was next to the Legion, where her boyfriend Arne would be drinking now. Respectable women didn't go to the Legion, so she could only imagine Arne in a row of men sitting at the bar, drinking Bud. She saw him only on weekends, when she had two high school kids do the milking. The kids were 4H, so they knew what they were doing with the animals, and she didn't have to worry about them. Now, with all that was happening, if Arne wanted to see her this weekend, he would have to come to her place, which he wouldn't do in the fall or winter because he couldn't watch football there. It was now summer, with no football, so he wouldn't have any excuse. But if he didn't want to come to her place, it would be all right. She liked Arne, and she had some good times with him, but Devon was the love of her life, and he always would be.

There was no self-service at the gas station, so the owner filled her tank. His name was Duane, and she talked with him through the open window of her car.

"I heard what happened to your dog," Duane told her, with his face at the level of the window. "And I know why they did it, but I can tell you, no one from around here would do a thing like that to you."

"I hope you're right," she said softly.

"I know I'm right. I know all these people, and they might have their flaws, but none of them would murder a dog that never did anything to them."

In thanks for his reassurance, she patted his hand, which was clamped on the door.

Continuing home, she thought about her conversation with Jordan. She decided that if her own children were living at home, she would hire armed guards for the month until the next board meeting, and she resolved to urge Jordan to do that. She would call him that evening when they were both done with the milking.

Being alone, without children to worry about, she would rely on the cameras to deter people who might come to harm her, or to take videos that could be used to catch them. She especially hoped to catch the guy who had murdered her dog.

But more than anything, she would rely on God to protect her since her position on the sand mining was supported by the pope's encyclical *Laudato Si'* about saving the earth, which gave her a universal reason beyond her personal reason for saving the valley. After reading the encyclical she felt as if she had been called to join a religious order whose mission was to save the earth, beginning with Franconia county. She had never imagined herself as a martyr, not even as a girl when she occasionally flirted with the idea of becoming a nun, and now she had absolutely no intention of being a martyr for this cause.

But if it happened, it would be God's will.

THREE

HER MOTHER AND her father met in St. Paul, where her father had driven with an army buddy looking for excitement. They were recently discharged from the military and were still adapting to civilian life. The girls they had known in high school were married or otherwise engaged, so they wanted to get out of Winona and try somewhere else, at least for a weekend. After being rebuffed in downtown bars they gravitated toward the Polish-American Club on Payne Avenue, which on Saturday night had a polka party.

At first the scene was as dull as Winona, with women in one group gossiping, men in another group drinking beer, and children in another group wishing they were somewhere else while a polka band played to an empty dance floor. But then, almost hidden by a matronly woman, he spotted a girl, a beautiful girl. With the look of serenity in her blue eyes she could have been the model for a painting of an angel, and though this wasn't the kind of girl he was looking for that night, he couldn't help being drawn to her.

Walking around the edge of the dance floor, he pretended not to be going toward her but only going by her, and he stopped near her as if something else had gotten his attention. He paused for a moment, and then he turned toward her. Up close, the power that had drawn him from across the room completely overwhelmed him, and he was at a loss for words.

She smiled at him with empathy, asking: *"Wszystko w porządku?"*

"Yah, I'm fine," he stammered. "I was looking for someone."

"Who were you looking for? I might know him."

"A guy from the army. He's from St. Paul."

"Are you from St. Paul?"

"I'm from Winona."

"I don't know where that is."

"It's about three hours south of here."

There was silence during which he couldn't think of anything else to say, but then she relieved him by asking: "Were you in the army?"

"Yah, I was discharged only a few months ago."

"Where did you serve?"

"In Europe," he said since he had seen action in more than one country.

Her eyes darkened. "I'm from Europe."

"Where in Europe?"

"What used to be Poland."

"How long have you been here?"

"Seven months."

"Are you with your family?"

She shook her head. "The Germans killed most of my family, and the Russians killed the rest. So I'm here alone."

"How did you get here?"

"It's a long story, and I don't want to tell it to you now. Can you do the polka?"

"Sure I can. Would you like to dance?"

"*Bardzo chciałbym, aby tańczyć,*" she said, offering him her arm.

He led her out to the dance floor, where they started doing the polka. He wasn't a good dancer, but she made him look good, and people watched them. The bandleader looked happy to see a couple dancing.

"What's your name?" he asked her.

"Aniela. What's yours?"

"Janusz," he said.

"That's a good name. It means God is gracious."

He knew that her name meant angel, so he didn't have to ask. In fact, he had known just by looking at her.

Aniela was eighteen, and she lived with an aunt and uncle in the city's Polish community. She spoke almost no English, so her job opportunities were limited to cleaning houses, offices, and schools. With the recommendation of the priest at St. Casimir's, she had gotten a job cleaning the church's school, and if all went well, she could get jobs cleaning other Catholic schools. In the meantime she was trying to learn English.

He didn't learn much more about her that evening, and he didn't hear the story of how she got to America until much later, but the next weekend he drove to St. Paul alone and had dinner at the house of her aunt and uncle, who asked him a lot of questions as if they were interviewing him for a job. Among the questions, her aunt asked him about his accent in Polish, and he explained that his family were Kashubians. From their response, he had a feeling that they would privately discuss this fact until they knew how to deal with it.

He saw her almost every weekend over the next three months, and then he brought her down to Winona to meet his family. His father immediately liked her, and his mother evidently saw how she could mold this young woman into the wife she wanted for her son, so all went well. Aniela spent the night in the guest bedroom, she joined them for mass the next day at St. Stanislaus, and she was subjected to a family dinner, which she survived. In fact, she more than held her own when the men started talking about how America should liberate Poland from the Russians, revealing a passion beneath her angelic surface.

Within three months they were engaged, and within another three months they were married. The only hitch was whether they should have the wedding at St. Casimir in St. Paul or at St. Stanislaus in Winona. It was customary to hold the wedding in the bride's church, but since there were far more members of the groom's family, his mother argued strongly in favor of Winona. As Lena well remembered, his mother was capable of arguing strongly and convincing people to do what she wanted. The grandchildren's word for her was Babcia but they also referred to her as Pani, which for them evoked more than its literal meaning in Polish (Mrs.)—in English it would have meant "matriarch." But the location of the wedding wasn't the only issue. The other issue for Aniela's aunt and uncle was whether St. Stanislaus, which had been founded by Kashubians, was a proper Polish church. To convince them that it was, Babcia invited them to attend mass at St. Stan's, and having no choice but to accept the invitation, they drove down to Winona on a Saturday and spent the night in the guestroom, with Aniela sharing a bedroom with one of the groom's three sisters. His being her only son of course intensified his mother's solicitude.

The aunt and uncle were satisfied with the church, and they got along with the groom's family at Sunday dinner, supporting the cause of liberating Poland from the Russians, so they agreed to have the wedding mass at St. Stan's on the third Saturday of September, with the homily in Polish, and the reception in a room of the church that was used for social activities. For their honeymoon the newly married couple went to Chicago, where Lena must have been conceived since she was born exactly nine months later.

Since there were complications with her delivery, and again with her brother Tony's delivery, their mother was told by the doctor that she wouldn't survive another delivery, and though she wanted to keep having children, she wanted even more to be a mother to the children she had, so she didn't have any more children.

Remembering back to the age of three, Lena could see what a good mother Aniela had been to both her children. She was loving, she was patient, and she was kind. She didn't get angry, and she didn't get upset. When there was a problem, she always tried to understand it before she offered a solution. The only problem that couldn't be solved was Lena's feeling that she could never be as good as her mother, which eventually led to her doing things as if to prove she wasn't as good as her mother.

When she got home from her meeting with Jordan she checked the cheese, and it was ready to be placed in the refrigerator. It was plain goat cheese, so it didn't need aging. From the seventy-two gallons of milk she had made about seventy-two pounds of cheese, which she would remove from the molds the next day. She would wrap the three-ounce buttons and label them and then arrange for the distributor to pick them up and take them to the Twin Cities. The distributor paid her ten dollars per pound for the cheeses, so she would collect about seven hundred twenty dollars for this shipment. With shipments every other day during ten months of the year, the business had annual income of about one hundred thousand dollars. Of course, that was before expenses.

She was in the compound, replenishing the hay feeder, when Arne's pickup rolled into the driveway. Arne was descended from immigrants who had come from Norway around the same time her great-grandparents had come from Poland, and they had established a dairy farm in a nearby valley. Arne's grandfather and his father had continued operating the farm, but Arne finally gave it up after several years of losing money, and he got a job as custodian at the county high school, where Lena met him years ago while serving on the school board. After being friends for a long time they became more than friends about two years ago, somewhat accidentally. It had changed their relationship, in some ways for better and in other ways for worse.

In the spring Arne had turned sixty-five, and he had retired from his job, so he didn't have enough to do, and he was spending more time at the Legion bar, where judging from the way he now walked toward the compound, he had spent the afternoon.

He was a tall man, with a body that was still in shape and silver hair that had once been blond. He had blue eyes which most of the time sparkled with humor. Unlike Devon, who was tightly wound and quickly reactive, Arne was loose and not easily upset. Today he looked more relaxed than usual, no doubt from having several rounds of beer.

Entering through the gate of the compound, he said: "I'm sorry about Grady. I heard about it from the guys at the Legion."

"I have a new dog," she said, pointing to Brady, who was moving with his nose along the ground as if he had picked up the scent of an animal other than a goat.

"I can see that," Arne said. "But you need more than a dog to protect you."

"Is that what the guys at the Legion think?"

"It's what I think," Arne said calmly. "I think you should have an armed guard. I mean, unless you change your position."

"I'm not going to change my position."

"I didn't think you would." He stooped down to scratch the head of Brady, who had come over to check him out.

"Would you like to be my armed guard?" she asked him facetiously. He had served a tour of duty in Vietnam, where he had been wounded invisibly, though he wouldn't admit it. From what he had told her about his war experiences, she assumed he knew how to fire an assault weapon and kill enemies.

"Naw, I don't like guns. You'll have to hire someone else for that purpose."

"Is there anyone you could recommend?"

He thought for a moment, stroking the dog. "There's a guy at the Legion who might be good for it. He did two tours of duty in Iraq."

"Well, I don't think I need an armed guard."

"Because you have God to protect you?" Arne had been raised as a Lutheran, but in the war he had lost his faith, and he couldn't understand why she still had her faith. That was an issue that separated them.

"I have more than that. I have surveillance cameras."

He looked around and said: "Oh, yah. I didn't notice them. Do you really think they'll protect you?"

"They'll take videos of anyone who comes here to harm my animals."

"But what if they come here to harm you?"

"The sheriff will have videos of them."

"Oh, that's great. He'll have videos of the guys who killed you. But even with videos he might not catch them, and in the meantime you'll be dead."

"So what do you advise me to do?"

"I advise you to change your position."

"You don't really mean that."

"Yah, I do," he said earnestly. "I don't want you to get killed."

"That's the nicest thing you ever said to me," she said, trying to make light of it.

"I'm serious. The guys who shot your dog are contract killers. They were hired by the mining company, and they'll do anything for money."

"How do you know that?"

"It's common knowledge. You think you're only up against the local farmers who want to sell their land and become millionaires, but you're also up against the guys who run the world, and you're no match for them."

"If we all stuck together, what could they do?"

"They could kill everyone who stands in their way, and then whoever inherits the land will gladly sell it to them."

"Would *you* sell your land to them?"

"I don't want to sell it to them, but if they held a gun to my head, I guess I would. I don't want to be a martyr for the cause."

"I don't want to be a martyr either," she said. "But I don't think it'll come to that. I think that when we pass our law, they'll go away and do something else with their money."

"If they kill you and Jordan and Neil, the remaining members of the board will vote to let them mine the sand."

"I don't think they'll go that far."

He sighed. "Okay. Well, let's change the subject. Do you have any plans for tonight?"

"I don't. I was only going to have dinner and go to bed."

"Will you come to my place?"

"I can't be away at night now. I have to stay here."

"But you'd be safer at my place."

"I'll be safer here if you stay with me."

He considered. "Okay. What's for dinner?"

She had some ribeye steaks in the freezer, which she knew he liked. She could take them out and let them thaw while they were doing what they did best together. "How about steaks?"

"That sounds good. We have a deal."

"You mean I feed you, and you protect me."

"Something like that." He took her hand and led her out of the compound.

Arne spent the night with her, which he rarely did. It was either because he was really concerned about her or because there was no football to watch. Whatever it was, she did feel safer having him there.

She left him in bed when she got up the next morning for the milking, and when she came back to the house around nine thirty, he was gone. He had a fear of being kidded about her by the guys at the Legion, so he carefully avoided being seen with her, which added a spice of secrecy to their relationship. Of course Heather would have seen his car in the driveway and would have guessed that he had spent the night there, but since Heather didn't hang out at the Legion, she wasn't a threat to his reputation.

Having some free time now, she called Vern about retrieving the body of Grady. He was about to leave on an emergency call, but he told her she could get the dog's remains from his assistant, so she drove to his clinic, which was in Arendal. The body was in a black plastic bag, which Lena took out and gently laid in the trunk of her car.

When she got home she carried the bag up the hillside to the cemetery she had created years ago for her animals. The graves were marked by ceramic bricks that a local potter made for her, with names and dates carved in them. She set down the bag in an empty space and went to the garage and got a spade and returned to the cemetery, where she spent the next hour digging a hole that was big enough to hold Grady. She kept him in the bag and put him in the hole and after saying a prayer for him she covered him with the loose earth. With a breaking heart, she softly told him: *"Spoczywaj w pokoju."*

She had an appointment to meet with Neil at eleven that morning, so after checking for phone messages she got into her car and drove to Passau, following the Gihon River. From a local pastor she had learned the significance of its name—the Gihon was one of the four rivers that according to the Book of Genesis flowed out of the Garden of Eden.

Neil's office was in Passau, above a bank that gave him a lot of business. Passau consisted of a main street with about a dozen side streets on which there were single-family homes. It was named after an ancient city on the Danube where a lot of early immigrants had come from, but with its population of less than three thousand and its position on a brown river instead of a blue one, it bore no resemblance to its namesake, as far as Lena could tell from pictures.

Other than the hospital, the bank building had the only elevator in town, which was a reason why Neil rented an office there—he had elderly clients for whom he did estate work. Seeing an opportunity to strengthen her leg muscles, Lena took the stairs and was pleased to find that when she reached the top she was breathing only a little more heavily than normal.

Neil was a sole practitioner, but he had an assistant to help him. She was a woman named Ruth who had earned a certificate as a paralegal and had been with him from the beginning. Neil had been a partner in a St. Paul law firm but after discovering the region on a trout fishing trip about fifteen years ago he sold his partnership, resettled in the county, married a local girl, and started a family. He now had two teenage children who were giving him problems, which he had shared with Lena, seeking her reassurance that his children would grow out of their current phase, and she had reassured him, sharing problems that her own children had given her and telling him how well they had turned out.

Ruth, who also served as a receptionist, greeted her with a friendly smile and told her she could go right into Mr. Krasnik's office, where she found him sitting behind a desk. He had features that her father would have labeled as Slavish, including a big forehead. He was very good at figuring out what clients needed and then figuring out how to use the law in their favor. For him the law was an instrument for solving problems, and his career as a lawyer was a means of getting rich. He was well on his way toward achieving this goal, having built a mansion on a hillside overlooking the Gihon River and acquired a lot of real estate. It was rumored that he owned more acres of land than the large corporate farms.

"Come in and sit down," Neil told her, rising from his desk.

"I have something for you," she said, opening her pocketbook. She took out a wheel of ripe Brie-style cheese, which she knew he liked, and offered it to him.

"Thank you," he said, taking it from her. "I love your cheeses.

Do I have to keep this in the refrigerator?"

"No, it'll be all right for a while at room temperature. It's still ripening."

"You can't buy a ripe Brie from the supermarket. And when we have guests, we never anticipate that problem."

She sat down on the sofa, and he sat down in one of the chairs. She had something else for him, and she wondered what would be the best time to give it to him.

"I heard about your dog," he said sympathetically. "I never thought they'd use violence to get their way."

"I never did either."

"I hope you've taken measures to protect yourself."

"I have," she said. "But what about you?"

"I have an electric fence around my property, and I have two German shepherds inside the fence, patrolling at night."

"They could kill the dogs."

"They could, but I also have an AR-15 that can fire ten rounds per second, and I have floodlights that'll show me where to point it, so if I hear a suspicious sound, I can turn on the lights and fire away."

"How would you hear them?" she said, surprised by his preparedness.

"I have a listening device with a monitor next to our bed."

She refrained from asking about his position on gun control. Instead, she took out pictures she had taken of the valley near the Mississippi where Jordan had shown her the devastation caused by sand mining. She handed them to Neil, saying: "You may have seen these pictures before, but it's always good to remind ourselves of why we're against sand mining."

He gazed at the pictures, shaking his head. "It's terrible. If they do that here, we won't have anything left of our county."

"We won't have anything for our children to inherit."

"Well, you don't have to worry about me changing positions. I have an idea of how much value my land would lose if they mined our valleys, and they couldn't pay me enough to offset that loss. And just so you know, they've made me some offers."

"They have? Who were they?"

"Agents representing the mining companies."

"Were you tempted?"

"Oh, yah. But I did the numbers, and what they offered was nowhere near what I can make by holding my land and selling it later."

"Who would you sell it to?" Lena asked out of curiosity.

"People who want to build single family houses. A lot of people in the Twin Cities are retiring, and they're looking for a place to live that's not too far away from their children and grandchildren."

"They wouldn't want condos?"

"No, they want houses with one floor, three bedrooms, and two bathrooms," Neil said as if he had done a market analysis.

"I can understand why they'd want to live here, but how would we benefit?"

"They'd bring money, and they'd spend it here. They'd support a supermarket in Passau, a pharmacy, and other stores, so you wouldn't have to drive to La Crosse to do your shopping."

"Well, I guess it would help our economy."

"It would help a lot. Our towns are dying, and they need new people to support them."

"But the young people will still leave and go to the cities."

"They will, but more of them will stay if they can get jobs here."

"I guess they will. So you're with us?"

"I am, and I think our law is stronger with the modifications. Porter did an excellent job." He had recommended Porter because of his experience as former counsel to the state legislature.

"You can keep those pictures," she said, getting up.

"Thanks," he said, also getting up. "I can use them to help people understand our position. And thanks for the cheese."

"I hope you enjoy it."

She left his office feeling she had accomplished her mission. But she had learned from his analysis that ultimately it was money he cared about, and there was still a risk that he would be offered enough money to change that analysis.

After lunch she went to the dairy barn and got out the cheese she had made the day before. She spent the next hour wrapping and labeling it, having arranged with the distributor to pick it up later than afternoon. She had just finished this task when she heard a vehicle come up her driveway. It wasn't likely to be anyone who intended to hurt her, but she still felt a twinge of anxiety, and going outside, she was relieved to see it was the pickup of a neighbor, Roy, who had a dairy farm a mile down the road.

Roy was a native of the valley, the fourth generation of his family to live in the house that his great-grandfather had built in stages after immigrating from Bavaria, beginning with a stone shelter. Like Arne, he had served in Vietnam, and they traded appalling war stories over rounds of beer at the Legion, though Roy, who had cows to milk daily, didn't go there as often as Arne did. His wife had passed away when his kids were still in high school, and they were long gone now, both of them living in the Twin Cities. The girl was a nursing assistant, married, with two children, and the boy was a construction worker, single, with a series of girlfriends. A year ago Roy had a hip replacement at Mayo, and though he swore that his hip was as good as new, he got out of his truck more slowly than he used to.

She called to him, walking across the compound to meet him. Meanwhile, he came to the other side of the gate and waited there for her.

"It's good to see you," she told him honestly, opening the gate.

"Well, it's good to see *you*," he told her with a smile in his blue eyes and a flicker of gold in his ragged teeth. He made fun of men with facial hair but he himself shaved only about once a week, so he always had iron gray bristles on his face, which was shaped like a cinder block.

"Would you like some coffee?"

"If you got the time, I got the time."

"Come on," she said, heading toward the house.

As they walked he said: "I'm sorry about your dog."

"Thanks. I got a new one," she added to fend off further condolences.

"Nothing like that ever happened in this valley. Things are in such a turmoil now."

She held the screen door open for him and led him up the stairs and into the kitchen, where she invited him to sit down at the table. She got the teapot off the stove and took it to the sink and filled it with enough water. She returned the teapot to the stove and turned on the burner underneath it. She got a filter out of a drawer and placed it into the hourglass coffee maker. Then she got the bag of coffee out of the refrigerator and put two heaping scoops into the filter. And finally she got a teabag for herself.

While she was making these preparations Roy didn't talk, as if he didn't want to distract her. But now he asked: "How're your kids?"

She had to smile. The girls, who were now in their early forties, were evidently still the teenage kids he remembered from when her family came to the valley for weekends. He had seen them on visits after they had grown up and moved away, yet they were still kids to him. "They're doing fine. How are yours doing?"

"The same as usual. Life is tough for them."

"It was tough for you."

"But not the way it's tough for them. I had a farm waiting for me when I came back from Vietnam."

"It's waiting for them, isn't it?"

"Yah. But they don't want the farm. And they're right not to want it. You can't make a living nowadays with a dairy farm."

"They could use it for something else."

"For what? Goats?"

"No, I already have enough competition." The water was ready, so she lifted the teapot off the stove and poured the right amount of water into the coffee maker.

"Are you making a living from those critters?"

"I'm not getting rich," she said, watching the coffee drip through the filter, "but I'm making enough to keep me afloat."

"I'm glad you are, but I'm not. I'd be better off financially if I wound down my farm."

"If you didn't have the farm, what would you do?"

49

"I'd spend more time at the Legion with Arne."

"Well, that wouldn't be good for you." She poured the coffee into a mug that said "Franconia 4H" on it, and she made her tea in the mug that had the prayer of St. Francis on it. Devon had given her that mug.

"If it's good for Arne, then why wouldn't it be good for me?"

"It's not good for Arne. He needs to get off his butt and do something."

"Like what?" Roy asked, blowing across the surface of his coffee.

"Like volunteering. There are a lot of people in this county who need help."

"Yah, there are, including me. My boy just gave notice." Roy was referring to the high school dropout who had helped him on the farm for the past two years.

"He did?" she said, sitting down at the table across from him. "What's he going to do?"

"Join the army."

"You mean knowing what happened to those guys in Afghanistan and Iraq, he still wants to join the army?"

"What else is there for him?"

"I don't know."

"At least in the army he'll get three square meals a day, he'll have a roof over his head, and he'll learn how to do things that might be useful."

"Like killing people?"

"Oh, don't give me that anti-war shit," Roy said with good humor. "Your father was in the army, and your brother was in the navy."

"But it's different now."

"How is it different?"

"The wars we fight now are to help the rich get even richer."

"That's how it always was. You think we fought wars to help the poor?"

"No, but we fought wars to save the world."

"Oh, yah. We fought the Vietnam War and the Korean War to

save the world from the Chinese, and we fought World War II to save the world from the Germans and the Japanese. But now we buy everything from China, Germany, and Japan."

She reconsidered. "Well, maybe it isn't that different now. I just wish the kids here had more opportunities."

"I do too," he said. He sipped his coffee, and then he came out with what must have been on his mind. "I think killing your dog was a warning."

"That's what the sheriff thinks," she said.

"Now, don't get me wrong. I'm totally against the use of violence, but I do understand why people don't want a law that limits what they can do with their land."

"You mean local people."

"Yah, I don't mean outsiders."

"So they don't want a law that limits what they can do with their land. But this law only limits the sale of their land for the purpose of mining."

"If the law can limit the sale of their land for that purpose, it could limit the sale of their land for other purposes."

"That's another issue. The issue now is sand mining."

"But I understand why they might worry about the law being extended to other issues."

"Okay." She thought about it. "We could say in the law that it won't be extended to other issues. Would that satisfy them?"

"It should," Roy said. "But they have reasons for not trusting the government."

"We all have reasons for not trusting the government. But do the people you're talking about see me as the government?"

"Of course. You're an elected official."

"But they elected me."

"You won an election, but those people didn't all vote for you. And you gotta understand that they still see you as an outsider."

"I've owned land here for twenty-seven years."

"Their families have owned land here for generations, so they see you as a woman from Winona who raises goats, which isn't what most people do here."

"I understand. And I don't have a problem with local people who don't want a law that limits what they can do with their land. I have a problem with outsiders who want to mine our land and leave us with deserts."

"Yah, I have a problem with them too. But if you could satisfy the concerns of local people, you might have more support from them."

"Okay," she said. "I'll talk with Jordan, and we'll have our lawyer modify the law so it doesn't limit the sale of land for other purposes."

"Well, thanks for listening and understanding," Roy said after finishing his coffee. "If you have more support from local people, it might help the sheriff catch whoever killed your dog."

She saw him out to the driveway, where she stood and watched him wheel his truck around and head for the road. She followed the dust behind his truck, conscious of having made a commitment to modify the proposed law. She tested her decision against what she believed Devon would have done, and she was reassured.

When she thought beyond what Roy had said about how having more support from the local people might help the sheriff, she hoped it also might help him stop the outsiders from doing more to hurt her.

FOUR

ANIELA WAS SERIOUSLY religious. She went to mass not only every Sunday at noon with the family but also every weekday morning alone. She contributed her time to the church, including service as a teacher in the religious education program. And her social life revolved around the church. In fact, all her friends and acquaintances were members of the church.

She lived in the house of her mother-in-law, Babcia, which had been designed for two families. Since her husband's three sisters were married and lived in their own houses, she took over the second floor and made it her own, with pictures of Jesus and the Blessed Mother in every room as well as a shrine at the entry. Babcia, who lived with her husband on the main floor, with a bedroom and a sitting room behind the kitchen, approved of these demonstrations of faith, and she herself had commissioned a grotto in the backyard upon moving into the house of *her* mother-in-law, thirty years ago. The two women mostly got along since Aniela showed respect for Babcia, and having lost her parents in the war, she let Babcia be a mother to her. She learned to cook from Babcia, whose stuffed cabbage was rated as the best in Winona, and when there was a church function that included food, the two women worked together to make trays of this delicacy.

Lena grew up in the closed world of her family, her church, and the Polish community. She went to the elementary school that was run by the church, and she played with classmates who were approved by her mother. Whenever as a child she ventured toward the borders of this world, her mother warned her of the dangers outside and reminded her of the blessings inside, and she didn't argue with her mother. She loved her mother, and she appreciated everything her mother had done for her. But at random moments she wondered what it would be like to belong to another family, another church, and another community.

After turning fifteen she started going to Cotter, the Catholic high school in Winona. There she encountered girls and boys with Irish, German, and English names who had trouble pronouncing Magdalena Jaszewski, so with them she used her nickname, Lena, which they could handle. But her world still hadn't expanded much beyond the Polish community, and by her sophomore year the random moments of wondering what it would be like to escape from the confines of her world occurred more frequently.

One afternoon in late May she was walking home from school with her friend, Agnieszka, whose nickname was Aggie, when a motorcycle approached from behind them and skidded to a stop at the curb beside them. She didn't know anyone who had a motorcycle—they were very rare in Minnesota because of the weather—and remembering what her mother had said about talking with strangers, she kept walking.

"Hey, girls," a brash voice called to them. "Don't be so unfriendly."

She snuck a look at him over her shoulder. He had straight black hair combed back with pomade and smoldering black eyes. He wore a tight black tee shirt that displayed his pectorals and tight jeans that suggested unmentionable attributes. The sight of him was like striking a match in a room full of flammable vapors.

"Stay and talk with me," the guy pleaded.

Aggie turned to her, silently asking what they should do.

Since she only intended to talk with him, Lena turned and faced him, asking: "What do you want to talk about?"

"I want to talk about how beautiful you are." Evidently, he meant both of them.

"Well, if you just want to give us a line," Lena told him, "we don't have time for you."

"I don't just want to give you a line. I want to give you a ride on my bike."

Of course the idea of riding on a motorcycle with a boy, especially a stranger, was absolutely unthinkable. But somehow it got into her mind.

"Who wants to be first?" he asked them as if he assumed they both wanted a ride.

She exchanged a look with Aggie, who shook her head, and she almost declined the invitation when the guy appealed to her with his eyes, and whatever was in them went directly to her heart. Against her mother's admonitions and against her own judgment, she said: "I do. But I only want to go around the block."

"Okay," the guy said happily. "That's enough to give you a taste of it."

"You're not really going to do it, are you?" Aggie asked her.

"Yah, why not? It's only a ride on a motorcycle."

"But it's dangerous."

She knew it was dangerous, but that was why it appealed to her. And the guy was like no one she had ever seen before. From what she had seen in movies, she guessed he was Italian.

"Sit here," he told her, indicating the back of the seat.

Since she was in her school uniform, she had to hike up her skirt in order to straddle the seat, and when she lowered her bottom onto it there was nothing between her and the seat but her panties. The seat was warm as if someone else had just been sitting on it.

Though the kickstand was down, he put a hand on her shoulder to make sure the motorcycle didn't tip over. Then he folded down the right footrest with the tip of his boot, saying: "Put your right foot here."

She did what he said.

Still with a hand on her shoulder, he walked around behind her and folded down the left footrest, saying: "Put your left foot here."

Again, she did what he said.

He gracefully slung a leg over the driver's area, sat down, and revved the engine.

"What do I hold on to?" she asked.

"Hold on to me. Put both arms around my waist and hold on tight."

She did, smelling the pomade on his hair, which at the back of his head was cut in what they called a duck's ass.

"Okay. Hold on."

She tightened her hold, feeling his hard abdominal muscles.

The motorcycle took off, and space opened up between them. She held on for dear life, already regretting her decision to go for a ride with him but at the same time feeling a thrill that she had never known before.

As they approached the end of the block he said: "When I turn, don't lean. Just hold yourself steady."

Feeling as if she was in a state of hypnosis, in which she would do whatever he said, she held herself steady as the motorcycle leaned into a turn. She prayed that it wouldn't lean so much that they scraped the pavement.

The next turn was easier, and she was beginning to enjoy riding a motorcycle.

On the straightaway he accelerated, and then before the next turn he braked harder than the first two times, and her body was thrown against his. She was aware of her breasts being squeezed against him, and she was glad he couldn't see her face.

"Sorry," he told her. "I forgot we're only going around the block."

"It's okay," she said with mixed feelings. Part of her suspected he had done it deliberately, and another part of her hoped he would do it again.

When they stopped at the point where they had started, he did do it again, and she let herself be squeezed against him.

He lowered the kickstand and politely helped her get off.

Aggie was there waiting for them, and she looked as if she was giving thanks that Lena had come back safely.

"You want to try it?" the guy asked her.

"Oh, no," she said definitely.

There was a silence during which the guy didn't seem to know what to do next. He finally said: "I'm Carlo. What's your name?"

"Lena," she told him after a moment of hesitation.

"If you want to take a longer ride, I can meet you on Saturday morning."

Aggie shook her head in warning, but Lena finally ignored her and said: "Okay. Where can me meet?"

"Here," he said. "I mean, if that's convenient for you."

"Yah, that's fine. What time?"

"Around ten?"

"Okay," she said, already wondering what she was going to tell her mother. Of course she couldn't tell her the truth, but she had virtually no experience lying to her mother.

She stood on the sidewalk with Aggie, watching Carlo roar away. It looked as if he was gunning the motorcycle to make a lasting impression on her.

"You're crazy," Aggie said. "You don't know anything about that guy."

"I know his name is Carlo, and I think he's Italian."

"But he could take you anywhere, and you wouldn't have any control over him."

"I'd like to go anywhere," she said as if she was in a trance. "And I wouldn't mind not having any control over him."

Aggie sighed. "Well, what are you going to tell your mother?"

"I don't know. I guess I'll have to tell her I'm doing something with you."

"You expect me to cover up for you?"

"I'd cover up for you."

"But I wouldn't ever do anything like this."

"You might. You never know."

Since Aggie agreed to cover up for her, she told her mother she was going to help her friend on a school project the next day. And her mother believed her, which made her feel bad. For a moment she wished she had the kind of mother who wouldn't worry about her daughter going for a ride on a motorcycle with a stranger, but then she felt worse for making such a wish, and she took it back.

The next day she arrived punctually at the spot where they had agreed to meet, and when he didn't show up after ten minutes she felt relieved—and disappointed. She wondered if he had only seen her as a dull girl in a Catholic school uniform who needed shaking up. She was about to head home when she heard his motorcycle in the distance, and she was greatly cheered by the sound. It promised a day of adventure.

"I'm sorry," he told her, skidding to a stop. "I had to do something for my mother."

"That's okay," she said, reassured by his being the kind of guy who would do something for his mother. It didn't go with his rebel appearance.

She waited for him to fold down the footrests, and then she mounted. Today she was wearing jeans, so she had more than her panties between her and the seat. She put both arms around his waist and braced herself for takeoff, feeling like an experienced rider.

They blasted off, and then they headed out of town.

"Where are we going?" she shouted to him.

"Wherever the road takes us," he shouted over his shoulder.

The road took them along the river, going north, into country she had never seen before. It wound around bluffs, so there were long curves that the motorcycle leaned into, and there were straightaways where they raced at high speed. They reached a wide body of water, which he said was Lake Pepin, and they slowed down going through the towns of Wabasha and Lake City and Red Wing and Hastings. And finally in the distance was the skyline of St. Paul, dominated by the green-tinged dome of the cathedral.

After crossing a high bridge they spent about a half hour exploring downtown, and they stopped to have lunch at a diner that was made of a former railroad car. When they finished eating it was already two in the afternoon, so she suggested that they head home.

Near Lake City he turned off the highway and went up a road to a hillside park, where they stopped to rest. The park overlooked Lake Pepin, the sun was benign, and the grass was soft, and after lying there for a while he rolled toward her and kissed her.

She had never been kissed by a boy before, and she found herself in a situation where she didn't have any control, at least until he slid his hand under her top.

"No," she told him, removing his hand. "You can't do that."

"What can I do?" he wanted to know.

"You can kiss me again. But that's it. And then you have to get me home."

He kissed her again, and he made it last as if he might never have the opportunity again.

She went along with him, forgetting what time it was.

By the time she got home it was after six, and even before she entered the house she knew she was in trouble.

She was met in the hallway by Babcia, who sternly demanded: "*Gdzie byłeś?*"

"I was with my friend Agnieszka," she lied.

"No, you weren't. Your mother called her house, and her mother said you weren't there. She said she hadn't seen you all day."

She stopped to think. She realized that it was good thing that Babcia was there to greet her since she would rather have been caught in a lie by her grandmother than by her mother. Now she would have to admit the truth or make up another lie.

"*Więc gdzie byłaś?*"

Unable to think of any lie that would stand a chance of being believed, she finally admitted: "I went for a ride with a guy on a motorcycle."

"You what?" Babcia said, with a look of disbelief.

"I went for a ride with a guy on a motorcycle," Lena repeated.

"I heard you the first time. Who was the guy?"

"It was no one you know."

"Well, that's the problem. You're not supposed to do anything with guys we don't know. And you're not supposed to ride around on motorcycles. So how do you explain it?"

"I can't explain it. I guess I just felt like doing something different."

"It was certainly different, what you did. I assume you know that your mother was worried sick about you."

"I'm sorry," Lena said, beginning to cry at the thought that she had upset her mother.

"You should have considered how much it would worry your mother," Babcia said, wagging a finger. "And what if something had happened to you? What if you'd had an accident?"

"I didn't think about that. I mean, I knew he was a good driver."

"How did you know he was a good driver? Did you go on rides with him before?"

"Only once, around the block."

Babcia shook her head in despair, muttering things in Polish and ending with the statement: "I always thought you were a sensible girl, but now I wonder."

At that moment her mother appeared, rushing down the stairs with a look of joyful relief in her eyes. "Thank God you're all right. I've been praying to the Blessed Mother, and she answered my prayers."

"I'm sorry," Lena told her, really meaning it.

Her mother threw her arms around her and held her tight, saying: "Thank God, thank God."

Lena cried her heart out, sobbing: "I'm sorry. I'm sorry."

Her mother never asked her where she had been. The only thing that mattered to her was that her daughter was home safe. Her father, who hadn't known she was missing, never asked her about it. But from then on she was under the power of Babcia, who had something on her, and when Carlo invited her for a ride a few days later when she was on her way home from school, she regretfully declined, and she never saw him again.

On weekends Heather was off, and the milking was done by two high-school students, Tara and Lori, who were members of 4H. For her 4H project Tara raised Angora goats, and Lori raised Himalayan rabbits. They were both planning to study animal husbandry at the university and return to their family farms, though Lena wondered if they would want to return after getting a taste of the Twin Cities.

They had finished the morning milking on Saturday when the man who helped her with maintenance arrived. His name was Otto, and during the week he did maintenance for the assisted living facility in Passau. He came every Saturday, and always spent a few hours working for her since he always found something that needed repairing or painting. Today it was the gate to the compound of the bucks, which they had butted to the point where it would almost no longer prevent them from getting to the does.

Otto was a short, compact man who could probably beat a man

twice his size in a fight, but he wasn't aggressive. Somehow he let people know not to mess with him. A veteran of Vietnam, like so many guys in the county who had grown up poor, he had learned a lot about machinery during his military service, and he was especially useful in maintaining the milking equipment.

"I'm sorry about your dog," he told her. "He was a good one."

"Yah, he was. I have a new one who I hope will be as good." She led him through the gate to the compound and introduced him to Brady.

As they continued walking toward the buck shed, he asked: "What kind of people would kill a dog in cold blood?"

"People who don't like me."

"Everyone likes you. I mean, everyone who knows you likes you."

"Well, I should have said people who don't like my position on the sand mining."

"You're on the right side. If they mine these valleys, we'll have nothing but deserts." He lived in Eden Valley, in a shack that a previous owner of the land had built years ago for weekends of hunting and fishing. The land was now owned by a doctor at Mayo who had granted Otto rights to the shack for his lifetime. And though he lived in a humble dwelling, Otto loved the valley as much as Lena did.

She left him at the buck shed, and she spent the rest of the day doing chores around the house and updating the books on her business.

On Sundays she went to church, either at St. Mary's in Passau or at St. Stan's in Winona. Since it was about forty minutes to Winona and only about fifteen minutes to Passau, she usually went to St. Mary's, but she tried to make it to St. Stan's at least once a month, and this Sunday she was overdue at St. Stan's, so while Tara and Lori were still working with the goats she left for Winona, planning to attend the ten o'clock mass.

It was a pleasant drive, mostly over farmland, and calmed by the peaceful scenery, she pushed the issue that divided her community to the back of her mind, and she enjoyed the journey.

When she came to the bluff that overlooked the city of Winona, the majestic dome of the Basilica of St. Stanislaus Kostka was the first thing she noticed on the skyline, and it made her recall some family history.

Her great-grandfather, who along with two brothers and one sister had fled from the Prussian takeover of their homeland in the 1860s, contributed his carpentry skills in building the first church on that site in the early 1870s. The church served the community of immigrants who belonged to an ethnic group that was closely related to the Polish but was also separate. They were known as Kashubians, and at that time they were the dominant local group of immigrants from Poland, a country that had been totally dismantled by the empires around it but still existed in the hearts and minds of its people.

The church was rebuilt in the 1890s to meet the growing needs of the community, with room for as many as eighteen hundred people, and when Lena had her First Communion in the mid-1950s the church was filled with people, many of whom spoke Polish or a Kashubian dialect of Polish. The mass was still in Latin then, but after Vatican II there was always a mass in Polish as well as two in English: three masses on Sundays, two on Saturdays, and one on weekdays. Now, with the shortage of priests and the dispersion of the community, St. Stan's was merged with St. John's, which had served the Czech community, and there was one mass at St. Stan's on Sundays, one on Saturdays, and one on weekdays except Mondays, with one at St. John's on Sundays.

Lena arrived at the church about ten minutes early, and she went to the pew where her family had sat, the fifth pew from the front on the left side. She genuflected and then took the place next to the aisle, kneeling to say a prayer of thanks before she settled onto the pew. To her left, there was no one sitting in the pew, where there had once been her grandmother, her mother, her father, her husband, and her two children. At that time they always went to the twelve o'clock mass, which was in English, instead of the ten o'clock mass, which was in Polish, since her husband and her children didn't understand Polish, and her grandmother could manage all right in English. From the time they were babies, Patty and Brenda went to mass with the family, and they were always at her side here until they went away to college. Once a month Devon served as the reader, and listening to his voice she was always inspired, as were other women in the congregation, who said he would have made a good priest. She smiled now, remembering this comment. Though she could imagine Devon as a priest, she felt that he had contributed more as a poet, a teacher, a husband, and a father.

Now, being the only person in the pew, she was conscious of how few people there were in the vast space of the basilica, which had once been filled by the Polish community, and she was concerned about the future of this church. By the time of the procession there were more people, mostly behind her, and she was encouraged by the sound of a family talking in Spanish.

Responding to the introductory phrases from the organ, she rose to sing the hymn for the procession, and when the music ended, along with the priest she began the mass by making a deliberate sign of the cross.

When people who didn't practice a religion asked her what she got out of going to mass, she said it nourished her. And today was no exception. When the mass was ended and she moved down the aisle, behind an old couple who could have been remnants of the Polish community, she felt renewed and ready to deal with whatever might happen. She thanked the priest, shaking his hand, and went out into the bright day.

Since the mass ended at eleven, she usually walked around for a while and then went to a Greek restaurant, where she had brunch. It wasn't part of her family tradition, it was something new, which she had started doing with Devon. Her family never ate at restaurants, and after church they had Sunday dinner, which usually included kielbasa, sauerkraut, pierogi, ham, stuffed cabbage, and pickled beets. They sat at the big round dining table: her grandparents, her parents, an uncle and aunt, two cousins, her brother Tony (whose actual name was Antonin, just as her actual name was Magdalena), and herself. They ate heartily, and they made a lot of noise, especially when the subject was politics. They all agreed that America shouldn't have let the Russians have Poland at the end of World War II, but they disagreed about tactics. Her father, who had served as a tank commander, usually argued that we should have kept moving our forces eastward to stop the Russians. Of course, her grandparents and parents talked in Polish, so she and her brother and her cousins were immersed in that language. In fact, it was Lena's first language since her mother had arrived at the end of the war as a displaced person without speaking a word of English, and she retained a heavy accent even after she gained some fluency in English.

Her family's house was only a few blocks from St. Stan's, and without any intention she walked there. On the outside it hadn't changed much, except that it had been painted carefully in different colors to accentuate its Victorian features, but on the inside it had been remodeled to create two condos, which were occupied by young professionals. She stood there remembering how Devon helped her remove the stuff accumulated by four generations of her family after her father passed away. Her father outlived her mother by ten years, during which time she saw him almost every day since he kept going to work at the lumberyard and she kept working in the office. She was there on the day when he had the heart attack that killed him, and she went with him in the ambulance to the hospital. It was the same floor where she had said goodbye to her mother, who had died of cancer. Her mother's last words were a blessing.

She turned away from her family's house and headed for the restaurant with her mind on the present. She wasn't worried about whether Tara and Lori would take good care of the goats since they loved animals and had experience raising animals. And she wasn't worried about anything happening to them since they weren't on the county board. She was only worried about what the people who had killed her dog would do next.

She entered the restaurant and took the booth that the hostess indicated. A waitress brought her tea and a menu, which had so many items it was hard to believe they had what was needed to cook them all. She perused the menu, thinking she might have something different, but she finally had the usual, eggs Benedict.

As she sipped her tea she thought about Neil with his electric fence, his two German shepherds, and his AR-15. She could imagine having an electric fence, though it would take a while for her goats to get used to it, and she could imagine having two German shepherds, though it would take a while for Brady to get used to them. But she couldn't imagine having an AR-15. She had never even fired a pistol, and since there had never been hunters in her family, the only member who had fired a weapon was her brother Tony, who had fired the guns of his fighter plane in Vietnam.

The thought of Tony made her miss him. After getting out of the navy he became a commercial pilot with Braniff and flew its routes to Latin America until it went bankrupt. He then flew these routes for Eastern until it went bankrupt, and he finally flew them for American. While flying for Braniff he met a young woman from Argentina who was working as a flight attendant on the route from Buenos Aires to Lima. They were married in Buenos Aires and that became his base, though the airlines he worked for had bases elsewhere. He retired two years ago, but he still had his own small plane, which he flew under contract with business executives and used for travel to a country place in the province of Cordoba. He was fluent in Spanish, and his two children both spoke Spanish as a first language, though he and his wife made sure they also learned English. Before he retired, he got Lena a free trip to Buenos Aires, and it was an amazing experience. But the flight took fourteen hours, with a stop in Sao Paulo, and he wouldn't get free trips anymore, so her only hope of seeing him was if he came for a visit to Minnesota, which he had done for their parents' funerals and for Patty's wedding.

After lingering over a second cup of tea she asked for the bill, paid it, tipped the waitress, and headed home. In the compound she was greeted by Brady, who rushed to her as if he was seeking recognition for the good job he had done in her absence, and she petted him gratefully. She made the rounds, and finding everything in order, she silently thanked Tara and Lori. They would come back in a few hours for the evening milking, but in the meantime she had the place all to herself, and she decided to go and sit on her deck with a book.

The deck was at the back of the house, facing the woods, which had grown over the spot where the fishing shack had been. In the shade of the tall trees the deck was a cool retreat during the summer. She had central air in the house, but she rarely used it, not only because she hated using energy for that purpose but also because she had trouble breathing the air that the system produced. When she was growing up, no one had air conditioning. It wasn't in cars, it wasn't in stores, and it wasn't in restaurants. It came first to the movie theaters, and then it gradually spread elsewhere. Devon was the one who had wanted it in the house, and she had gone along with him.

She was partly reading, partly dozing, when the phone rang. She got up and answered it, thinking it might be Patty, calling early. Patty always called her on Sundays around seven, which was eight Eastern time. By then Patty had done the dishes and cleaned up after feeding her husband and her children. She never missed calling on Sunday, and it was one of the things in her life that Lena could depend on.

It wasn't Patty, it was Heather, who said: "How're you doing?"

"I'm doing fine. I went to church in Winona today."

"How was Winona?"

"The same as usual. I had brunch at the Greek restaurant."

"They make a good club sandwich. It has real turkey instead of that yucky roll."

"I should try that sometime."

There was a pause, and then Heather said: "Well, I just called to make sure you're all right. I mean, I worry about you."

"I'm all right." She sensed that Heather wanted to talk, so she opened a subject that was on her mind. "Do you know Neil Krasnik?"

"I know who he is. He's a lawyer, isn't he?"

"Yah. He has an office in Passau."

66

"He did some legal work for my parents, something about the deed to their house."

"He's also a member of the county board."

"Oh, yah. I voted for him."

"So far he's with us on the sand mining issue. And you know what he has to protect himself? He has an electric fence, two German shepherds, and an AR-15."

"He has an assault weapon?" Heather said as if she was shocked.

"It's the weapon they use in mass shootings, isn't it?"

"Yah. It's the weapon of choice."

"Well, I don't want to live in a world where we need assault weapons to protect ourselves."

"I don't either. But I think it's becoming that kind of world. I mean, we have a mass shooting every week."

"So we could solve the problem by arming ourselves with assault weapons?"

"We could according to the gun manufacturers. If we all had assault weapons, then no one would dare to attack us."

"It would be like it was when I was a kid. We had nuclear weapons, and then Russia got nuclear weapons, so we got more nuclear weapons, and Russia did too, until between us we had enough nuclear weapons to destroy the world. And because we both had so many weapons, we didn't dare to attack each other."

"Maybe it'll be like that with assault weapons."

"Maybe it will. But of course there's another solution."

"There is? What?"

"Love and let live."

There was another pause. "Yah, that would work if people tried it. The problem is, they won't try it. They have too much fun killing each other."

"But if they tried it, they'd have even more fun loving each other."

When they ended the call she thought about what she had said, and she considered calling Arne and suggesting that he come over for the night. But she knew he would feel embarrassed if he arrived while Tara and Lori were still there tending the goats, so she put off calling him, and by the time the girls were gone it was too late.

Around seven Patty called. She gave brief reports on the children, who among other activities were going to a sports camp and learning how to play tennis. Patty was teaching a summer course at St. Catherine, the college in Yonkers where she was a professor of English literature. She taught the summer course for extra income since her husband Carmine didn't make a lot of money working for his older brother, who owned a body shop in Yonkers. When she first met him, Lena couldn't understand why Patty was attracted to him, other than physically, which she *could* understand from her fling with Carlo. Intellectually, they were worlds apart since Patty had a doctorate from St. John's University and Carmine had barely finished high school. But once she got to know him, Lena realized that he was just what her daughter needed, and as far as she could see, they had a happy marriage.

"What's happening there?" Patty asked.

"Oh, nothing much. The goats are fine." She refrained from telling Patty what had happened to Grady, even though Patty had left home years before the arrival of Grady and had only seen him during visits, so it wouldn't be a personal tragedy for her. The reason she didn't tell Patty about the dog was that she didn't want her daughter to worry, just as she hadn't told her parents about things that would have made them worry. She only said: "We're still working on the mining law."

"When is the vote?"

"July twenty-first."

"That's only about three weeks from now."

"Yah, but it seems like a long time."

"I know you're going to win the vote," her daughter said, "and when it's over, you should come and visit us."

"But who would take care of the goats?"

"You have Heather and the 4H kids. They can handle the goats for two weeks."

"You mean you're inviting me for two weeks?"

"Of course I am. You should stay long enough to make the trip worth it. And you should think about flying."

She always went by train. It took more than twenty-four hours, but it was less stressful, and the views from the train going across the country were beyond words. The only problem with the train was that the tracks were owned by the freight railroads, so the passenger trains had to pull aside and let the freight trains pass, which could add hours to the journey. "Thanks, but I'm happy with the train."

"So how about in August? The kids would be done with the sports camp, and we could all go to the beach."

The idea appealed to her, though she would have to work out the logistics. "Okay. I'll look at my calendar and let you know what would be a good time."

They talked for another ten minutes, and then they ended the conversation. After these phone calls, Lena always felt there were things she hadn't mentioned and should have mentioned, and this time wasn't any different. Still, she justified not telling her daughter about Grady on the grounds that she didn't want her to worry.

Lena was in a deep sleep when she was awakened by the cry of an animal in pain. Since things happened in the woods at night, it wasn't unusual to hear such a cry, but something told her it hadn't come from a wild animal.

She jumped out of bed and rushed to the monitor, which had multiple views including one of the compound that showed two men in balaclavas holding a goat in front of the doe shed. She immediately called the sheriff, who ordered her not to go out and confront the men but to keep watching them in the hope of spotting something that would help him to identify them. She knew he was right, but she couldn't bear doing nothing while she waited for the sheriff to arrive, and now she wished she had an assault weapon so she could go out there and spray those fucking bastards with bullets.

She didn't have much time to watch them because suddenly they stopped what they were doing, raised their heads as if to listen, and then bolted out of the compound. The monitor showed them running to a car, which was parked in her driveway with its front heading out, and in almost no time they were roaring out of her driveway. At the road they turned left as if they knew that the sheriff would be coming from the right, and they sped away.

When the sheriff arrived, within fifteen minutes of the time she had called him, the only sign of the two men was the dust from their car lingering over the road. She had already gone into the compound, where the first thing she encountered was Brady, curled up in a fetal position. She was relieved to find that he was still breathing, and there were no visible wounds, so they hadn't shot him. Remembering the cry of pain, she supposed that one of the men had kicked him, hard enough to knock him out and maybe break a rib.

She stayed with him until he was conscious, and with her hand gently but firmly on his back she told him not to move. He seemed to understand, and he lay there whimpering in pain. She tried to comfort him, saying: "It's all right, it's all right."

She was still at his side when the sheriff and his deputy came through the gate.

"Did they shoot him?" Earl asked her.

"I don't think so. I think they kicked him."

"What the fucking hell!" the deputy exclaimed. He had continued walking toward the doe shed.

It got her attention, so she left Brady and rushed to where the deputy was standing over the body of a doe. There was blood all around her.

"Oh, my God," she cried. "What did they do to her?"

"It looks like they cut her throat," the deputy said, kneeling beside her.

Ignoring the blood, she knelt beside the fallen doe, whom she immediately recognized. "Oh, my God, it's Tulia."

"They killed her," the deputy said.

"My poor baby," she sobbed, stroking her back.

"I'm sorry," Earl said as if he understood how she felt.

"She was a stubborn creature," Lena cried, "but she was my

favorite. Maybe because she was so much like me."

After a moment of respectful silence, Earl asked: "Did you see them on your monitor?"

"Yah. I didn't see what they did to Tulia, but I saw them in the compound. They were wearing balaclavas."

"That figures. They're professionals, and they knew you have cameras. Did you notice anything else about them?"

"No, not really. Except that they were men."

"How do you know they were men?"

"I know because women wouldn't do such things."

"There've been women suicide bombers," the deputy quietly pointed out.

"They were victims of terrorism," Lena said. "They weren't acting on their free will."

"I'll go with your instincts," Earl said. "Well, there's no point in calling Vern, unless you want him to look at your dog."

"Let's see how he is," she said, her attention back on Brady. She walked to where she had left the dog lying on his side. It was as if he was still obeying her order not to move. He was breathing regularly, and he was no longer whimpering in pain. She knelt down beside him and gently asked: "How are you doing?"

His tail flickered.

"If they kicked him," Earl said, "they could have broken a rib or two."

"Then I shouldn't move him. But I can't leave him here."

"I'll call Vern. I haven't bothered him for a while at this time of night. And he knows what happened to your last dog."

Unlike everyone else, the sheriff was able to get mobile phone service in the valley, and he called the vet and explained the situation. After ending the call he reported: "He said he'll be here in about twenty minutes, so let's have a look at your videos."

She repeated her order to Brady not to move, and then she led the sheriff and his deputy into her house and upstairs to the living area. The deputy, who was in his late twenties, seemed to know about surveillance systems, and the sheriff deferred to him. Like a kid going to a machine that played video games, the deputy went to the monitor and began playing with it.

"I don't know shit about that stuff," the sheriff said. "But he acts like he was born with it."

After a while the deputy said: "We have nothing of their faces, and they covered the license plate of their car with a piece of cardboard."

"What kind of car was it?" the sheriff asked.

"A Toyota Camry."

"Can you tell the color?"

"It looks like black or dark blue. If we work with the video, we can determine the color."

"Anything particular about the car?"

"It has a dent near the right tail-light."

"Does the tail-light work?"

"Yah, there's light. But the dent is recognizable."

"It's possible that someone repaired the light without pounding out the dent."

"They don't pound out dents anymore," the deputy said. "They replace the whole unit."

"No wonder we buy everything from China," the sheriff said. "No one in this country knows how to do anything."

"Well, pounding out dents isn't exactly high-skilled labor."

"It takes some skill, but replacing a whole unit?" The sheriff shook his head. "Okay. Can you send the videos to our office?"

"Sure, but I need a time period."

"When did you wake up?" the sheriff asked her.

"Around three," Lena said.

"We got here around three fifteen, so send all the videos from two until three fifteen."

"Okay," the deputy said. He added: "I have a video of a man kicking your dog."

Lena looked over his shoulder while he played the scene again, which showed Brady challenging the men and then being kicked. She was proud of him, but she felt bad about putting him in a situation that exposed him to injury and even death.

It made her wonder where the vet was, and when she looked

out she saw his van in the driveway. He must have arrived while they were absorbed in the videos. Since he knew his way around, he must have gone straight to the compound.

"Vern's here," she said. "I'll go out and see how he's doing."

"Okay. We'll join you in a minute."

She found the vet kneeling by the dog. He was a tall angular man in his late fifties, with thinning hair that was still blond and placid blue eyes. Like Arne, he was of Norwegian descent, with the common last name of Olson. He wasn't the only vet in the region, but he was the only one she trusted with her animals.

"How is he?" she asked, kneeling beside him.

"He'll be okay. He could have a broken rib or two. I'll know from an X-ray."

"Will you take him with you now?"

"Yah. He'll be safer with me."

She felt that with this remark he was somehow blaming her for what had happened, though she knew he strongly supported her on the mining issue.

"I'm sorry," he said. "I didn't mean to be critical. You take good care of your animals. But you *are* exposing them to harm."

"You saw what they did to Tulia?"

"Yah. It looked like she was the victim of a blood sacrifice."

The image resonated strongly with her. "Well, I don't want my animals to be the victims who redeem our community."

"I don't either. And I don't want *you* to be the victim, though I guess you already are the victim, indirectly."

"So what should I do to protect my animals?"

"I think you should hire an armed guard, at least until the board votes on your law."

"That's three weeks from now."

"Well, the cost of a guard would be offset by a reduction in vet costs."

His wry humor helped to detach her from the emotions that had boiled up in response to the latest attack. "Okay. I'll think about it."

After helping him put Brady in the back of his van, which served as a kind of ambulance, she went into the house, where Earl and his deputy had just finished with the monitor. While the deputy was making some adjustments in the machine, she took Earl aside and asked: "Do you think I need an armed guard?"

"I advised you to get one after they killed Grady, but you wouldn't consider it."

"Well, I'm considering it now."

"Why? Because they killed your favorite doe?"

"Because Vern advised it."

Earl cocked his head. "You mean his advice carries more weight than mine?"

"No. It's a second opinion, which supports your advice."

"I thought hiring an armed guard was against your principles."

"It still is. But I guess I have to bend them."

"I understand," the sheriff said, looking at her with empathy. "I assume you want him only until the vote on your law."

"Yah, after that they wouldn't have any reason to hurt me."

"Unless they want to get revenge."

Having considered this possibility in her conversation with Jordan, she said: "That's possible, but it's not likely. I mean, if these guys are professionals they're only doing it for money. And whoever's paying them won't pay them to get revenge."

The sheriff nodded as if he agreed. "So you need an armed guard for about three weeks. Do you need him round the clock?"

"No. I only need him from the time we finish the evening milking to the time we start the morning milking—from eight-thirty in the evening until six-thirty in the morning."

"That's ten hours a day. And it would be seven days a week, right?"

"Right. How much do you think he'd charge per hour?"

Earl shrugged. "Depends on who you get. You could probably get a dumb kid to do it for ten dollars an hour. But if you want someone with experience, you'll have to pay as much as thirty an hour, especially since there's risk involved."

"I'd do it for thirty an hour," the deputy offered. He had drifted over and evidently heard the last part of their conversation.

"You're not allowed to moonlight," the sheriff told him.

"I wasn't serious. I saw what they did to that poor doe, and I don't want to end up like that."

"I have someone in mind," the sheriff said. "He served in Iraq, and he's had trouble finding a job that pays him anything."

"Does he hang out at the Legion?"

"I assume he does, along with our other veterans. Is that a problem?"

"No, it's not. I associate with guys who hang out there. I just wondered if he was the same guy that someone else mentioned for the job."

With a knowing look, the sheriff said: "Okay. I'll see if he's interested."

Since they agreed that the men who had killed Tulia and wounded Brady had done their damage for the night, they believed that she would be all right from then until after the evening milking. It was now four thirty in the morning, and the sun would be coming up soon, so with nothing more to do at that point, the sheriff and the deputy left.

With only a half hour left before the time she usually got up, Lena didn't go back to bed. She made tea and took it to the dining table, where she sat and reflected on what had happened. She was resigned to hiring a guard, and she thought about how she might pay for him. On a piece of paper from her notepad she figured that at thirty dollars per hour it would cost her six thousand six hundred dollars for the twenty-two days remaining until the board voted. She didn't have that kind of money. In fact, she had only about three thousand dollars in her savings account, which she needed to cover occasional deficits in her cash flow. Years ago she had resisted the bank's offer for a line of credit, secured by her house, on the principle that she didn't want to owe the bank anything. But now she wished she had a line of credit, and she wondered if the bank would still be open to the idea. It occurred to her that the strategy of the people behind the attacks was to ruin her financially, either by making her pay for protection or by killing off the animals she needed in her business. And if that didn't work, they still had the option of killing her.

She had just finished drinking the tea when an uncomfortable fact emerged from the jumble of her thoughts. Somehow they had known that Tulia was her favorite doe, and they had killed her favorite doe to inflict maximum damage on her. But how had they known that Tulia was her favorite doe? The people who knew were Heather, Arne, Tara, Lori, Earl, and Vern, and she couldn't imagine any of them giving that information to a stranger. So they must have learned it by spying on her. They must have been collecting information on her since the time she began her campaign for the county board with a promise to stop the sand mining. And she wondered what else they knew about her.

FIVE

THERE WASN'T MUCH debate in her family about where Lena would go to college. It had to be a Catholic college, it had to be for women only, and it had to be close enough to home so she wouldn't have to board there, which left two possibilities: St. Theresa in Winona, and Viterbo in La Crosse. Since she didn't have a car and her father couldn't afford to buy her one, her only remaining possibility was St. Theresa, which she could walk to.

Lena was the first in her family to go to college, so her parents made a big deal of it. They had great expectations of her, though they didn't give her any clear ideas about what she should get out of college, or what career she should pursue. She had the impression that her mother wanted her to be a teacher and her father wanted her to work in his business, which supplied lumber and other building materials to contractors. But they left it open for her to decide what she wanted to do, so she didn't feel they would be disappointed if she pursued another career. She only felt they would be disappointed if she didn't do well academically.

In high school she was a solid "B" student, which wasn't bad considering all the distractions she had while going through her teens, and she figured that her parents would be satisfied if she did that well in college. She just had to choose a major that wasn't too challenging and one that might be useful if she did pursue a career in education or business. After a few meetings with her advisor she decided to major in English, which at that time was a popular major, so she figured that she couldn't go too far wrong with it.

As things turned out, her decision to major in English would have life-changing effects on her. Its first effect was to put her into a Shakespeare class with a girl who became her new best friend. The girl, who had long red hair and impish green eyes, arrived at the classroom a few minutes late. Instead of wearing the expected skirt and conservative blouse she wore black pants and a black cotton tunic, and instead of retiring quietly to the back row, she plopped herself down conspicuously in an empty desk next to Lena in the front row.

The professor had begun calling the roll, and when she came to the girl's name she had trouble pronouncing it. As if she was asking a question, she said: "Sye-oban?

"Shivahn," the girl corrected her. "It's an Irish name."

"Well, I don't speak Irish."

"I don't either, but that's my name."

When she had determined who was present and who was absent, the professor handed out a syllabus and explained what they would do in the course. There were questions from students, which included how long the papers had to be and how long she would take to grade them. Since it was a fifty-minute class, it was over by the time the professor had given them an assignment for the next class.

Emerging from the classroom, Lena found Shivahn by her side, and she introduced herself, saying: "Hi. I'm Lena."

"I'm Shivahn, the girl with a name that no one can pronounce."

"I have a last name that no one can pronounce."

"What's your last name?"

"Yashevski."

"That's not hard to pronounce."

"It is if you read it. Can you guess how it's spelled?"

"No, how is it spelled?"

"J-a-s-z-e-w-s-k-i."

"Wow. How do you get Yashevski out of that?"

"It's Polish," she said as if that explained it.

"My name is spelled S-i-o-b-h-a-n."

"How do you get Shivahn out of that?"

"It's Irish."

They both laughed.

Since they were both free until the afternoon, they went to the cafeteria, where Siobhan got a coffee and Lena got a Coke.

"This isn't good coffee," Siobhan said as they sat down at an isolated table. "But it's better than nothing. I wish they had espresso."

"What's espresso?"

"It's strong coffee in a small cup. It's what artists and writers drink."

"Do you know a lot of artists and writers?"

"I know a few, but no one famous. I'm from St. Paul, and the last famous writer to come from there was Scott Fitzgerald."

"What made you go to college here?"

"Well, I had to go to a Catholic college for women, and there's a good one in St. Paul, but my sisters went there, so I wanted to try something different."

"I had to go to a Catholic college for women," Lena said. "But I didn't have the option of going away, so that's why I'm here."

"You're from Winona?"

"I was born and raised here."

"Then you must know all the cool places."

"I don't know any cool places."

Siobhan smiled. "Then we can discover them together."

They talked until it was time to go to their next class. From the conversation, Lena learned that Siobhan was the youngest in a family with ten children that lived in the Crocus Hill area of St. Paul, attended St. Luke's Church, and went to Catholic schools. She had four older sisters and five older brothers, who were all out of college except the brother who was two years older than her. Three of her brothers were working in the family business, which supplied concrete to contractors, and one of her sisters was in the process of becoming a nun.

She also learned that Siobhan was majoring in English because she wanted to be a writer, and that she had read books that were on the list of books condemned by the Catholic Church, including novels by D.H. Lawrence, William Burroughs, Henry Miller, and Jack Kerouac. She had just finished reading *On the Road* for the second time, and she offered her copy to Lena as a present to initiate their friendship.

Siobhan had a car, which gave her a mobility that other students could only dream of, and over the next few months they did a lot of things together. They went to parties given by boys at

St. Mary's, they drove to La Crosse and went to bars, where they could drink legally since they were in Wisconsin, and they took a trip to Minneapolis and went to the pizza place in Dinkytown, near the university, where Bob Dylan had performed when he was still Bob Zimmerman.

After putting off her mother, who wanted to meet her new friend, Lena finally invited her to Sunday dinner, though not without some trepidation. Siobhan arrived in a nice dress, which she must have worn to church, and she made a good impression, at least at first. When Lena went into the kitchen between courses, her mother said: "She was raised well, and she dresses well, though her hair could be shorter."

"Long hair is the style now," Lena told her.

"Well, I hope you don't grow your hair longer."

She hadn't intended to grow her hair longer, but she was at an age when being advised not to do something made her want to do it.

All went well until the conversation after dinner. The trouble began when Babcia told about watching the television report on the anti-war demonstrations by students at the university in Madison. She said: "It was awful seeing the police beat them up."

Lena held her breath, hoping that no one would pursue this topic since it was controversial.

"The students had it coming," her father said.

"Why did they have it coming?" Siobhan asked mildly.

Her father looked at Siobhan as if she had no right to question him. "They had it coming because they're supporting the other side."

"The other side of what?"

"The other side of our war against the Russians."

"I thought we were fighting in Vietnam."

"We *are* fighting in Vietnam, but we're fighting the Russians there. Don't you know? It's a proxy war between us and the Russians."

"Maybe it is. But it's also a war of liberation for the Vietnamese people."

"A war of liberation from what?"

"From the colonial powers," Siobhan said precisely, "who have oppressed them for centuries."

"We are not a colonial power. Russia is a colonial power. Look what they're doing to the countries in Eastern Europe."

"I know what they're doing. But if that's the issue, then why don't we send our troops into Eastern Europe and drive the Russians out of there? Why are we wasting them in Vietnam?"

"We have to stop the Russians somewhere."

"Why don't we drive the Russians out of Poland?" Lena asked, entering the conversation with the hope of defusing the issue between her father and Siobhan.

Her father shook his head, saying: "A direct war with the Russia would be very destructive."

"You mean we'd use nuclear weapons?" Siobhan asked him.

"Maybe we would. But even if we didn't use nuclear weapons, a lot of people would be killed in a direct war with Russia, including a lot of civilians."

"A lot of people are being killed in this war, including a lot of civilians."

"I know they are, but—" Her father didn't complete the argument, which could have been that the civilians being killed in this war were Asians.

Siobhan looked as if she was ready to counter that argument, but instead she said: "Whoever they are, the victims of war are children of the same God."

It was a statement to end the conversation, to make peace, and Lena wondered where it had come from. She knew that Siobhan had been raised as a Catholic, but after this statement she realized that she didn't know much about her friend's personal beliefs.

Of course her parents had a long discussion about Siobhan after she left. They were in the kitchen, speaking Polish, and Lena was going back and forth from the dining room to the kitchen, clearing the table and helping them clean up. Her mother liked the girl's point about using our troops to liberate countries in Eastern

Europe instead of wasting them in Vietnam, but she didn't like her long hair. Her father liked the girl's interest in current affairs, but he didn't like her anti-war position. They had mixed feelings about whether Siobhan would have a good influence on their daughter, but they agreed to wait and see.

As their friendship developed Lena learned that Siobhan read not only secular writers but also religious writers, though most of the latter were radical in the sense that they wanted to push the church into doing more to promote peace and social justice. The most prominent among these writers was Dorothy Day, the founder of the Catholic Worker Movement. Siobhan also liked the writings of Thomas Merton, who after a turbulent youth became a Trappist monk, a social activist, and a pacifist. She especially liked his autobiography, *The Seven Storey Mountain*. And she admired Jim Forrest and Tom Cornell, who wrote for the *Catholic Worker* and founded the Catholic Peace Fellowship, a movement that was committed to non-violent opposition to the Vietnam War. It was through their involvement in the Catholic Peace Fellowship that Siobhan and Lena got into trouble.

Siobhan went home for Christmas break, but a few weeks after she returned to college the North Vietnamese launched the Tet offensive, which raised the war to another level. The anti-war movement was energized by a photograph of a South Vietnamese security official executing a Viet Cong prisoner, an image that became a rallying point for protesters. A few weeks later the government announced the highest casualty toll of the war, and Walter Cronkite, who had gone to Vietnam to see first-hand what was happening there, advised the government to negotiate for peace. In early March a friend of Siobhan from St. Paul who was attending a Catholic college came to Winona and talked with students from St. Theresa about the Catholic Peace Fellowship. By the end of that week Siobhan and Lena had formed a chapter of CPF, with only the two of them as members but with the hope of recruiting more members.

The events of that spring completely disrupted the status quo. Eugene McCarthy, who campaigned with the support of thousands of students, almost defeated President Johnson in the New Hampshire primary. Within that week Robert Kennedy announced that he would enter the Presidential race. At the end of March the President announced that he would take steps to limit the war in Vietnam, and that he had decided not to seek reelection. The following week Martin Luther King, Jr. was assassinated. Two weeks later students at Columbia University occupied several buildings to protest the university's participation in a military project. In early May students in Paris battled police, and a month later Robert Kennedy was assassinated. By then the spring semester had ended, but Lena and Siobhan still had CPF meetings, one of which resulted in a march in downtown Minneapolis to protest against the war.

With ten other students whom they had recruited from St. Theresa, Siobhan and Lena carried a banner that read: "End the War." Like the other protesters they practiced non-violence, but a few obnoxious guys in the group ahead of them disturbed the peace by squirting water at a group of hostile bystanders. That would have been harmless, but they squirted the two police officers who came to stop them. The police responded by detaining them, which was exactly what they wanted, and from there the scene degenerated to the point where a platoon of police officers surrounded the protesters.

"Take down the banner," a police officer ordered Siobhan.

"We're not doing anything wrong," Siobhan told him. "We're only exercising our right to free speech."

"I know what you're doing, but I'm ordering you to take down the banner and go away."

"You don't want people to get our message?"

"They got your message."

"Are they giving you a hard time?" another police officer asked.

"No, they're all right. They're only kids."

"We should arrest them to teach them a lesson."

"We don't have to do that. They'll do what I told them." He waited for Siobhan and Lena to take down the banner, but they resisted for a moment too long.

"We're getting their names," the other police officer said. "And if they don't cooperate, we're arresting them."

With no alternative but jail, they took down the banner and gave their names to the police. They convinced the police that they didn't need the names of the other ten girls. If they had the names of the two leaders, that was enough.

As they walked away with the rolled-up banner, Siobhan said: "We should have stood firm and made them arrest us."

"No, we shouldn't have. We protected our members. We did the right thing."

"But the leaders I admire stand firm and make the police arrest them."

"We're not at their level. I mean, we're not famous, so no one would notice if we were arrested. Except our parents."

"I have to admit, I thought of how my parents would react if they heard I was in jail."

"I did too. And I'm thinking of how my parents will react if the police contact them and tell them we were disturbing the peace."

"We weren't disturbing the peace. We were trying to make peace."

"Well, I hope our parents see it that way."

Her parents didn't quite see it that way. What they saw was their daughter misbehaving to a point where the police had to intervene, and they made her promise not to get involved in any more anti-war demonstrations. They were reassured when Siobhan came to the house and promised the same thing, and they were pleased when Lena received three A's in her courses that semester, which they correctly attributed to the influence of her friend. But until the fall of her senior year, when she got involved in another kind of relationship, they worried about what the two girls might do next.

Heather arrived the next day at the usual time for the morning milking, and she burst into tears when Lena told her about Tulia. Sobbing, she sought comfort in the arms of Lena, who summoned all her resources to console the girl.

"Those creeps," Heather cried. "To kill a sweet defenseless animal."

"They don't have hearts," Lena said.

"But who *are* they?"

"I don't know. I only know they live for money."

"You mean money from sand mining?"

"It goes beyond sand mining. It goes to fracking, and ultimately it goes to oil."

"Then they're oilmen?"

"Yah. I guess that's as good a name for them as any."

Without the antics of Tulia, the milking took a bit less time, but it was sad work without her, and Lena thought she detected a state of mourning in the body language of the does, who were certainly not dumb animals.

When Heather had left for her other job, Lena went into the house and called Vern to find out how Brady was doing. Vern wasn't there, but his assistant told her that Brady had a broken rib but was otherwise all right. She told the girl that she would come by and pick up Brady in about a half hour.

Then she called Jordan, who took a while to answer his phone. She let it ring since she didn't know what kind of message to leave.

"Sorry," he said. "I was out in the driveway saying goodbye to my family."

"Where are they going?"

"They're going to St. Paul to stay with Anna's mother until after we have the vote. I want them to be safe," he added unnecessarily.

"You heard that they killed one of my goats?"

"I heard it from Vern. He was here this morning to treat a sick cow."

"Well, he convinced me that I should hire an armed guard."

"I should do that too, but I don't have the money."

"I don't have the money either," she said. "I'm going to ask the bank for a loan."

"Have you been to the bank lately?"

"I was there a month ago."

"They have all new people there, including a smooth guy who offers money management services."

"I think they're in the wrong market. Who has money in this county?"

"Maybe they're anticipating sales of land for sand mining."

"You mean they're betting that we'll lose the vote?"

"They might know something we don't know."

"I can't imagine what. I know how you and I will vote, and I think I know how Neil will vote. Did you talk with him?"

"Yah. From what he told me, I think he expects to make more money from his real estate investments if we don't allow sand mining."

"That's what I think," Lena said. "So I don't know what the bank could be thinking."

After a pause Jordan said: "I'm meeting with Porter this afternoon. We're going to review his final draft of the law. Would you like to join us?"

"Yah, sure. Where are you going to meet with him?"

"At my place. There's no one around, so we won't have any distractions."

"What time?"

"At two."

"I'll see you then." She ended the call, seeing the meeting as an opportunity to get Porter to insert language into the law that would satisfy the concerns of her neighbor.

Since it wasn't quite ten, she had time to pick up Brady and bring him home and then go to Passau and talk with the bank before she met with Jordan, so she got her pocketbook and left the house, locking the door behind her.

When she arrived at the animal clinic Vern was still out doing rounds, so his assistant went and got Brady, bringing him in an animal carrier. The assistant told Lena she could take the carrier, and she could return it at her convenience. Lena peeked into the carrier and saw Brady, who acted very glad to see her.

She put the carrier on the passenger seat of her car and drove home, being especially careful not to hit any bumps or holes that would make Brady feel discomfort, as the doctors called it. They all seemed to have acquired this word in medical school as a euphemism for pain, and she remembered cursing the doctor who had used it to describe what Devon was feeling as his lungs were imploding.

She had thought of putting Brady in the house but decided against it because the cats would stir him up, so she made him comfortable in his doghouse, confident that the does wouldn't bother him.

Before going to the bank, she checked the phone for messages, hoping to hear from the sheriff about his progress in finding an armed guard for her, but there were no messages, so she left again and headed for Passau.

She parked her car behind the bank and entered from the back. Immediately she noticed the changes: from an open platform, they had gone to closed offices with windows framed in dark wood, which projected an upscale image. From habit she went to the corner office, where she had last talked with the manager, but instead she found a young man in a dapper gray suit with the kind of blue tie that politicians liked to wear. He had neat brown hair and engaging blue eyes, and he welcomed her into his office as if she had a trust fund.

"I'm Scott," he said, extending his hand. "I'm a personal banker."

"I'm Lena," she said, taking his hand.

They sat down in comfortable chairs that faced each other.

"Do you already have a banking relationship with us?"

"Yah, I've had one for a while." She thought back in time. "My husband and I opened accounts here twenty-seven years ago."

"What type of accounts?"

"Checking and savings. And later we opened a business account."

"What type of business do you have?"

"I raise goats, who produce milk that I make into cheese and sell to a distributor."

"Is your business doing well?"

"It's doing well enough. But lately I've been having political problems."

"Political problems?"

"I'm on the county board," she explained, "and we're about to vote on a law that will make some people unhappy. And to put it mildly, they're harassing me."

"Can you be more specific?"

"Yah, I can. They're killing my animals."

"You're kidding," he said as if he hoped she was kidding.

"So for the next three weeks I need to hire an armed guard to protect my animals. And that will cost money."

"Why only for the next three weeks?"

"Because on the third Tuesday of July we'll vote on the law, and after that they won't have any reason to hurt me."

"What's the law about?"

"Sand mining."

He looked blank.

"In this area we have rich deposits of the kind of sand they need for oil fracking. In fact, these deposits are the richest in the country. And the people who benefit from the mining are willing to pay a lot of money for our land."

"That sounds like a good thing," he said. "So what's the issue?"

"The issue is that if they mine our land, they'll turn it into a desert that no one can use for anything. They'll destroy our county."

"But they'll pay a lot of money for the land."

"They won't pay enough for the land to be restored to its natural state. And the people who get the money from them will leave us with the mess."

He shook his head slowly. "I had no idea that this was happening."

"How long have you been here?"

"Only a month. I live in La Crosse, and I commute here."

"If you live in La Crosse, you should have known it was happening. But anyway, it is. So I need a loan to pay for an armed guard."

"How much do you need?"

"About five thousand dollars."

Scott nodded. "How would you repay it?"

"With cash flow from my business. I figure I could pay you back in about three years."

"Do you have assets to pledge as collateral?"

"I have two hundred acres of land, plus a house, a milking barn, and sheds for my animals, not to mention the animals."

"Okay. Now, what do you think those assets are worth?"

"I have no idea. But I know they're worth more than five thousand dollars."

"I'm sure they are," he said with a smile. "Well, our main business isn't making loans, but since you've had a relationship with us for twenty-seven years, we'll consider it. But we'll need a cash flow and copies of titles to your property."

"I can bring you a cash flow tomorrow," she said, wondering what their main business was if it wasn't making loans. "The titles are here in a safe deposit box."

"Do you have any liquid assets?"

"Yah, I have goat milk."

He smiled. "I meant financial assets."

"I have a retirement plan with TIAA. My husband was a college professor."

"Is he retired?"

"No, he passed away ten years ago."

"I'm sorry," Scott said politely.

Far beyond responding to condolences, she said nothing, and she braced herself for being categorized as a widow.

"How is the money invested?"

"It's all in bonds."

"How much are you earning on them?"

"About four per cent."

"That's not bad, but if you let us manage your money we could do better."

"I really don't want to do better. I want to be safe."

He let it go, at least for now. "Well, if you have a fund with TIAA, you could get the money you need from them."

"I could? Would there be a penalty?"

"It depends. How old are you?"

"I'm sixty-six."

"Then you're entitled to take money out of your fund without a penalty, though you might have to pay taxes on it."

"I'll call them and ask them about it," she said, getting the impression that he didn't want to give her a loan but only wanted to manage her money.

After a pause he asked: "What kind of cheese do you make from goat milk?"

"I make goat cheese."

He smiled again. "What kind of goat cheese?"

"I make plain goat cheese, and I also make cheese in the styles of Brie, Camembert, Gouda, and Tomme."

"And you sell them to a distributor?"

"Yah. There's a market for them in the Twin Cities."

"I've never tasted goat Camembert. Is it good?"

"It's excellent. I'll bring you a button with my cash flow."

"Okay." He didn't comment further, but he looked as if he was more disposed to giving her a loan, and she wondered if he was influenced by the prospect of tasting her Camembert or the possibility of managing her retirement fund.

Driving home, she felt better about her ability to pay for the armed guard, believing that if she didn't get the money from the bank she could get it from the retirement fund. The contributions had come from Devon and his employers over almost forty years, beginning with St. John's University and ending with St. Mary's University. The accumulated balance, with annual interest, was more than she had ever imagined, but it wasn't enough to make her rich. In fact, as a young man at TIAA (whose name was also Scott) recently explained over the phone, it was only enough to provide an annual income that was slightly higher than what she received from Devon's Social Security, and following her husband's advice, she hadn't touched the retirement fund, so now when she might need it, the money was there for her.

When she got home she went to the compound to check on Brady, and he came out of his house to greet her as if there was nothing wrong with him. She patted him gently on the back and let him tag along with her while she checked on the does, who were grazing in the far pasture. She counted them going from left to right, and there were fifty-five of them, as there should have been. They all looked fine, so she headed for the house, leaving Brady in the compound.

In the kitchen she made herself a tuna sandwich which she ate at the table while reading the local weekly newspaper, which had come on Friday. It had an editorial that supported her position on sand mining, and she made a mental note to thank the woman who owned and managed the paper. Most people only read the paper for stories about their kids playing sports, and since school was out for the summer, there weren't many stories of interest to them. But if only a few people read that editorial, it would help the cause.

She filled the bowls of the cats with water, and she changed the litterbox, noticing that she was getting low on litter. She added that item to a growing list of groceries, and then she left the house for her meeting with Jordan and the lawyer.

The pickup wasn't in the driveway, which made her wonder if Jordan was home until she realized that Anna must have taken it to St. Paul. And then she wondered how he was getting around without a vehicle.

She found him in the kitchen, drinking herb tea out of a mug. The tea smelled like it had licorice in it.

"Hey," she said. "How are you doing?"

"Not so well," he said. "I miss Anna and the kids."

"I understand." When her own kids left she missed them more than she had expected, having been misled by people who said how relieved they were when their kids finally left.

"Would you like some tea?"

She knew he didn't drink anything with caffeine in it, but he had tea and coffee available for guests. "No, thanks. Where's Porter?"

"He should be here soon. Did you go to the bank?"

"I went there this morning. You were right—it's changed. I met with a young man named Scott who was more interested in managing my retirement fund than in giving me a loan. But he did give me a good idea. He said I could take money out of the retirement fund."

"Would that be better than getting a loan?"

"I don't know. I know Devon wouldn't like it. He told me not to touch the retirement fund."

"But if you can't get a loan, at least you have a backup."

At that point there was the sound of a car in the driveway, and assuming it was Porter, they got up and went to the front hall.

Porter was dressed in a suit and was carrying a briefcase that could have been a travel bag. He was a short man, with nubbly hair and slitty eyes. And he walked with purpose, like a cat going to its food dish.

Jordan welcomed him, and they sat down at the kitchen table, where Porter opened his briefcase and began handing out papers, saying: "This is my latest draft of the law. It's not my final draft, but it's almost there."

Lena began to peruse her copy, focusing on the items that were underlined, which indicated that they had been changed.

"Let's take the changes one at a time," Jordan suggested.

So they went through the changes one at a time, with Porter explaining each change. He had a flat accent, which he must have acquired during his years at Harvard Law School since he was born and raised in St. Paul. And he went into the minutest details as if he was doing an exegesis of holy scripture.

When they had finished, Lena said: "One of my neighbors, who I think is representative of the community, is worried about this law being extended to restrict uses of land other than for sand mining."

"There's no implication of that in the law," Porter said.

"Well, I think he'd be satisfied if you wrote something into the law that says it can't be extended to restrict other uses."

Porter rubbed his chin, thinking. "What I think you want is an explicit statement that the application of the law will be limited to sand mining."

"What about coal mining?" Jordan asked.

"Are there coal deposits in this region?"

"No, but I think the law should state that its application will be limited to any kind of mining, oil drilling, or extractive activity."

"I could add a statement to that effect. Would it satisfy your neighbor?"

Lena thought about it, trying to see it from Roy's perspective. "It might satisfy him, but I think the law should also state that its application will *not* be extended to commercial or residential development."

"If we say its application will be limited to any kind of mining, oil drilling, or extractive activity, then we leave land use open to commercial and residential development."

"I understand, but I want it to be absolutely clear that if people want to sell their land for that purpose, the law won't stop them."

"I wish it *would* stop them," Jordan muttered.

"Our mission isn't to stop development," Lena reminded him. "Our mission is to stop sand mining or anything that destroys the environment."

"Development destroys the environment."

"We can't go that far," Porter said. "If we do, then the law won't stand up in court, and it won't stop the sand mining."

"I know. I was only wishing."

They agreed that Porter would draft a statement to satisfy people like Roy who were afraid the law might be extended to prevent them from selling their land for commercial or residential development.

When she got home the light on the phone was blinking, and there was a message from the sheriff, who said: "The guy I told you about is interested. His name is Rodney. I think you can get him for twenty an hour. I told him to be at your place by five since you do the milking at six thirty. After you've met him, call me and let me know how it went."

It was four thirty, so she didn't have much time to prepare questions for an interview. Without much thought she decided that the main qualifications for the job, besides being able to use a weapon effectively, were reliability, loyalty, and trustworthiness. If the guy had those three qualifications, then she could accept his hanging out at the Legion. After all, she could accept her boyfriend's hanging out at the Legion.

When an old car rattled into her driveway at quarter to five, she assumed it was Rodney, demonstrating the virtue of punctuality. She went out and met him, immediately struck by how young he looked, like the guys from Fort McCoy who sometimes appeared on the streets of La Crosse. They were so young, it made her want to cry.

He was medium height and wiry, with brown hair probably as short as it had been during his military service. In his eyes there was evidence of an invisible wound.

"Hi, I'm Rodney," he said, offering his hand. "Are you Mrs. McLean?"

"Yah. You can call me Lena."

"I'm pleased to meet you," he said as they shook hands. "The sheriff told me you're looking for an armed guard."

"I am, and he recommended you."

"I have some experience as a security guard, mainly at stores. And I served for three years in the military."

"Then I assume you can use a weapon effectively."

"What kind of weapon do you have in mind?"

"A pistol, a rifle, or—" She hesitated.

"I have an assault weapon if that's what you have in mind."

"Do you have experience with it?"

"It's the same kind of weapon we used in the military."

"I guess it was a dumb question. Then maybe that's the weapon you should use."

"I'm also good with a rifle. I used to hunt rabbits when I was a kid."

"Whatever you feel would be most effective." She paused and then asked: "Did the sheriff tell you why I need protection?"

"He told me there are guys who come here in the night and kill your animals."

"That's what they do. And they're not bothered by surveillance cameras."

"Can you tell me how many guys there are?"

"So far there've been only two, but there could be more the next time."

"Then I better use my assault weapon."

She wanted to ask him questions that would test his reliability, loyalty, and trustworthiness, but she couldn't think of any, so she finally relied on her instincts, his military service, and the sheriff's recommendation. When she offered him the job, at twenty dollars an hour, he looked elated, and he said he was ready to start that evening. He only had to go home and get his assault weapon, which he didn't keep in the trunk of his car.

As she watched his car leave the driveway she felt relieved of a major anxiety, but at the same time she was disturbed by the realization that she was exploiting this young man, using the skills that he had acquired at a terrible cost and also putting his life in danger.

SIX

THERE WAS TALK of a merger between St. Theresa and St. Mary's, which would have created a co-educational Catholic university. Most of the students at both colleges were in favor of it, especially the girls at St. Theresa, who believed that the rules at St. Mary's governing student behavior were not as strict as the rules they had to live under. There was also the prospect of being in a classroom with boys, which some of them had never experienced. While the discussions were under way, the two institutions began to share faculty resources, so if one of them had an outstanding professor in some area, students from both would have access to him—in those days it was usually a man. So it happened that at the urging of Siobhan, who always seemed to know what was happening at the other college, Lena enrolled in a course at St. Mary's in the fall of her senior year. It was a course in her major, on the Romantic Poets, and it was being held in a classroom there. According to Siobhan, the professor was one of the best in the field, he was from New York, and he had taught at St. John's University.

On a warm day in early September, which still felt like summer, the two friends walked to the St. Mary's campus and found the building where the class was being held. When they entered the classroom they weren't disappointed to find that they were the only two girls in a class of about twenty students. Lena was conscious of being checked out as they headed for desks in the front row, which was empty. It looked as if boys preferred the back rows in classrooms.

As they waited for the professor, the boys behind them bantered away, and from the words that Lena caught, the topics were sports, cars, and girls. It made her anxious having all those boys behind her, with an unprotected view of the back of her head, and more than once she reached back with her right arm and made sure that her hair was in order. She had let it grow long, like Siobhan's hair, and it fell below her shoulders.

She was reaching back when a man suddenly entered the room, carrying a portfolio. At the sight of this man, who was evidently the professor, her arm froze and her heart stopped. He was by far the most attractive man she had ever seen, and she lost her mental balance when in passing by her on his way to the desk at the front of the classroom he glanced at her.

He stopped behind the desk and stood for a moment surveying the class. He was dressed in black pants and a black turtle-neck, which almost made him look like a priest. He had a trim body, without the slightest trace of a bulge where other men had bellies. And when he turned to look at the clock above the blackboard, she could tell from the way he filled the seat of his pants that there were muscles instead of flab.

"Hello," he finally said. "I'm your professor. My name is Devon McLean, and you can call me Professor McLean, Dr. McLean, or Professor, but you can't call me Devon or Hey-you. Is that clear?"

There were murmurs of assent.

From his accent Lena could tell that he was indeed from New York, having heard it from actors in the movies.

"I see we have two students from St. Theresa," he said, looking at her and Siobhan, "so I expect you guys to act like gentlemen, even if you're not."

She bowed her head to avoid engaging with his tender brown eyes.

"Now, I'll tell you what we're going to do in this class. We're going to read poetry, and we're going to learn to appreciate it. We're going to study the poetry of a group that we call the Romantics, not because they were romantic in the sense that we use the word today, but because they had a different view of the world than the previous generation. They lived at a time of social upheaval, like the present time, and we'll see in their poetry how they dealt with what was happening."

She listened, spellbound by his voice. She wouldn't have had to see him, she only would have had to hear his voice to be overwhelmed by him.

"I'll give you the syllabus," he said, opening his portfolio. He took out some papers, and since Lena was sitting closest to him, he took a few steps and handed them to her, asking: "Please pass these around, okay?"

"Okay," she said in a faint voice. Keeping a copy for herself, she passed the syllabi to Siobhan. She noticed that unlike the syllabi of other faculty, his syllabus was only two pages. There were no exams, but there were weekly papers and weekly discussions.

"I don't believe in exams," he said as the syllabi went around the class. "I don't want you to cram your heads with useless facts. I want you to demonstrate that you know how to read a poem, and that you can explain it to each other as well as to me, so you're going to write papers, and you're going to have discussions."

She liked the approach. She was good at writing papers and good at discussions, but she hated exams, which for her were instruments of torture.

He went over the syllabus, and he gave them their first assignment, which was to read a poem by Wordsworth and write a paper on it, following a process that was in the syllabus. And then, to get them started, he recited the following lines:

The clouds that gather round the setting sun
Do take a sober coloring from an eye
That hath kept watch o'er man's mortality;
Another race hath been, and other palms are won.
Thanks to the human heart by which we live,
Thanks to its tenderness, its joys and fears,
To me the meanest flower that blows can give
Thoughts that do often lie too deep for tears.

In the silence that followed, Lena felt that a whole new world had been opened for her, and it wasn't only the world of poetry.

As they walked out of the building Siobhan said: "I think you have a crush on him."

"Why do you think so?"

"I could feel your vibrations."

"Well, I do like him."

"I like him too. And I think it'll be a great course."

"Do you think he noticed me?"

"Sure, he noticed you. He gave you the syllabi to pass around."

"He only did that because I was sitting closest to him."

"It wasn't only that," Siobhan said. "I saw how he looked at you."

"How did he look at me?"

"He looked at you as if he liked you."

"Well, I didn't see how he looked at me. I didn't want him to know how I felt."

"I think he could guess how you felt. He's had experience with women."

"How can you tell?"

"I can tell by looking at him."

They walked in silence for a while, and then Lena asked: "Do you think he's married?"

"I don't think so. He doesn't wear a ring." Siobhan always noticed things like that, while Lena hadn't looked to see if he wore a ring.

"How old do you think he is?"

"About thirty."

"So he's ten years older."

"That's all right."

"I guess it is. My father's ten years older than my mother. But he was in a war," Lena added as if that explained the age difference.

"Professor McLean might have been in a war."

"You mean in Vietnam?" she said. "It's possible. But I have a feeling he wasn't there."

"We'll find out soon enough," Siobhan said. "If he was in Vietnam, he'll tell us war stories."

In the following classes they found out that he wasn't in Vietnam. He had been deferred while pursuing his doctorate at St. John's, and by the time he completed it he was too old to be drafted. So he hadn't served in the military, and he had mixed feelings about not serving while guys who couldn't afford college were being drafted and sent to war. But he was firmly against the war, and he advised the boys in the class to avoid being drafted by any means, short of leaving the country and going to Canada.

They also learned that he had grown up in Brooklyn, the fifth in a family with nine children. His parents were immigrants from Ireland, and he was the first member of his family to go to college. He had taught part-time at St. John's while working on his doctorate, but when they offered him a full-time position he decided it was time to get out of New York—he didn't say why, which led to speculation. Lena believed he left New York to get away from his family, while Siobhan wondered if he left New York to get away from a relationship. In any case, he had nothing but good things to say about Winona.

Though in the classroom he seemed to favor the girls over the boys, he never crossed the line that prohibited him from having any kind of personal relationship with them. In fact, he was very strict with them, and he held them to higher standards than the boys.

For Lena the high point of the course was when they read the poems of Keats, who could have been a character in a romantic tragedy. She would never forget the professor's recitation from "The Eve of Saint Agnes," which included the following stanza:

Anon his heart revives: her vespers done,
Of all its wreathed pearls her hair she frees;
Unclasps her warmed jewels one by one;
Loosens her fragrant bodice; by degrees
Her rich attire creeps rustling to her knees;
Half-hidden, like a mermaid in sea-weed,
Pensive awhile she dreams awake, and sees,
In fancy, fair St. Agnes in her bed,
But dares not look behind, or all the charm is fled.

While reciting the poem, which reached the depths of her body and soul, he didn't look at her more than at any other student, but Lena felt that the story about the lovers was about him and her, and that was when she knew for sure that she was in love with him.

They wanted to take a course with Professor McLean in the spring semester, but he was only teaching courses that they had already taken, so they had to find another way to see him. For several weeks during the winter Siobhan and Lena plotted different ways of encountering him, ranging from the ploy of just happening to be outside the classroom building when his class ended to the ploy of positioning themselves in the path he normally traveled to his office. But not wanting to be so obvious, Lena rejected these ideas, so all she could do for a while was think about him, dream about him, and imagine being with him.

Then one day in March, before spring break, Siobhan told her she knew where Professor McLean hung out. While doing an errand in town she had seen him go into the Kool Kat, a coffeehouse that attracted creative types. Siobhan had disdained it because she felt that the people who hung out there were trying too hard to act like artists and writers, but now there was a reason to go there, and if Professor McLean hung out there, it couldn't be all bad.

Siobhan had seen him go into the Kool Kat around five, so they went there at four-thirty and found a table and ordered espressos and sat there with a copy of *Ulysses* on the table. Lena was disappointed when he didn't show up around five, but she was willing to sit it out, and they ordered another round of espressos while "The Times They Are a-Changin'" played in the background. The place was about half filled with students, and there were even a few professors, one of whom she recognized as the strange but entertaining professor who had taught the course on Chaucer. There were posters on the walls about ending the war, saving the environment, and giving equal rights to women, and there was the fragrance of coffee and cinnamon in the air, not to mention cigarette smoke.

They had planned to be having an intense discussion about *Ulysses* right at the time when Professor McLean walked into the shop, but he surprised them—they were talking about hair when he finally did walk in, and since that subject wouldn't have impressed him, they quickly changed subjects. Siobhan opened the book to a random page as if it would provide an answer to the question that they were discussing. In a loud enough voice, she said: "In this passage, it's very clear that Joyce is rejecting some key elements of his Irish heritage."

Professor McLean smiled as if he had overheard the comment, but he kept walking toward a table in the corner, accompanied by an older man who looked like a professor. Lena had been hoping he would stop and at least say hello, and now she felt humbled by the fact that he evidently hadn't noticed her. She didn't see any point in staying, so she asked the waiter for the check, and she left without looking behind her.

"Why did I ever think he might be interested in me?" she asked Siobhan as they trudged back to the campus of St. Theresa.

"He *is* interested in you," Siobhan said with certainty.

"Then why didn't he stop and say hello?"

"He was with another professor, and he didn't want his colleague to think he's interested in students. In case you didn't know, there's a rule against professors having relationships with their students."

"But I'm not his student."

"His colleague doesn't know that, and you *could* be his student, which would be enough for the old fart to draw conclusions."

She thought about it, wanting to believe Siobhan. "Then going to the Kool Kat won't do any good if he always goes there with a colleague."

"But he was alone when I saw him go there, so maybe next time he'll go there alone."

"Then you think we should try again?"

"I think we should. You have nothing to lose by trying."

She felt that she had a lot to lose, starting with her self-respect and ending with her dream of love. But she went along with her friend's suggestion. "Okay. We'll try again."

The next day they were sitting in the Kool Kat, again with a copy of *Ulysses* on the table, when Professor McLean walked in, alone. Instead of walking by them, he stopped at their table, saying: "Hello, ladies."

It might have been her imagination, but she thought that on entering the shop his eyes lit up at the sight of her, and that he had been hoping she would be there.

"Hello, professor," they both said.

"Do you mind if I join you?"

"Not at all," Siobhan said, moving her chair to make room for another chair.

Immobilized, Lena watched him bring a chair from another table and sit down with them and light up a cigarette.

"I see that you're working on *Ulysses*," he said, reaching for the book.

"We're trying to understand it," Siobhan said.

"It's pretty basic, but it comes with a lot of literary trappings, which obfuscate things. Joyce was a great obfuscator."

Lena had been looking for something to say that wouldn't embarrass her or make her look stupid, and she decided it was okay to ask: "Do you like Joyce?"

"I love him," the professor said, looking directly at her with his tender brown eyes.

It made her feel that he might be talking about her instead of Joyce.

"What do you love about him?" Siobhan asked.

"I love how he wrote about Ireland as if everything about its culture broke his heart. And of course I love the language he used."

"Are you a writer?"

"I'm not a writer of fiction," he said. "I believe that Joyce took fiction as far as it could go. But I am a writer of poetry."

"Could we read your work somewhere?"

"Sure, you could." He gave them the names of several journals that had published his poems, and Siobhan made a note of them while he ordered an espresso. Then he said: "Believe it or not, I remember your names. You're Siobhan, and you're Lena."

"Right," they both said.

"I remember your names because you were the only two females in the class, and because you were the best students."

"We worked hard for you," Siobhan said. "Would you rather teach females or males?"

"I'd rather teach females any day."

"Why? Because you like them?"

"I do like them, but I also think they're better students, at least in my discipline. They do the assignments, they come to class prepared, and they sit in front where they can participate in the class. Of course there are exceptions, and I've had some very good male students. But generally the females are better."

"You know," Siobhan said. "You're the only teacher I ever had who could pronounce my name from the roster."

"That's because I'm Irish. But," he said, looking at Lena, "I would have had trouble with your last name if I'd tried to pronounce it."

"Yashevski," she said, meeting his eyes.

"Yashevski," he repeated, making it sound like poetry.

"Oh, my God," Siobhan said, looking at her watch. "I'm going to be late for my appointment. Excuse me, professor, but I gotta run."

"I understand," he said as if it was all right for her to go.

Lena knew that Siobhan didn't have an appointment, and that she was leaving in order to give her a chance to be alone with the professor. At first it scared her, but then she realized that it was the chance she had been waiting for, and with a look she thanked her friend.

"Are you from around here?" he asked after a silence.

"Yah, I'm from Winona." She was conscious of her accent, which sounded so much less refined than his. But she couldn't pretend to be from somewhere else.

"I like Winona. I'm glad I came here."

"But don't you miss New York?"

"No. It's stimulating, but I couldn't get anything done there. Too many distractions."

"Well, there aren't too many distractions here."

He sipped his coffee, and then he asked: "Do you live in the dormitory?"

"No, I live at home. With my parents and my grandmother," she added without knowing why.

"Do you have a big family?"

"I have a lot of aunts, uncles, and cousins, but I only have a brother. His name is Tony."

"Is your mother Italian?"

"No, she's Polish. My brother's actual name is Antonin."

"What's your actual name?"

"Magdalena."

"Magdalena Yashevski," he said as if he liked the sound of it. "But shouldn't it be Mary Magdalene?"

"It is. My full name is Marya Magdalena Jaszewski."

He nodded, saying: "That's how it should be. My full name is Devon Patrick McLean. And you can call me Devon now since you're no longer my student."

"Okay," she said, feeling that he had shifted the relationship to another ground.

"You're a senior, aren't you?"

"Yah, I am. I'm graduating this May."

"What are you planning to do after you graduate?"

"I'm planning to go to New York with Siobhan," she said, though she was only thinking about it.

"What are you hoping to do in New York?"

"I'm hoping to get a job with a publishing company."

"You don't want to be a writer?"

"No. Siobhan wants to be a writer, and she has talent. But I don't have talent for writing."

"You wrote some very good papers in the course."

"Well, I should have said I don't have talent for writing fiction or poetry."

"You could be a critic," he suggested. "But that's a hard way to make a living. It's almost as hard as it is to make a living as a poet."

"Is that why you teach?"

"Oh, yeah. But I also teach because I love it. I love the energy I get from students."

They talked until it was time for her to go home for dinner, and they were back on the subject of Joyce when he opened the book and found a passage that he read to her. It was the soliloquy of Molly Bloom, which ended with her saying: "I was a Flower of the mountain yes when I put the rose in my hair like the Andalusian girls used or shall I wear a red yes and how he kissed me under the Moorish wall and I thought well as well him as another and then I asked him with my eyes to ask again yes and then he asked me would I yes to say yes my mountain flower and first I put my arms around him yes and drew him down to me so he could feel my breasts all perfume yes and his heart was going like mad and yes I said yes I will Yes."

She listened enthralled by his soft Irish accent and his way of expressing what the woman felt, as if he really understood her. By the end he had made her feel like Molly Bloom, and with all her heart, body, and soul she was saying yes.

She was still in the compound that evening after the milking when Arne arrived. He came through the gate and paused to check on Brady, who was still staying close to his house, and then he joined her at the hay feeder, which she was replenishing.

"I hear you hired Rodney," he muttered as if he had lost the competition for the job.

"You said you didn't want the job," she reminded him. "And you recommended Rodney."

"I didn't recommend him. I just mentioned him."

"Do you have doubts about him?"

"No. I think you made a good decision. I don't know anyone who could do a better job."

"You know, the sheriff recommended him."

"Then he'll be fine."

"So what's your problem?"

"I don't have a problem. Why do you think I have a problem?"

"The way you said you heard I hired Rodney."

"Well, maybe it was jealousy. This guy is going to spend the night with you."

"He's only going to spend the night with my does."

Arne looked as if he was about to make a ribald comment, but instead he said: "Yah. I know. But he'll be here all night."

"If you want to spend the night with me, you're always welcome."

He considered this invitation. "If I did, then you'd have two guys protecting you."

"I'd have one guy protecting me. Rodney's job is to protect the animals."

At that moment Rodney's car rattled up the driveway.

They waited for him in the compound. As he approached, the two guys acted like two male bucks in the presence of a doe, and the air was thick with testosterone.

"Hey, Arne," Rodney said.

"Hey, Rodney. I see you have your weapon."

"From what the lady said, I might need it."

"Where are you going to station him?" Arne asked her.

"I hadn't thought about it. What do you guys think?"

"Well, he shouldn't be in plain sight. But he should be able to see them coming."

"What about that shed?" Rodney asked, pointing toward the doe shed.

"Yah, that might work—if you don't mind the smell of does."

The two guys exchanged a look but they didn't say what they were thinking.

"Let's go and see," Rodney said.

Together they walked to the shed, where the does were getting settled for the night.

"It's not bad," Rodney told them. "It's not as bad as being in a Humvee with guys who are scared shitless."

"You need a chair," Lena said. "I have a folding chair in the house that's pretty comfortable. Have you had dinner?"

"I had a slice of pizza. That's enough."

They left him and went into the house, where Lena got the

chair and handed it to Arne. While he was taking the chair and a bottle of spring water to Rodney, she opened the freezer and found a steak that she had been saving for no particular occasion. She could see that having Rodney there at night gave Arne a reason, however misguided, for staying with her, so she was getting something extra for her money. She had to laugh at the way the two guys had behaved. In thrall to their gonads, men did such stupid things.

She had peeled potatoes, sliced them, and put them into a hot skillet when Arne returned from the compound, saying: "He's in the doe shed, sitting in the chair."

"I think it's the best place for him. I mean, since they come after the animals."

"What if they come after you?" he asked, opening the refrigerator to get a bottle of beer.

"I have you to protect me," she reminded him.

"Yah, you have me," he said, laughing. He opened a drawer and looked for the opener, which always migrated toward the back. He finally found it, opened the bottle, and took a swig. Of course the beer was Budweiser, the only brand that he would drink because it was American, though she had pointed out that the company was no longer owned by Americans, which he didn't believe. "What's for dinner?"

"I have a steak, which you can grill."

"Good idea. I could use a steak."

She handed him the platter on which she had put the steak, and while he went out to the deck, she turned the potatoes in the pan.

By the time she joined him on the deck with a glass of red wine, the potatoes were done, and he had a fire going on the grill. It was a gas grill, which she had bought to replace the grill that used charcoal, not only because it was easier but also because it was friendlier to the environment.

It didn't take long to cook the steak, which they both liked medium. While he sliced it on a wooden cutting board and put it on a clean platter, which she had brought from the kitchen, she went and got the potatoes, which she put in a serving bowl. They weren't having a vegetable, but they would have a salad with lettuce from the garden of a neighbor.

They ate the steak and potatoes at the table on the deck. It was a beautiful evening, still light, and since it hadn't rained for a while, there were no mosquitoes.

"You know, I was thinking," Arne said, chewing on a bite of steak. "I was wondering why they go to the all trouble of killing your animals when it would be easier to pay you off."

"They couldn't pay me off," Lena said, surprised that he would suggest the possibility.

"If they offered you a million dollars for your land, what would you do?"

"I wouldn't take it."

"A million dollars? Think about it. You could retire on a million dollars. You could go to Florida and live in the tropics, instead of freezing your ass off here."

"I don't want to retire," she said. "I want to keep working."

"If you retired, you wouldn't say that. You'd know what it's like to get up in the morning and not have to work."

"But I wouldn't have anything to do."

"You'd have plenty to do. For one thing, you could relax and enjoy life."

"You mean I could go and hang out at the Legion?"

He shook his head. "You couldn't go there. You're a woman."

"Then what would I do?"

"You'd go to the beach. You'd be in Florida."

"I don't like beaches," she said. "I have fair skin, so I can't be in the sun."

"I have fair skin, and I have no problem being in the sun."

The fact was, she had noticed some unusual marks on his skin that should be examined by a dermatologist, and she had advised him to go and see one, but he hadn't taken this seriously. "Well, I have a problem being in the sun, so I wouldn't have anything to do in Florida."

"Just think about it. A million dollars."

"I wouldn't sell my land to them for ten million dollars, for a hundred million dollars. I don't want money."

"What do you want?"

"I want to save this valley."

"For who?" he asked. "Your children won't ever come back and live here, and their children won't either. So who do you want to save it for?"

"For future generations."

"Why do you care about people who aren't related to you?"

"We're all related to each other."

"You mean we're all descended from Adam and Eve?"

"I mean we're all children of God."

He made a noise that sounded like a clearing of his throat. "Oh, that's too much."

"It's not too much. In fact, it's not enough." She was tempted to quote from St. John about how we must love one another, and how if we do, then God remains in us and his love is brought to perfection in us. But instead, she simply said: "If we don't care about future generations, there won't be any humans left on earth."

"That might not be such a bad thing," Arne said. "We've really fucked up the earth."

"We have, but we've also done some good things."

"Name one good thing."

"Have you tried my goat cheese lately?"

He made a motion with his hand as if he was going to throw his napkin at her.

While she cleaned up after dinner, Arne went to the compound to see how Rodney was doing, and he returned with the report that everything was okay.

By then it was time to go to bed, where they put into practice what she hadn't said about loving one another. There were all kinds of love, and this was a kind that worked for them, even when other kinds didn't work.

She got up at the usual time the next morning, and after making tea she went into her office, turned on the computer, and checked her email. There was nothing but the usual spam, which she deleted. Then she composed an update on the situation for Siobhan, who was living in New York, in an apartment in the West Village that she had bought years ago. With her writing talent and her commitment to social justice, she had built a relationship with the *New York Times* writing about the suffering that women and children endured around the world as victims of political violence. Lena always got together with her during her visits to Patty, and on the last visit she had told Siobhan about the issue of sand mining. Siobhan was interested, seeing the issue as representative of the global issue that Pope Francis had addressed in his encyclical *Laudato Si'*, and she was working on an in-depth story about it. Her major theme was the use of corporate money and power to stop any meaningful steps toward saving the earth. Her plan was to finish her story when she knew how the vote came out, and Lena was feeding her information on events as they developed.

When she had sent an email with the latest developments, she went back into the kitchen and grabbed a muffin and went out to meet Heather for the morning milking. She found Rodney in the doe shed, ready to leave and go home and get some sleep. He reported that the night had been peaceful, except for the yipping of some coyotes.

The milking went smoothly, and when Heather had left for her other job, Lena returned to the house and spent the next two hours at her computer reviewing the accounts of her business and preparing a cash flow for the bank.

At eleven thirty she left for Passau, where the county board was having a special meeting at noon. With only three weeks left before the meeting when they would vote on the mining law, they had to review the final draft. They met in a conference room of the town hall, which was furnished with a long table and ten folding chairs.

Jordan had sent a copy of the draft to each of the board members, so they would all have a chance to review it. Jordan, Lena, and Neil agreed with the changes made by Porter, and they were there to hear objections by their opponents, Gary and Lester.

Gary owned land on the ridge and in a valley. He rented his land on the ridge to a corporate farm that grew corn for ethanol and soybeans for China, and he lived in the valley in a modern house that he had built after tearing down his family house, which had been there for three generations. He was a Lutheran, a good example of the Protestant ethic. He had worked hard and built a fortune, and he was in principle against the government interfering with his rights as a landowner, even though he had no intention of selling his land to the mining company. At least that's what he said, and Lena believed him.

Lester was something else. He had moved to the county from Minneapolis, where he had been a broker in the securities industry. He had been laid off from his job, and like so many people who lost their jobs, he became a consultant. He offered his services to farmers and small businesses, but it was hard to see how he made a living at it. He was evidently being supported by his wife, who worked as a nurse at the assisted living facility in Passau. During the past year he had displayed some tokens of success, including a new Lexus, which made Lena suspect that he had become a paid lobbyist for the mining company.

The meeting focused on the change that limited the application of the law to mining, oil drilling, or other extractive activities. Gary had no problem with it, presumably because it left open the possibility of selling his land for real estate development, but Lester had a problem with it, presumably because it didn't leave open the possibility of sand mining—which was absurd because the purpose of the law was to prohibit sand mining.

"You're not being clear," Neil told him patiently. "Could you explain to us again why you object to this clause?"

"I object to this clause because it's unconstitutional," Lester said. In other situations he was affable, a natural salesperson, but in this situation he was edgy, as if he was out of his element. He had been elected to the board by effectively selling himself to people, but without explaining the specific benefits that they would get from him.

"Maybe it is, but I don't think so. It was drafted by an attorney who has a lot of experience in writing legislation."

"I know who drafted it," Lester said crossly.

"You still haven't told us exactly why you object to it."

"All right. I object to it because it leaves open the possibility of real estate development."

"What do you mean?" Lena asked.

"I mean that if you want to save your precious valleys, this law shouldn't allow real estate development."

"That would change our valleys, but it wouldn't destroy them."

"Mining won't destroy them. After mining the sand, the company will restore them to their original state, and you won't even know they were mined."

"Yah, like they did for the valleys in the next county."

"You've seen the pictures of those valleys," Jordan said. "How can you pretend that the mining company would restore our valleys?"

"That was another company," Lester said. "The company that wants to mine these valleys has a different set of values."

"I don't believe it. I don't even think it's possible to restore land that's been mined."

"They have the technology to do it."

"This discussion isn't productive," Gary said, glancing at his watch as if he had another appointment after this meeting.

"We're adding this clause," Jordan said, "so the law can't be extended to prohibit people from selling their land for purposes other than mining, oil drilling, or other extractive activities. The only question is, does the clause do what we want it to do?"

"I think it does," Neil said.

"I'm satisfied with it," Gary said.

"What about you?" Jordan asked Lester.

"I still think it's unconstitutional," Lester said querulously.

"The courts can decide that," Neil told him.

"Are there any other issues?" Jordan asked them.

No one had any, so the meeting was adjourned.

By then it was dark, and when Lena got home she went into

the compound to see how Rodney was doing. He was seated in the folding chair, with his weapon leaning against the doorway, within easy reach.

"How are you doing?" she asked him, conscious of how hard it must be to sit there for hours, alone and with nothing to do. She supposed he had learned to deal with such conditions from doing guard duty in the military, but she still felt sympathy for him.

"I'm doing fine," he said. "I'm getting to know some of the animals."

"They all have names. If you point to one of them, I'll tell you her name." Of course she might have trouble identifying them in the dark, so she hoped he would point to one that she knew especially well.

"What's her name?" he asked, pointing to a large doe who hadn't yet settled with the others.

"That's Regina. She's the queen."

"I figured that. She acts like a queen."

She was leaving him when she saw Arne's pickup coming into the driveway. Two nights in a row, which was a record.

A week passed without any incident. It looked as if having an armed guard effectively deterred the killers. But then, on the eighth night that Rodney was on duty, they were awakened around three in the morning by a shot, followed by a rat-a-tat-tat. They jumped out of bed, and Lena ran to the monitor. The view of the doe shed showed Rodney kneeling on the ground, holding his weapon in one hand and his other arm dangling. It looked like he had been wounded.

She raced to the phone and called the sheriff, conscious of being a regular caller at this hour in the morning. After two rings the sheriff answered.

"They shot Rodney. We need an ambulance."

"Oh, jeez," the sheriff said as if there was no end to the occurrences at Eden Valley Farm.

"It sounded like he shot back at them, so I think they went away."

"You shouldn't go out until I get there," he told her, sounding like her father.

"I'll take the risk. I have to attend to him."

"You're not a nurse. You don't know how to attend to him."

"Just get here," she said, "as soon as you can. And bring an ambulance."

Arne was already dressed by the time she got off the phone, and she threw on some clothes and headed out.

"Where are you going?" he asked her.

"I'm going to attend to Rodney."

"They might still be around."

"I don't think they are. It sounded like he shot back at them."

"All right," Arne sighed. "If you're going out, I'm going with you. They can't be worse than the Viet Cong."

Before going out she checked the monitor, and none of the cameras showed anyone except Rodney, who was still kneeling in front of the doe shed.

She carefully left the house, praying to the Blessed Mother for protection, and she went through the gate into the compound, followed by Arne.

Seeing them, Rodney let go of his weapon.

"What happened?" she asked him.

"They got me in the shoulder. It's not serious, but it hurts like hell."

"I called the sheriff, and he's bringing an ambulance."

"I shot back at them," he said with pride. "And I'm pretty sure I hit at least one of them. I sprayed the fuckers with a magazine of bullets."

"Where were they?"

"They were in the woods. I had to pee, but as soon as I left the shed they hit me. I saw where it came from, and I had my weapon with me, so I was able to shoot back at them."

"You remembered your training," Arne said. "Never go and pee without your weapon."

Rodney forced a smile.

"Let me see the wound," Lena told him.

He sat up from his kneeling position and displayed his left shoulder, which was dripping blood.

"Did it hit a bone?" she asked him.

"I don't think so. I think it passed through my shoulder."

That was lucky. An inch or two either way, and it would have shattered his shoulder or killed him.

"Where exactly in the woods were they?" Arne asked.

Rodney pointed with his right hand.

"Don't go after them," Lena said.

"I wasn't about to. I only wanted to know where the sheriff should look for blood. If Rodney hit one of them, it'll leave a trail."

Lena went into the shed and found Rodney's bottle of water and brought it to him. She helped him shift from a kneeling position to a sitting position, and she handed him the bottle, which he took in his right hand and drank from.

A few minutes later they saw the flashing lights of the sheriff's cruiser, with the ambulance behind them. A girl, whom Lena recognized as the daughter of Duane, the owner of the gas station in Arendal, came into the compound and immediately attended to Rodney. Her partner followed her with a stretcher, which they laid down next to Rodney. They carefully got him onto the stretcher and looked ready to take him away.

"Can he stay here for a moment while I question him?" the sheriff asked.

"Yah. But the sooner we get him to the hospital, the better."

"I won't take long." The sheriff turned to Rodney and asked: "How did it happen?"

Rodney repeated what he had told them, ending with the information about the area of the woods where the shot had come from.

"You can take him away," the sheriff told the paramedics.

While they carried him away on the stretcher, Lena said: "They could have killed him."

"They meant to kill him," the sheriff said. "If they'd only wanted to scare him away, they would have shot him in the leg."

"So you have a case of attempted murder," Arne said.

"You bet I do. And they won't get away with it. Jim," the sheriff said to his deputy, "take the big light and go into the woods and see if there are any signs of blood. We'll go into the house and see what the cameras tell us."

While the deputy headed for the woods, the rest of them headed for the house.

"Rodney left his weapon on the ground," Lena told the sheriff. "Should I pick it up?"

"Only if you intend to use it. I'll take it." The sheriff stooped and carefully picked up the assault weapon.

Inside the house, the sheriff reviewed the film on the monitor, looking for clues. It was slow going, and Lena felt useless. She paced around, praying for Rodney.

After what seemed like a long time the deputy returned and said: "I found a lot of blood. There's a trail of it that leads to the road, where they must have left their car, so one of those guys needs medical attention."

"Where would he get it?" Lena asked.

"He wouldn't get it at a hospital," the sheriff said. "He'd have to find a doctor who wouldn't report it."

"Or else make a doctor treat him," the deputy said.

"Yah, that's likely. So we'll put out a notice to all doctors within a hundred miles of here. If the guy's seriously wounded, they probably won't get any farther."

When the sheriff and the deputy had left, Lena had time to reflect on what had happened to Rodney, a young man from a poor family who had survived the war in Iraq but almost hadn't survived the war in Eden Valley. She thanked God that he hadn't been killed or more seriously wounded, but she blamed herself for putting him in harm's way.

SEVEN

AS SHE LEARNED from subsequent meetings, Devon went to the Kool Kat only a few times a week since he had other commitments, which included office hours between four and six on Mondays and Wednesdays, and he only went there on weekdays. Later, she realized that he must have cut his office hours on the Wednesday when he met her and Siobhan there, which indicated how much he had wanted to see her. On weekends he spent the mornings working on his poems and the afternoons taking short trips in the area, north to Red Wing, east to La Crosse, and south to Passau, often with a colleague from his department, a woman, who was only a friend. He didn't go west because the landscape flattened and had no features of interest. He especially liked the country around Passau, which reminded him of the Pyrenees.

From that comparison she learned that he had spent a year in Europe after receiving his bachelor's degree from St. John's, and that his favorite countries were Ireland, France, Italy, and Spain. He said he might have remained in Europe if he could have found a way to make a living there, but he faced reality and returned to New York. He confirmed what he had suggested in that first meeting with her and Siobhan, that he hadn't left New York to get away from his family or to get away from a relationship, he had left New York because he couldn't get anything done there. After hearing about his life in Greenwich Village, she understood why he couldn't get anything done there. It wasn't only the endless nights in Village bars drinking and talking, it was also the dreary mornings waking up with a hangover and knowing that in less than an hour he had to take a subway out to Queens and teach a class.

She also learned that his parents still lived in the house in Brooklyn where he had grown up, refusing to follow the Irish of their generation out of the city, which from their perspective was changing for the worse. When he went back there, he had trouble recognizing the neighborhood where he had played with all the kids from those Irish families. Not that he minded the fact that other immigrants were moving into the neighborhood, but he was sorry that his parents were losing the community that nourished and supported them. And there was no solution for them since the people who left the neighborhood dispersed to towns the length of Long Island and even over to Westchester, so there was no concentration of the people who had been their neighbors and friends. When he heard that the Polish community in Winona was still cohesive, he said he envied Lena for that, though she couldn't understand why since as far back as she could remember she had wanted to escape from that community.

During spring break he went to a conference in Chicago that had been scheduled months ago, and while he was gone she missed him badly. She confided her feelings to Siobhan, who helped her through the period of his absence, and when he returned, she tried to hide how happy she was to see him—until she saw how happy he was to see her.

That day they met as usual at the Kool Kat, but after only one cup of espresso he suggested that they go to his apartment. She could only guess what he had in mind, and it didn't deter her. She held his arm while they walked there as if they were a longtime couple, and she put out of her mind the fact that her parents expected her home for dinner by six o'clock.

He lived in a building of garden apartments, on the ground floor, which gave him access to a patio in back. One wall of the living room was lined with books from the floor to the ceiling, and the opposite wall had a print of a Matisse that she recognized from her art history course. There were two easy chairs and a sofa on a mostly red Persian carpet, and there was a cabinet for his stereo equipment.

"Do you drink wine?" he asked her.

"Oh, yah," she said, though she had sipped it on only a few occasions other than Communion. Beer was the beverage of choice in her community.

"I have a bottle of Chardonnay in the refrigerator," he said, heading into the kitchen.

She remained on her feet in the living room, moving closer to the bookshelves and inspecting the titles. They were mostly collections of poems, with the authors ranging from John Donne to Dylan Thomas. On a middle shelf were several volumes of William Butler Yeats.

He returned from the kitchen with two glasses of white wine, one of which he handed to her.

"Thanks," she said, taking it. "I gather you like Yeats."

"I love Yeats," he said. "I love how he evolved with the events of his time."

Not knowing how to comment on that, she took a small sip of wine. She liked the taste, and she could see how she might enjoy drinking wine.

"I assume you're at the legal drinking age," he said with a twinkle in his eyes.

"Yah, I just turned twenty-one," she said.

"When was your birthday?"

"It was last week." It had gone by without much notice since her mind was all on him.

"What date?" he asked.

"April third," she said.

"Then let's drink a toast to your being at the legal drinking age."

They gently clinked their glasses together, looking into each other's eyes. She felt that in a way they were drinking a toast to their future.

"My birthday is April twenty-fourth," he said. "The date of the Easter Rising."

"What was the Easter Rising?"

"It was a failed attempt by Ireland to gain independence from Britain."

"Do the Irish celebrate that date?"

"Oh, yeah. For some reason we celebrate failures."

After thinking about it, Lena said: "The Polish only celebrate religious holidays. We don't have an independence day."

120

"Someday you will. And speaking of independence, do you like Chopin?"

"Of course I like him. My grandmother has records of his music."

He went over to the cabinet and found an album. He lifted the top of the player and carefully put on a record. In a moment she heard a piano playing something she recognized.

With glasses of wine in their hands and romantic music in the air, they sat down on the sofa, where she listened to him explain what he knew about Polish history. He concluded that Irish history and Polish history had a lot in common. And then he got up and went into the kitchen and returned with the bottle of wine.

She was very relaxed when he leaned over and tenderly kissed her. It was as if a spark ignited something compressed inside of her. She kissed him back, and they kept kissing until other things started happening.

She could have stopped him, and foreseeing the possible consequences, she almost did stop him, but finally instead of stopping him, she encouraged him, saying: "Yes, yes."

Later, he lifted her from the sofa and carried her into the bedroom and set her gently on the bed and lay down with her. She curled up next to him with her face against his chest, kissing him softly and in almost no time falling asleep.

When she awoke she could see through the window that it was dark outside, and then she looked at her watch and saw it was after six thirty. She sat up quickly, saying: "Oh, my God. I was supposed to be home for dinner at six."

"I'm sorry," he said. "If I'd known, I would have waked you."

"I wouldn't have wanted you to wake me. It was the sweetest sleep I've ever had." She gave him a kiss, and then she got up. She was naked, and she had no idea where her clothes were.

"They're in the living room," he said as if he had read her mind. He got up and led her there.

She found her panties on the floor in front of the sofa, and she started getting dressed. She didn't hurry because getting home five minutes sooner wouldn't help her.

"Will you be in trouble?" he asked her with concern.

"Oh, yah. They expect me home for dinner on time, and if I can't make it, they expect me to let them know in advance."

"What are you going to tell them?"

"I don't know. I could tell them I was with Siobhan, and that we were so busy studying we lost track of the time."

He smiled. "Would they believe that?"

"No. I have a history of lying to them, so they won't believe anything I say."

"Would they believe the truth?"

"Oh, yah. But I can't tell them the truth."

"Why can't you?"

"I just can't. They'd make me feel bad," she said, knowing how they would react to the truth. "They'd tell me I committed a sin."

"I understand. I was raised in the same church."

By now she was dressed and ready to go. "Well, wish me luck."

"I'll do more than that. If you tell them you were meeting with a professor, I'll back you up. I mean, it's the truth—you *were* meeting with me. And maybe what happened between us will never occur to them."

"But how would I have lost track of the time?"

He thought for a moment. "I gave you a writing exercise. No, even better, I had you take a Myers-Briggs test, and then we analyzed the results."

"What's a Myers-Briggs test?"

"It's a personality test based on concepts of Jung. You studied Jung, didn't you?"

"Yah." She could see how her parents, who hadn't gone to college, might be impeded by the reference to Jung. "And what were the results?"

"The results were that you get your energy from within, you see the details of a situation, you make decisions based on your feelings, and you act to achieve your goals."

Impressed, she asked: "Does that apply to what happened between us?"

"I think it does. I got it from what happened between us."

122

"Okay. I'll try that story on them. Will you be at the Kool Kat tomorrow?"

"I'll be there," he said, putting an arm around her shoulders and drawing her toward him for a goodbye kiss.

When she got home her parents, her grandmother, and her brother were sitting at the dining table, waiting for her. They had gone ahead with dinner, which they had finished, but they were still at the table, waiting for her.

"*Jesteś dwie godziny późno na kolację,*" her grandmother said.

"I'm sorry," she said. "I was meeting with a professor, and I lost track of the time."

"What was so fascinating," her father asked, "that you lost track of the time?"

"He had me take a Myers-Briggs test, and then we analyzed the results."

"What's a Myers-Briggs test?"

"It's a personality test based on concepts of Jung," she said as if it was something they should knew about.

"Who's Jung?" Babcia asked.

"He was one of the founders of psychology. He was Christian," she added, believing it would help.

"What was the purpose of this test?" her father asked.

"To determine what kind of personality I have."

"And what did it determine?"

Unable to remember exactly what Devon had said, she improvised, saying: "It determined that I'm not as considerate of other people as I should be, I'm not responsible, and I'm not thankful for the blessings of my life."

"Are you sure you weren't with a priest?" her brother said.

"I was with a professor," she said, wanting to kill him.

"The test was right about you," Babcia said.

"All right," her mother said after a silence. "I accept your explanation. But next time please let us know if you're going to be late."

"I will, mom." She wasn't sure about the rest of them, but she was sure that her mother believed her, and she felt bad for lying to her.

By the early summer, after weeks of lying to her parents to conceal her relationship with Devon, she made the decision to tell them about him. She waited until after her graduation, which her parents and her grandmother attended. She knew they were very proud of her since she was the first in the family to go to college, let alone graduate with honors, and she took advantage of their being on a cloud of contentment to float the news that she had a boyfriend.

"A boyfriend!" Babcia said as if it was an infirmity.

"Where did you meet him?" her mother asked.

"I met him at college. Wasn't that a reason for going to college—to meet a husband?"

"We didn't send you to college to meet a husband," her father said. "We sent you to college to get an education."

"I thought he was only a boyfriend," her brother said.

"He *is* only a boyfriend. I mean, I'm not planning to marry him."

"Is he a student at St. Mary's?" her mother asked.

"No, he's a professor at St. Mary's."

"Maybe I know him," her brother said. He had just finished his sophomore year there.

"How old is he?" Babcia asked.

"In his late twenties," Lena said, though she knew he was thirty-one now.

"Isn't he kind of old for you?" her father said.

"He's only seven years older than me. And you're ten years older than mom."

"I was in the war," her father said as if this explained everything. "Did this professor serve in the military?"

"No, he didn't. He was getting his doctorate, and by the time he finished, it was too late."

"Too late to serve?" Her father shook his head. "It's never too late to serve our country. And why wasn't he drafted?"

"As long as you're in college," her brother said, "you're deferred from the draft."

"Well, that doesn't sound fair to me."

"I hope you don't want your son to go to Vietnam," her mother said.

"Whether or not he goes to Vietnam, I want my son to serve our country."

"What *is* this young man?" Babcia asked.

"What do you mean?" Lena said, bracing herself.

"Is he Polish?"

"No, he's Irish."

"Irish!" He might as well have been an alien from outer space.

"If he's Irish, then he's Catholic," her mother said, coming to the rescue. "Is he from Ireland, or was he born here?"

"He was born here. His parents came here from Ireland."

"Is he from Winona?" her father asked as if he might know the parents.

"No, he's from New York," she said, thinking it sounded better than Brooklyn.

"They're a lot of Irish in New York," Babcia said.

"How long have you been seeing him?" her mother asked her.

"I don't know. For about a month."

"Then we should meet him. We should have him to dinner next Sunday after church. I assume he goes to church."

"Oh, yah. He goes to the chapel at St. Mary's," she improvised, intending to make it true by the time her parents met him.

The next afternoon she told Devon about the invitation, realizing that it was a test of how serious he was about her. When his response was affirmative, she was relieved, and she felt that it had significantly advanced their relationship. She asked him to go to mass on Sunday, whether or not he had planned to, and she explained why. He said he understood, which left her with one less thing to worry about.

The rest of the week went slowly, and by Sunday after church her insides were churning with anxiety. After going to the bathroom yet another time, she positioned herself near the front door to prevent Babcia from being there ahead of her when the doorbell rang.

When it finally did ring, she jumped at the sound of it.

She opened the door, and there was Devon with his hair combed and his face cleanly shaven. He was wearing a white shirt and a striped tie, under an open blue blazer that had gold buttons. For the first time since she had met him, Devon looked like other professors.

Conscious of Babcia hovering behind her, she didn't greet him with a kiss. She said: "Hi. Come in."

"I would have been here earlier," Devon said, "but the priest delivered a long homily."

She gave him an approving look that Babcia couldn't see, and then she turned to introduce him. "Babcia, this is Dr. McLean."

"I'm pleased to meet you," Devon said, taking her hand.

Babcia nodded awkwardly as if she lacked the proper words in English.

"Come and meet my parents," Lena said, leading him toward the dining room.

Her father and her brother were at the table in their usual places, her father at the head and her brother to his right. As she introduced them, Devon went from her father to her brother, shaking their hands and saying: "I'm pleased to meet you."

"You should sit here," Lena told him, indicating a chair that would be next to her mother, who always sat at the foot of the table, opposite her father.

Lena then went into the kitchen, where her mother handed her a platter with a ham on it. There were other platters with kielbasa and pierogi as well as bowls of kapusta and beets. She carried the ham into the dining room and set it down in front of her father, who would carve it, and then she returned to the kitchen. She and her mother brought the rest of the food into the dining room, and then she introduced Devon to her mother.

Her mother slightly inclined her head in deference to the professor as they shook hands, and she said: "Thank you for joining us."

"Thank you for inviting me," Devon said.

When everyone had sat down, there was a silence. Then as usual her mother said grace: "*Szanowny panie, dziękujemy za ten pokarm i każde błogosławieństwo, został przyznany na nas. W imię ojca i syna i świętego ducha. Amen.*"

Lena refrained from giving Devon a look to see how he reacted to this strange language.

After the grace they all spoke English as well as they could.

"Are you from New York?" Babcia asked him.

"Yes, I'm from Brooklyn," Devon said.

"Have you been to Greenpoint?"

"I've been there a few times. It's a Polish neighborhood."

"Are you from an Irish neighborhood?" her father asked, carving the ham.

"It's mostly Irish. It's also Italian."

"I guess you have everything in New York."

"But you have a variety of people here."

"We're mostly Polish, German, and Norwegian."

"You have two beautiful Polish churches."

"My grandfather helped to build St. Stanislaus in 1872. That was the original church."

"What brought him here?"

"The lumber. Winona was a major lumbering town. It's not anymore, but we still do a lot of building with wood."

"I understand from Lena that you own a lumber yard."

"Yah, we deal in lumber and other building materials. It's not a bad business."

"What do you teach?" her mother asked.

"I teach English literature."

"That was Lena's major. Did you have her as a student in a course?"

"I had her in a course last fall. She was an excellent student."

"Were your parents from Ireland?"

"Both my parents were from Ireland. They were both from County Clare, and they met on the boat coming over."

"Do you have any brothers or sisters?"

Devon smiled. "I have four brothers and four sisters."

"How wonderful," her mother said since she had wanted to have more children. "Where are you among them?"

"I'm the fifth child. I'm right in the middle."

"Do your brothers and sisters live in Brooklyn?"

"No, only my parents live in Brooklyn. My brothers and sisters mostly live on Long Island, so they're not very far from Brooklyn."

"Brooklyn is actually on Long Island," Lena explained.

"Do you miss your family?" her mother asked.

"I do miss them, and I go back to see them now and then. But I don't miss New York."

Her mother looked content with the last statement as if it was an assurance that if he married her daughter, he wouldn't take her away to New York.

Of course they discussed him after he had gone. Her grandmother was negative. She hadn't understood much of the conversation, but she didn't like the fact that Devon was Irish, though she couldn't explain why. Her father was less negative, though it bothered him that Devon hadn't served in the military. And her mother was positive. In fact, she had nothing but good things to say about Devon. But then she had nothing but good things to say about everyone.

At the end of June he flew to New York to see his parents and siblings, and while he was away she missed him. She wished she had gone with him, but he hadn't asked her, so he probably wasn't ready to have her meet his family.

One evening she got a phone call from Siobhan, whom she hadn't seen since graduation. At that time Siobhan was definite about going to New York and working there, whereas Lena was still only thinking about it. The major event since then was Devon meeting her parents, and that had made her think less about New York, though she hadn't decided against it.

"I'm going there in the middle of July," Siobhan told her. "Do you want to come with me?"

"I do," she said honestly. "But I also want to stay here with Devon."

"Well, if you were in New York, then he might move back there to be with you."

"He might, but what if he didn't?"

"Then you could always go back to Winona."

It was tempting. She had wanted to get out of Winona as far

128

back as she could remember. But the thought of getting out and then going back because Devon hadn't followed her was somehow worse than never getting out. She finally said: "I'll stay here for a while and see what happens, and if nothing happens, I'll join you in New York."

"Okay," Siobhan said. "I'll wait to hear from you."

When Devon returned from New York he had a ring for her. It was a diamond in a simple setting, and it sparkled beautifully in the light.

"Will you marry me?" he asked holding the ring at the tip of the appropriate finger.

"Then he asked me would I yes and yes I said yes I will Yes," she said.

With joyful laughter he slid the ring on her finger and kissed her lovingly.

They scheduled the wedding for October. The mass would be at St. Stan's, and the reception would be in the lower level of the church, where the Polish community had parties.

As soon as they had set the date she called Siobhan and told her what was happening. She asked Siobhan if she could make it to the wedding, and Siobhan said yes, she wouldn't miss it. She then asked Siobhan if she would be her maid of honor, and Siobhan said yes, she would love to be her maid of honor. And she told Siobhan that there would be no bridesmaids, there would only be the maid of honor and the best man, and since Devon had four brothers, three of whom would be unhappy if he asked one of them to be his best man, he had asked his father to perform that role, and his father had said yes.

Since neither she nor her mother had a driver's license, her father drove them to a store in St. Paul where young women from the Polish community bought their wedding dresses. She found a dress that both she and her mother liked, and it was within her father's budget. They booked a room in a modest hotel, which they all shared, and then they went to the Polish-American Club, where her parents had met twenty-four years ago. They showed her how they had danced the Polka that night, and when they came off the floor her mother said that nothing had changed, except that her father was now a better dancer.

Siobhan arrived two days before the wedding in a car she had rented in St. Paul, having stopped there for a while to visit her family. She stayed in the guestroom, which was seldom used and doubled as a sewing room for Lena's mother.

The day before the wedding Devon's family arrived in a minibus that they had rented at the airport in La Crosse: his father and mother and all except one of his eight siblings along with their spouses. A younger brother who was injured on his job as a linesman for Con Edison couldn't make it. His family virtually took over the hotel that was closest to the church.

That night her mother cooked a Polish feast for them with kielbasa, kapusta, pierogi, szynka, wołowina, chrzan, gołąbki, and buraki, which they devoured while consuming an unbelievable volume of Polish beer.

At the wedding mass the next day the priest did the homily both in English and in Polish, and when the bride and groom entered the reception hall they were greeted by Lena's parents with the tray of bread, salt, and wine. As she knew from attending previous weddings, her parents offered them bread in the hope that they would never hunger, salt to remind them that their life would be difficult at times, so they must learn to cope with troubles, and wine in the hope that they would never thirst and would have a life of good health and good cheer, and would share the company of many good friends.

"That was very nice," Devon said after she had explained the ritual to him.

Her father had the first dance with Lena, and as they whirled around the room she could feel how proud and happy he was. With grace, he handed her over to Devon, who attempted to continue the Polka. For a while the band only played Polkas, but then the oldest of Devon's brothers got the band to play Irish music, and the four brothers demonstrated an Irish dance while their laughing wives and sisters watched them.

After a riotous send-off by their families and friends, the couple spent their wedding night at an inn that Devon had discovered on his trips in the region of Passau, and they had two days of peace before returning to Winona and bidding goodbye to Devon's family. Siobhan left with them, and the two friends exchanged a special goodbye, promising to stay in touch.

Two months later Lena discovered that she was pregnant and due in July. Since she had done nothing to avoid getting pregnant from all the times they had made love before the wedding, and since she wouldn't have wanted Devon to marry her because she was pregnant, she was very thankful for the timing.

The next morning, when Heather arrived for the milking, Lena told her what had happened to Rodney. She had previously learned from Heather that they were in high school together, though Heather was two years older than Rodney so they hadn't dated. Rodney was like a younger brother, and she had tried to stop him from joining the army.

"Where did they take him?" Heather asked.

"To the hospital in Passau," Lena said. "I'm going to visit him later this morning. Do you want to go with me?"

"Yah, sure. I'll tell them at work that I have an emergency."

After they had finished the milking, Heather left for her other job and Lena went into the house, where she saw the light flashing on the phone. It was a message from the sheriff, who said: "Please call me. I have some news."

She called him immediately.

"We caught them," he told her.

"You did?" She thanked God. "Where?"

"They went to La Crescent, where they found a doctor who has his office in his house. It was around four in the morning, and they woke him and held him at gunpoint and made him treat the guy who was wounded. A neighbor noticed that the lights were on and called to see if everything was all right. When the doctor didn't answer the phone, the neighbor got suspicious and called the police."

"Is the doctor all right?"

"Oh, yah. He's fine. And so is his wife, who the other guy held a gun on while the doctor performed surgery. There were three bullets in the wounded guy's leg."

"Are they being held in La Crescent?"

"No. We brought them here. And guess what."

Unable to guess, she waited for the sheriff to continue.

"The gun the other guy was holding on the doctor's wife was a Glock, and I'll bet it was the same gun they used to kill Grady."

"What about the gun they used to shoot Rodney?"

"It was in the trunk of their car, and it's being dusted for fingerprints. I'll bet they match the prints of the guy who was wounded."

"Why not the other guy?"

"Rodney fired at the spot where he saw the flash of the gun that shot him, so he probably hit the guy who held that gun. We'll know soon."

After reflecting, Lena asked: "Does this mean that my animals are safe?"

"No, it doesn't. Whoever hired these two thugs can hire more thugs. Your animals won't be safe until you vote on the law. So we need to talk. I think I know what they're trying to do."

"You mean the people who hired these thugs?"

"Yah," the sheriff said. "And if I'm right, then we know what to expect from them."

"When would be a good time for you?"

"Around noon"

"Should I go to your office?"

"That would be best. We have a lot of balls in the air."

"Okay. I'll see you around noon."

When the call had ended, Lena went into the kitchen and ran some water into the teapot and put it on the stove. She wondered what the sheriff thought the people who had hired those thugs were trying to do. To her it looked like they were simply escalating to the point where if necessary they would kill her to stop her from voting for the law. But the sheriff had experience that she didn't have, and maybe he also knew something that she didn't know.

Whatever it was, she was anxious to hear what he had to say.

The hospital was in Passau, near the middle of town. Though it had replaced the previous hospital more than fifteen years ago, people still referred to it as the "new" hospital as if they had better memories of the old one.

Since Lena had a meeting with the sheriff at noon and Heather had to return to work after the visit, they came in separate cars and met in the lobby of the hospital. Heather knew her way around since back in the days before she was rehabilitated, she had been treated in the emergency room multiple times for overdoses. People in cities had no idea how bad the drug problem was in small towns and rural areas. The main difference was that the addicts here couldn't afford upscale drugs like cocaine and heroin but instead relied on home-made brews of methamphetamine.

"He's on the second floor," Heather said after talking with the receptionist as if she knew her.

They took the elevator to the second floor, where they stopped to verify Rodney's room number. The nurse at the desk asked Heather how she was doing and looked glad to hear that she was doing fine, meaning that she was drug free.

They found Rodney propped up in a bed with his left arm cradled in a sling.

"Hey, guys," he said brightly.

"How are they treating you?" Heather asked him.

"They're treating me better than they would in a VA hospital."

"Have you ever been in a VA hospital?"

"No, but I heard they suck."

"Have they told you how long you'll be here?"

"Yah. I'll be here for a few days."

"Well, give yourself enough time to heal."

He nodded as if he understood. "Do you have my weapon?"

"The sheriff has it. Don't worry, he'll take good care of it. You got one of those guys with it."

"I thought I did. I thought I heard a cry of pain."

"You put three bullets into his leg. Because he was wounded, he had to see a doctor, and that's where the police caught them."

"The police caught them?" Rodney said with a look of delight.

"The sheriff has them in custody," Lena told him, "and he thinks he'll have enough evidence to put them away."

"That's great." He frowned. "Then you don't need a guard anymore."

"I might still need one. But you can't do it. You have to rest and recover."

"I can use my right arm. I only used my right arm when I fired at them, and I hit one of them, so I can handle my weapon with my good arm."

"We'll talk about it later," Lena told him. "Whatever I do, I'm paying you two thousand dollars. That's for eight nights plus a bonus."

"You're paying me a bonus for getting shot?"

"I'm paying you a bonus for helping the sheriff catch those guys. So it's really a reward, it's not a bonus."

"You're a good person, Mrs. McLean."

It usually made her feel old being addressed that way, but coming from this young man who almost could have been her grandson, it made her feel great. She leaned over and kissed him on the forehead.

She parted with Heather in the parking lot, and instead of using her car, she walked to the sheriff's office, which was in the back of the town hall. Since she was early for their meeting, she expected to wait a while, but the sheriff had her go right in. He didn't have much of an office, but it was appropriate for the county, which didn't have much in terms of resources. People made do with what they had, and they didn't complain.

"Have you had lunch?" he asked her.

"No, but I can have it later."

"You're not going to watch me eat alone, so I'll order you a sandwich. How about ham on rye with mustard?"

"As long as it's Polish mustard," she joked.

"I'll ask for that if you tell me how to pronounce it."

"Koshchooshko," she told him.

"What a language," he said, shaking his head. "I'm glad we spoke Norwegian."

"You speak Norwegian?"

"Only a few words that I remember from my grandmother. *Ikke noen gang gjøre det igjen.*"

"What does that mean?"

"It means don't ever do that again."

"Were you a bad boy?"

"I was a normal boy. You know how boys are."

"I only had girls, so I don't know. But I did have a brother."

Earl got out his phone and ordered the sandwiches, and then he said: "As I told you, I think I know what they're trying to do."

"So what *are* they trying to do?"

"They're only trying to make you change your position on the mining law. They're not trying to kill you because that wouldn't help them. If they killed you, then we'd have an election to fill your position on the board, and most likely it would be someone who's as strongly against the mining as you are."

"I guess that makes sense," she said after thinking about it. "I mean, it explains why they haven't killed me. But why did they try to kill Rodney?"

"To hurt you. Whatever they've done, it was to hurt you. They knew you cared about Grady, so they killed him. They knew you cared about your goats, so they killed that stubborn doe. What was her name?"

"Tulia."

"That's what I mean. Your goats all have names, which shows you care about them in a way that most farmers don't care about their animals. And somehow they knew you care about Rodney, so they tried to kill him."

"But how could they have known I care about Rodney?"

"They could have known from your body language by watching you with him."

Something occurred to her. "If I had a boyfriend, would they kill him?"

"Do you have a boyfriend?"

"That was a hypothetical question."

"You think the whole county doesn't know?"

"I hope they don't know. The hypothetical boyfriend would be embarrassed."

"Well, the answer is, if they thought you really cared about him, they probably would kill him. Or at least they'd threaten to kill him."

"The only threat I've received was from that guy at the town meeting last week."

"I haven't forgotten about that," the sheriff told her. "I want you to have a look at these thugs and see if either of them was the guy who threatened you."

"I'd be glad to look at them." She thought for a moment, and then she said: "You said that if you're right about what the people who hired those thugs are trying to do, then we know what to expect from them. So what should we expect from them?"

"We should expect them to keep trying to kill your animals," the sheriff said, "and we should expect them to keep trying to kill people you care about."

"People I care about?" she said, with a list beginning to form in her mind.

"Yah, people you care about. And that would include the hypothetical boyfriend."

"I guess it would. It would also include other people." She thought of Heather, Tara, and Lori but she stopped short of including her children, who luckily lived far away and were therefore presumably safe.

"So you need to keep protecting your animals, and you need to think about how to protect people you care about."

"You mean other than by changing my position on the sand mining."

"I'd never advise you to change your position, though that would be the easiest way."

"You agree with my position, don't you?"

"Of course I do," the sheriff said. "But my job is to maintain law and order in this county. It's not to save our valleys from sand mining."

"No, that's *my* job."

"Yah, it is. But I'll do everything in my power to help you do your job."

"Thanks," she said. "Can I ask you a question?"

Looking as if he knew what it was, he said: "Go ahead."

"Did you make a promise to my husband?"

"Yah. I told him I'd watch out for you. I had no idea what I was getting into, though he did warn me."

"How did he warn you?"

"He told me you were a stubborn Polack."

She laughed in recognition. "Well, he was right. I *am* a stubborn Polack. But he was a superstitious Mick. We both carried a lot of baggage from our ancestors."

"I understand," the sheriff said. "I come from people who in Norway had no land, no boats, and no way to make a living. Yet somehow they got here and survived."

The sandwiches arrived, and they stopped talking for a while.

Then Lena said: "So how can I protect my animals?"

"I think you can protect them without posting an armed guard in the compound. I think you only need to have someone in the house who can watch the monitor, and if he sees a threat, then he can deal with it."

"I wonder if Rodney could do that. He said he could handle his weapon with his good arm."

"I wouldn't use Rodney for that purpose. I'd only raise the possibility of using him for that purpose with the hypothetical boyfriend."

"I don't understand."

"It was one thing to have Rodney outside in the compound," the sheriff told her, "but if you were going to have him inside your house every night then the hypothetical boyfriend would have more reason to volunteer."

"I guess he would," Lena said, marveling at the sagacity of the sheriff.

The sheriff took her to the jail cell where they were holding one of the suspects so that she could have a look at him, and he showed her a picture of the other suspect, who was in the hospital. She didn't recognize either of them, so it was someone else who had threatened her at the town meeting, which didn't surprise her since even people she had known for a long time and been friendly with had turned against her.

Before heading home, she stopped at the co-op, which during the summer had produce from local farms as well as the usual household products. It was too early for corn, but the carrots and the zucchini looked good, so she bought a bunch of carrots and two zucchinis along with a roll of paper towels.

On the way home she remembered that she was supposed to give Scott, her personal banker, the cash flow of her business, which she had completely forgotten about. Since she had enough money in her savings account to pay Rodney what she had promised him, she decided that she wouldn't need a bank loan. If she scrimped on things, she could get by, unless there was an unforeseen emergency.

When she got home she left the bag from the co-op at the back door, and she went into the compound to check on the animals, beginning with Brady. The dog greeted her and pranced around her as if his broken rib was already healed, though it couldn't be. It encouraged her that he was able to ignore whatever pain he was still feeling.

He accompanied her while she mingled with the does, who were eating hay or munching on alfalfa pellets. She counted them to make sure there were fifty-five. She then went and checked on the bucks, who were grazing in their own compound. On seeing her, Rex raised his head and gave her a skeptical look as if he doubted her ability to protect the does. She patted his back, saying: "You belong with the guys at the Legion."

After doing the rounds she went to the house, picked up the bag, and unlocked the door. Inside, the cats were waiting for her, and they went up the stairs with her. She went to the kitchen and put the vegetables in a ceramic colander that she had bought years ago from a potter in another valley. She checked the water dish, and then she did what she almost never did: she went into her bedroom and lay down. She had gotten almost no sleep last night, and it finally caught up with her. She set the alarm for four, giving herself enough time for a nap, and she rolled over and closed her eyes.

She was dreaming about a cat tickling her nose with its whiskers when she woke up and found herself face to face with Katiuska, whose head she cupped in her hand and gently pulled against her face, saying: "You thought I should wake up, didn't you."

She reached over and shut off the alarm, which had about ten minutes to go. She felt a little groggy, but it didn't take long after she got up for her to feel the benefits of the nap. It was like starting a new day.

She made herself a cup of tea, which she drank at leisure out on the deck, and then she headed out to the compound, just in time to meet Heather.

While they were rounding up the goats for the milking, Heather asked: "Are you going to get another guard?"

"Yah. The sheriff thinks I should have the guard in the house and station him at the monitor, so if he saw a threat, he could deal with it."

"He'd be there all night?"

"Yah, from eight in the evening to six in the morning."

"But who could you trust to be in the house all night with you?"

Lena laughed. "You think the guard might come into my bedroom?"

"He'd have the opportunity. And you're a very sexy woman."

"Thanks," she said, patting Heather on the shoulder. "I thought of hiring Rodney. He said he could handle his weapon with his good arm."

"You could trust Rodney."

"But the sheriff advised me not to hire Rodney."

"Well, who else could you trust?"

"I could trust Arne."

Heather gave her a knowing look. "Then why not hire him?"

"I offered him the job before, and he turned it down."

"He did? I wonder why."

"I think he had enough war in Vietnam."

"Are you sure it wasn't because he would have had to sit out here in the doe shed?"

"It might have been. It might be more appealing for him to be in the house. Of course he has to sit at the monitor."

"Of course," Heather said, smiling as if they were in a conspiracy together.

Arne arrived shortly after they finished the milking. He walked from his pickup to the house carrying a paper bag in one hand and a rifle in the other. It looked as if he wasn't going to spend another night there without a weapon.

"What's that?" she asked as he came into the living area.

"It's my hunting rifle. It's not an assault weapon, but it's enough to stop one of them."

"What about the other one?"

"I have this," he said, pulling a pistol from his belt.

"I guess we're lucky we don't have strict gun control laws in this state."

"The rifle is for hunting," he said, leaning it against a wall.

"What's the pistol for?"

"Self-defense."

"You mean you have no intention of robbing a bank with that thing?"

"I wouldn't even rob a gas station with it. Robbing banks and gas stations is a piss-poor way to make a living."

"Yah, the real money's in sand mining."

He set the pistol and the paper bag on the table and went into the kitchen and opened the refrigerator to get a beer. He took out a bottle, saying: "You need to get more beer."

"Why don't you get it? You're the one who drinks it."

"I brought a bottle of wine for you," he said as if she wasn't being fair.

"Where is it?"

"It's in the bag."

"So I get beer for you," she said, taking a bottle of red wine out of the bag, "and you get wine for me. Does that make sense?"

"I think it does. We're each doing something for the other."

"That was sweet." She went and kissed him for it.

"What's for dinner?"

"I can make pasta."

"Can you make those hollow noodles with meat sauce?"

"Yah, sure. I can also make zucchini sauce."

He made a face. "No, I'd rather have meat sauce."

"Are you hungry now?"

"I'm always hungry."

He always was, but he didn't gain weight. His body maintained a good tone, and his limbs were strong. His secret was that he worked out three times a week at a gym in Passau, which gave him a preferential rate as a veteran.

She half-filled the pasta pot with water and turned the flame to high under it. She got a package of ground beef from the freezer, and a can of whole tomatoes from the cabinet where she kept canned food.

She was cooking chopped onion in her medium cast-iron skillet when she broached the subject, saying: "I talked with the sheriff today, and he thinks I should have the guard in the house instead of in the compound."

"That makes sense," Arne said. "In the house he wouldn't be a sitting duck."

"Well, I didn't mean to put Rodney in that position."

"I know you didn't. And don't feel bad about it. We all went along with him being in the compound. But it would be better to have the guard in the house."

"He could sit at the monitor, and if he sees a threat, he could deal with it."

"That makes sense," Arne said again.

"I could have Rodney in the house," she said after a pause. "I saw him in the hospital this morning, and he's doing fine. He said he could handle his weapon with his good arm."

"Oh, I don't know. Have you ever tried to fire an assault weapon with one arm?"

"I haven't fired an assault weapon with two arms, but he was firing his weapon with one arm when he hit that guy."

"It was a lucky shot."

"Maybe it was. But he hit the guy, and he helped the sheriff catch them."

There was a long silence. "So he'd be in the house all night?"

"Yah. He'd be sitting at the monitor."

"So if I came over, he'd be here?"

"Yah." She stirred the onions.

"And if I didn't come over, he'd be here?"

"Yah." She added the tomatoes to the skillet.

"Well, I don't like the idea."

"What don't you like about it?"

"I don't like having a one-armed guy protect you."

"I need someone to protect me," she said, turning up the heat, "and I don't know any two-armed guys who are willing to do it."

"Why do you think I brought my rifle and my pistol?"

"I don't know. I guess you didn't want to spend another night here without a weapon."

"I brought them to protect you."

"Actually, the sheriff thinks I don't need to be protected. He thinks it's the animals that need to be protected."

"I could protect the animals."

"Are you willing to sit all night at the monitor?"

He hesitated. "From when until when?"

"From eight at night until six in the morning."

"If we could spend some time in bed before eight, I'd be willing to do it."

"Some time in bed?" she teased him.

"Yah. But I don't see how we could swing it. You have the milking from six thirty to eight thirty, and by then I'd be on duty."

"We could spend some time in bed during the afternoon. In fact, I took a nap today, and it was delicious."

He thought about it. "I'd have to cut out the Legion in the afternoon."

"You could make that sacrifice. It would only be until the board votes on our law."

"When is that again?"

"Thirteen days from now."

He looked as if he was weighing thirteen days without going to the Legion against thirteen days of spending time in bed with her during the afternoon. It might have been close, but he finally said: "Okay. We have a deal. I'll be your armed guard."

Later, while she was lying in bed and Arne was sitting at the monitor, doing guard duty, she felt that the animals were safe. She trusted Arne to stay awake and respond to any threat by firing a warning shot and calling the sheriff.

Then she remembered how during her conversation with the sheriff she hadn't included her children on the list of people who were in danger. At the time she believed that whoever was threatening her wouldn't know where her children were, but now she wondered, and she debated whether she should warn them or simply trust in God to protect them. If she warned them and they really weren't in any danger, then she would upset them unnecessarily. But if she didn't warn them, then she might leave them exposed to danger that could have been avoided, though she didn't see what practical measures she could take, other than having them fly to Argentina and stay with her brother for the next thirteen days. Her last thoughts before going to sleep were calculating the airfare to Argentina for her children and her grandchildren, and concluding that she would need to withdraw money from the retirement plan to pay for their trip.

EIGHT

THEY WERE LIVING with her parents when Patty was born. By then her brother Tony had graduated from St. Mary's and joined the navy, so there was room for them in the house, and having her mother and Babcia on hand to help with the baby was a major benefit. Among other things, it enabled her after a few months to resume working in her father's office, where she answered the phone, attended customers, and assisted the bookkeeper. She worked about twenty hours a week, which got her out of the house for a while and gave her some income to contribute to their fund for a down payment on their own house.

From then on, the baby was the main subject of her letters to Siobhan, who was doing well at her job with a publishing company and was living in Greenwich Village. There were times when Lena wished she had other things to write about, and there were times when after reading a letter from Siobhan she wondered what her life would have been like if she had gone with her friend to New York. But when she picked up her baby, she knew without a doubt that she had made the right decision.

Two years later she got pregnant again, and at that point they decided to look for a house. It took them a long time to find the right house, get a contract on it, secure a mortgage, and do the closing, and they were still living with her parents when Brenda was born. In fact, Brenda was three months old when they finally moved. Since their house was only two blocks away from her parents' house, they still had her mother and Babcia nearby to help with the baby, so they had some independence now without giving up all the benefits of living with her parents.

Lena hadn't known what to expect from Devon as a father, especially with two girls, but her instincts about him as a person must have been right since he was a warm and loving father, first with Patty and then with Brenda, from the day they were born. Of course, since Patty had Devon all to herself for three years, she probably couldn't help being envious of the new rival for her father's affection, but somehow he was able to make her feel that she meant as much to him as ever, which went a long way toward achieving peace.

It helped that the girls were so very different. With her dark hair and shimmering white skin, Patty looked like she came from the Irish side of the family, and she was like her father in other ways, especially in having his love of words. When she vied for his attention, she would ask him to read a book to her, or ask him a question that she knew he would enjoy answering, drawing on his store of knowledge. At the age of three she was already an ideal student. In contrast, with her blond hair and rosy complexion, Brenda looked like she came from the Polish side of the family. Whereas Patty was delicate, Brenda was sturdy. And when she vied for her father's attention, instead of using words as Patty did, Brenda would do something physical, like take his hand or give him a nudge.

As they grew up, they continued being different. Patty was very good at school and Brenda was very good at sports, so they had different goals, with Patty wanting to become a scholar and Brenda wanting to become an athlete. Since they weren't competing for the same thing, other than their father's affection, they got along fine. It helped that Devon spent as much time watching Brenda play softball as he did talking with Patty about books, and that he praised them equally for their accomplishments.

The girls were in elementary school when something disrupted their happy life. It started with a phone call from a girl who after hearing Lena's voice said she was sorry, she had the wrong number, and then hung up. It wasn't unusual to get a call from someone who had the wrong number, but it was typically an older person who had misdialed. The caller this time sounded like a young female. It could have been a student from St. Theresa taking a course with Devon, or it could have been any of the large number of female students at St. Mary's, which by then had become co-educational. Whoever it was, she was a young female.

Not wanting to jump to conclusions, Lena tried to put the

phone call out of her mind, but she had just turned thirty and had begun to notice lines in her face. She realized that with all those female students at the college Devon was exposed to temptation every time he walked into a classroom. And he had a history of falling in love with a female student.

With the kids in school, Lena was working about thirty hours a week in her father's office, and the day after the phone call she left work around three, and on a hunch, she walked over to the Kool Kat. It had new owners, but it hadn't changed. It was still the place where students and faculty from the liberal arts hung out, drinking coffee and smoking cigarettes and discussing works of fiction, philosophy, and theology. It was also still the place where Devon went a few times a week to have an espresso.

She could have peered through the window, but if he was there, she didn't want him to see her checking on him, so she walked into the place as if she was going to buy a coffee to take out. She got as far as the register when she saw Devon at a table in back. He was facing away from her, so unless he turned around he wouldn't see her. But the girl was facing her, young and pretty and gazing at him with rapturous eyes.

Overcome with anger and despair, she left the shop, and she spent the next hour wandering the streets asking over and over how he could do such a thing to her. She loved him as much as she ever had, and she had always been faithful to him. So why was he betraying her with this slut?

By the time Devon got home that evening she had almost convinced herself that he was only having coffee with a student, helping her with a paper or a reading assignment, and if she asked him what he was doing in the Kool Kat with that girl, it would reveal an insecurity that she dreaded admitting, not to mention a loss of self-respect. So she didn't ask about the girl, and during dinner with the kids he didn't display any guilty behavior. In fact, he acted as if some weight had been removed from his conscience.

Two days later as she was returning from the stationary store after buying supplies for the office, she saw him drive by with the girl in the passenger seat of his car. The girl had a palpable look of contentment, which made Lena wonder if they had come from the sleazy motel outside of town that rented rooms by the hour. And that put Lena over the edge. She stopped and glared at the back of the car wishing she had a bomb to hurl at it.

That evening, after dinner when the kids were upstairs supposedly studying, she confronted him. They were in the kitchen, where she had just finished cleaning up.

Turning from the sink and facing him, she said: "I saw you today with a girl in your car."

"You did?" He didn't look a bit upset. "I didn't see you. Where were you?"

"I was on my way back to the office from the stationary store."

"Well, I can explain," he told her. "But let's sit down. It's a long story."

"It better be a good one," she said, fuming. She sat down at the table, and he sat down across from her with his hands clasped as if he was going to say grace.

The story began with his year in Europe. He was in Madrid, staying at a hotel that cost only two dollars a day and eating at restaurants for even less. One night he was in a bar on Plaza Santa Ana when he met two girls from Boston who had just graduated from Salve Regina. After sixteen years of Catholic schools they were letting off steam, and they were hopping from bar to bar in search of action. They were joined by a guy from Notre Dame, who was attracted to one of the girls, the redhead, and when the four of them moved on, Devon paired up with the other girl, the brunette. Eventually, the two of them split from the other couple, and they ended up in his hotel room, where the girl let off a lot of steam.

She didn't spend the rest of the night with him, and she didn't come to Plaza Santa Ana the next evening. But he ran into the guy from Notre Dame, who told him that the girls had left that day for Barcelona.

He never saw her or heard from her again. And then a week ago he got a phone call from a girl who thought she might be his daughter. She lived in a suburb of Philadelphia with her adoptive parents. When she finished college she embarked on a quest to find her biological parents. With the cooperation of her adoptive mother, who understood her need for the quest, she tracked down her biological mother, who lived in a suburb of Boston and had no idea who her daughter's biological father was. When pressed, she came up with the names of several guys she had slept with during her trip to Europe after graduating from Salve Regina, plus a few nameless ones, which included an Irish guy from New York who had gone to St. John's University and claimed to be a poet. After six months of investigation, the young woman finally tracked Devon to Winona.

"So is she your daughter?" Lena asked him.

"There's no way of knowing," Devon said. "I only know that I slept with her mother, but so did a lot of other guys."

"From what I could see of her, she doesn't look like you."

"She doesn't. She looks like her mother."

"You remember what her mother looked like?"

"I remembered what she looked like when I saw her daughter, but I hadn't thought about that night since the morning after."

At least this was reassuring. "Has she found her other possible fathers?"

"She found them all. I was the last."

"Well, after meeting you, does she think you're her father?"

"She doesn't know what to think," Devon said. "But after we talked, she felt that it really didn't matter who her biological parents were. She decided that her real parents were the couple who adopted her."

"That's nice," Lena said, meaning it. "Where were you taking her in your car?"

"I was taking her to the airport in La Crosse so she could fly home to Philadelphia."

She knew that he was being totally honest with her, and she realized that she should be totally honest with him. "Well, I must admit, I thought you were having sex with her, and I was really pissed at you."

"I should have told you sooner, but it was so bizarre. I mean, after more than twenty years a girl appears out of the blue who thinks she might be my daughter."

"I would have understood."

"I'm sorry. I was going to tell you, but I wanted to see how the story ended."

"I like the way the story ended," Lena said. "If we'd had to adopt kids, I would have liked them to feel that way."

"You know," Devon said, "it's complicated enough having our own kids, so I'm glad we didn't have the additional complication of adopting them."

"I agree. Do you think they're really studying?"

"No. I think they're only pretending to study. But I don't know what the hell they're up to."

"I don't either. But at least I can stop worrying about *you* now."

"I'm sorry," he repeated. He reached out and took both of her hands and drew them toward him and kissed them.

In bed with him that night she didn't worry about anything, not even the kids.

The next day, after the milking, she called her brother in Buenos Aires. The time was two hours later there, so he and his wife Sylvia would be up. In fact, Sylvia would be at work in the bank where she ran the department of human resources. Unless he had a contract to fly somewhere, Tony would be at home reading the paper, with a game of squash scheduled for later that morning, followed by lunch at a downtown restaurant. They lived in a house in Palermo which they had bought in the early 1980s after the generals were driven out of office by their disastrous war in the Falkland Islands, which Argentines called Las Malvinas. Despite the patriotic refrain "Las Malvinas son Argentinas," the islands were still British. But the war had served the purpose of getting rid of the military government, which had run the country for the past seven years, or even longer according to people who said they were behind the scenes of the previous regime.

Tony's older child, Rosa, was married and living in the nearby suburb of Vicente Lopez, while his younger child, Mateo, was working in Sao Paulo at the branch of an Argentine company that did infrastructure projects. So their bedrooms would be empty.

"Hola?" her brother said, answering the phone.

"Hi, it's Lena." They talked on the phone about once a month. It was less expensive now, and the phone system worked much better. In the old days, it was hard to hear the other person, and the line was often cut off.

"Hey, it's good to hear from you. How are you doing?"

"I'm doing fine. How are Sylvia and the kids?"

"They're doing fine. And guess what? Rosa's finally pregnant." Rosa had been trying for several years to get pregnant, and recently she had undergone fertility treatments.

"That's great! I'm so happy for her," Lena said, remembering thankfully how easy it had been for her to get pregnant.

"She's due in January, so Sylvia will be able to help her. She always takes her vacation then."

Lena had to remind herself that since the seasons were reversed, January was in the middle of summer there. "So it's good timing."

"It's perfect timing," Tony said, "though of course the due date is immaterial."

She collected herself, and then she broached the subject. "I'm calling because I wondered if you could have some guests there for the next twelve days."

"Sure, we could. We're not going anywhere until early August. Are you planning to visit us?"

"I'm not, but I'm hoping my children and my grandchildren can visit you."

"That would be fine. But what about you?"

"I have to be here for the vote on the mining law." They had discussed the law in previous conversations, so he knew what she was talking about. He also knew that as a supporter of the law she had made a lot of enemies.

"When is the vote?"

"In twelve days."

There was a silence at the other end, and then Tony finally said: "I have a feeling it's not a coincidence that you want them to visit us between now and the day of the vote."

"You're right. It's not a coincidence. I should have told you before," she continued, "but the people who don't want a law against mining have been trying to get me to change my position. The first thing they did was kill my dog, and then they killed my favorite doe, and then they tried to kill the young man I hired to protect my animals."

"Holy shit. It sounds like Argentina when I first came here. So you're worried that they'll kill your children or grandchildren?"

"Yah, I am. I want to get them out of the way until the vote."

"But aren't you worried that they'll kill *you?*"

"The sheriff thinks they have nothing to gain by killing me since I'd be replaced by someone who would take the same position on the mining. What they want is to make me change my position. And if they think they can make me change my position by threatening my children or my grandchildren, then I have something to worry about."

"I understand. But are they right in thinking they could make you change your position by threatening your children or your grandchildren?"

"I don't know. And I don't want to let them test me on that question."

"Well, we have two empty bedrooms here, so we have room for all of them. And maybe I can get them a deal on the flights. When would they come?"

"The sooner, the better. But I haven't talked with Patty or Brenda yet. I wanted to make sure that you could do it."

"*No hay problema,*" Tony said. "I just wish you were coming too."

The next thing she did was call Patty. It was an hour later there, and since Patty's class was on Mondays and Wednesdays, she should have been home. But she didn't answer, so Lena left a message and then called Brenda on her cell phone since they used the land line only for business. But Brenda didn't answer, so Lena left another message. It was frustrating not to reach people when she wanted to, and if the situation hadn't been urgent, she would have understood, as she did at other times. But now she didn't have any patience.

She was about to go into the kitchen and find something to kill time when the phone rang.

It was Patty, who said: "I'm sorry I missed you. I was doing the laundry."

"That's okay. I called you because—" She paused, looking for the right way to put it. "I'm worried about you and the kids."

"You're worried? Why?"

She explained why.

"Hey, are you all right, mom?" Patty asked as if she was afraid her mother was losing it.

"I'm perfectly all right. I want to get you and the kids out of the way, so I just talked with your uncle Tony, and he has plenty of room for you to stay with him for the next twelve days."

"You want us to go to Argentina?"

"Yah, I do. You should be safe there."

"In case you forgot, I'm teaching a course."

"You can give them a special online assignment." She knew that in all her courses Patty had her students do things online. "You can stay in touch with them through email."

"Students don't read email."

"Then text them or however you communicate with them. But I want you to go to Argentina for the next twelve days."

There was a long silence.

"Are you still there?" she asked her daughter.

"Yeah, I'm here, mom. But this whole thing is crazy. I mean, people might kill for gold or diamonds or emeralds or rubies, but they don't kill for sand."

"They already *have* killed for sand," she said, raising her voice. "They killed my dog and my favorite doe. And they tried to kill the young man who was protecting my animals. So don't tell me people don't kill for sand."

"But they don't know where we are."

"They have global resources. They know everything."

There was another long silence. "Well, I have to talk with Carmine about it."

"I understand. But we don't have much time. If they're going to do anything, they're going to do it within the next twelve days."

"Okay," Patty said as if she still thought her mother was crazy.

After ending the call, Lena wandered into the living area, reflecting on the conversation, which hadn't gone as well as she had hoped. But she knew her daughter, so she should have known that Patty would resist the idea of taking her children to Argentina just because her mother was worried. Patty was stubborn, like her mother, but in most ways she was like her father. She had his brains, and she followed in his footsteps by getting her doctorate at St. John's and taking a job at a Catholic college that didn't have a national brand name. So out of respect for her father she would have listened to him. But he wasn't there to help his family in this situation, which made him even more keenly missed.

Lena was still waiting to hear from Brenda when the sheriff called to give her an update. There was a match between the Glock found in the glove compartment of the car driven by the two thugs and the bullet that killed Grady. There was a match between the rifle found in the trunk of their car and the bullet that wounded Rodney. And there was a match between fingerprints found on the rifle and one of the guys, so the sheriff had a very strong case against them. With the help of the prosecutor he was trying to get them to reveal who had hired them, but they were refusing to talk. He would keep trying, using the stick of fifteen years in prison for attempted murder and the carrot of a reduced sentence for cooperating with law enforcement.

When he had finished updating her, the sheriff asked: "Do you have an armed guard?"

"Oh, yah. And he's doing fine. At least they haven't killed any more animals."

"They won't stop at killing animals. Look what they did to Rodney."

"I know. I'm trying to get my kids out of the way."

"Where would you send them?"

"To Argentina."

"Well, that's out of the way," the sheriff said. "I'll get back to you on whatever progress we make with those two thugs. Take care."

After ending the call, she tried calling Brenda again, and this time she got her. She explained to Brenda why she wanted her to go to Argentina, and unlike her sister, Brenda didn't act like she thought her mother was crazy. But she offered an alternative.

"Look, mom," Brenda said. "I'd love to go to Argentina and see Uncle Tony, but we have so much business here I just can't take the time off. But we have a friend who owns a cabin in the north woods, and if it would make you happy, I could go there tomorrow and stay until you have the vote. There's no way anyone could find me up there."

"What about your business?"

"I can handle my side of the business from anywhere. All I need is my computer and access to the internet."

"You have access to the internet from a cabin in the north woods?"

"It has a dish, so I have access to everything. I can even watch crappy TV shows."

"I hope you don't go to a cabin in the north woods and watch crappy TV shows there."

"Of course I don't. I was only saying what I *can* do. So the cabin would work, as long as Jane can stay here and handle her side of the business. They wouldn't hurt Jane, would they?"

"No. They'd only hurt my children or my grandchildren."

"So Carmine isn't going to Argentina?"

"To tell you truth," Lena said, "I don't know if Patty is going to Argentina. You know how your sister is."

"Yah, if you want her to do something, she'll do the opposite."

"Well, I'm working on her, and I'm hoping she'll come around soon."

"If she doesn't want to go to Argentina, she could always bring the kids up to the cabin."

"How big is the cabin?"

"It's big enough for two sisters and two kids."

"Thanks. You've given me a backup plan. So you're going to the cabin tomorrow?"

"Yah. I'll leave in the morning. It's a three-hour drive."

"How can I reach you there?"

"By email. You can even text me. I told you, I have access to everything."

"Well, I don't have access to everything. We don't have cell phone service in the valley."

"Oh, that's right. Then you can reach me by email."

After ending the call, Lena reflected on this conversation. She was always amazed at how different her daughters were when they had the same parents and the same upbringing. Brenda was like her grandfather in knowing how to build things. She could have been an engineer, but she dropped out of college while having an identity crisis. After emerging from that crisis with the acceptance that she was gay, she enrolled in a construction management program at a community college and learned her trade. She managed the projects while her partner Jane managed the guys who worked on them, so it was plausible that Brenda could handle her side of the business from a cabin in the north woods with access to the internet. And it was gratifying that she would go there just because her mother was worried.

By now it was noon, and Lena had to go into town: first, to see her personal banker, and second, to visit Rodney in the hospital. So after eating a sandwich and an apple for lunch, she headed into town. On the way she decided to give Patty until that evening to make a decision, and if she didn't hear from her by nine, she would call her.

Scott was meeting with a client when she arrived at the bank, so she went to the counter and withdrew two thousand dollars in cash. By the time she was done, Scott was available, so she accepted his invitation to sit down with him.

"I decided not to borrow the money," she told him. "I'm going to withdraw it from the retirement fund, as you suggested."

"That's a good decision," he said, looking happy that she had taken his advice. "Just be sure you talk with someone at TIAA about the tax consequences."

"I will. I need to learn more about taxes."

"I assume you have an accountant."

"No. I've always done my taxes myself. Before we started the business," she said, "I took a course on taxes at the community college."

"Your husband didn't handle the taxes?"

"Oh, no. He didn't like numbers."

"Well, I'm impressed. But managing your retirement fund takes knowledge and experience."

She smiled. "Yah. I got the message. And since you helped me, I promise that if I ever need help in managing my retirement fund, I'll come to you."

"Fair enough," he said.

With the meeting over, she took a button of goat Camembert out of her pocketbook and gave it to him, which she hoped he would enjoy more than reviewing her cash flow.

As she went out she wondered if he would ever find money to manage in the county. As far as she knew, the people who had money were outsiders, and they would have personal bankers in the cities where they lived.

She walked from the bank to the hospital, where she took the elevator to the second floor. She found Rodney lying in bed and watching an old movie on television.

"Hi," he said, immediately muting the television.

"How are you doing?" she asked him, approaching the bed.

"I'm doing fine. I'm being released today."

"That's good. Are you going home?"

"Yah." He looked as if the thought of going home completely depressed him.

"I brought you the money I owe you," she said, taking the envelope with the money out of her pocketbook. "But maybe I shouldn't give it to you now unless you have a safe place to put it."

"I have a safe place to put it," he said. "Do you want me back as a guard?"

"No. I have a new guard. It's a guy you know from the Legion. And I think you can do more with your life than being a guard."

"You do? But I don't know how to do anything."

"You can learn how to do things. But you have to think about what you like."

He stared blankly across the room.

"What do you like?" she prompted him.

"I don't know. I like your goats. And I like your dog."

Remembering how he had wanted to know the names of her does, which seemed to confirm what he had just told her, she had an idea. "Then maybe you should pursue a career in taking care of animals."

"You need a degree to do that, don't you?"

"To be a veterinarian you do. But you could start helping a vet, and if you like the work, you could get a degree. You have benefits that pay for college."

"Yah, I do. But I didn't see how I could use them."

She thought of asking Vern if he could use an assistant who might learn as an apprentice, but she didn't mention it, not wanting to get Rodney's hopes up, so she only said: "I'll see if I can find a position for you."

"Okay," he said, for a change looking hopeful.

She handed him the envelope and leaned over and kissed him on the forehead, praying that Vern would hire him as an assistant. She was even willing to pay Vern to hire him, and now that she was at the point of breaking Devon's rule against touching the retirement fund, she felt that she could afford to subsidize him.

As soon as she got home she called Vern and left a message. It was after two, so she had just enough time to check the animals before Arne arrived. She had noticed that when he arrived yesterday he smelled of beer, which indicated that he had stopped at the Legion for a round or two before reporting to duty. She smiled at the thought that he had found a way to have it all: the Legion, her, a nice siesta, and a home-cooked dinner before he sat at the monitor all night. She could see how it might be sustainable, at least for the next twelve days.

When she returned to the house after checking the animals, she saw the light on the phone flashing. It was a message from Vern, who said he would be at his office until three-thirty. It was just after three, so she called him immediately.

"I hope it's not about an animal," Vern said wryly.

"It's about a human being," she said.

"I only treat animals."

"He doesn't need to be treated. He needs to be helped."

There was a long pause. "I hope it's not Arne."

"It's Rodney, the young veteran I hired as a guard." She was appealing to Vern's solidarity with veterans since he too had served in the military before he went to veterinary school. The only thing he didn't do as a veteran was hang out at the Legion.

"How can I help him?"

"You can hire him as an assistant."

"Why should I hire him as an assistant?"

"He likes animals, he's reliable, and he's trustworthy, so I think he'd make a good assistant."

"You do, uh? Well, it just happens that the girl who's been working as my assistant got into veterinary school, and she's leaving me at the end of the summer."

"Then there'd be an overlap between them. The girl could help him learn the job."

There was another long pause. "How well do you know this young man?"

"I feel like I know him very well. I mean, he risked his life for me, and he risked his life for our country."

"Okay. I'll see him," Vern told her. "He's still in the hospital, isn't he?"

"Yah, but he's being released today. I'll tell him to call you and make an appointment."

"Tomorrow would be good." There was yet another long pause. "So how are *you* doing?"

"I'm doing fine. I hired Arne to guard the animals."

"Well, he must be doing a good job since there haven't been any more calls in the middle of the night."

"He's doing a great job," she said, seeing his car appear in the driveway. "And thanks for being willing to see Rodney."

"Thanks for trying to help him," Vern said.

When he came into the house Arne was carrying a six-pack in one hand and a bottle of wine in the other hand. After only two days he was buying beer and bringing wine, and she wondered what heights he might attain by the end of his tour of duty.

"How was your day?" he asked her.

"Busy. How was yours?"

"It wasn't busy, but it was fine." He gave her a beery kiss, and then he put the six-pack into the refrigerator.

"Did you hear anything today at the Legion?"

"No, nothing important. A lot of grousing about the Twins."

"Nothing about sand mining?"

"They don't care about sand mining."

"They're not for it or against it?"

"No. They don't understand what all the fuss is about."

"I hope you don't mean that," she said, suspecting that she was being teased.

"I don't mean it," he said, grinning. "I only mean that they're not passionate about it."

"Are they passionate about anything?"

"Yah, they are. They're passionate about beer."

She gently flicked him in the chest with her forefinger. He grabbed the finger, brought it to his lips and kissed it, and from that point on there was no stopping them.

Arne extended his siesta through the time of the evening milking, and when Lena returned to the house she had to wake him up. While he sat at the table with a bottle of beer, she prepared a dinner of pan-fried chicken cutlets, rice, and green beans.

"You know," he said as he chewed on a bite of chicken, "I have a feeling they won't do anything more to the animals."

"I have that feeling too," she said.

"Then why do I have to guard them all night?"

"You said you would. And if you stopped, they'd probably kill another animal."

"They wouldn't know if I stopped. They can't see me."

"Somehow they'd know. I think they know everything we do."

"Everything?" He looked embarrassed. "Oh, that's paranoid. They can't possibly know everything we do."

"Well, they know everything that involves them."

"So if I stopped sitting at the monitor, they'd know?"

"Yah. I think they'd know.

He made a face that expressed doubt. "Well, even if they knew I wasn't sitting at the monitor, I still think they wouldn't do anything more to the animals. I think they've moved on."

"Moved on to what?" she asked, though she knew exactly what he meant.

"To people," he said. "The last thing they did was to try to kill Rodney, so the next thing they do will target someone else."

"Are you worried about yourself?"

"No. If those fuckers in Vietnam couldn't kill me, no one can. But I *am* worried about you."

"You shouldn't be worried about me. They don't want to kill me. They want to make me change my position on sand mining."

"If they killed you," he said, "then you couldn't vote against sand mining."

"But someone would be elected to replace me, and that person would vote against it."

"How do you know?"

"I don't know. But it's very likely, so they have nothing to gain by killing me."

"Okay," he said. "Well, if they have nothing to gain by killing you, then what are we worried about?"

"We're worried about what they might do to the animals. Or to someone I care about," she added, feeling it was time to share this concern with him.

He frowned. "Do you care about me?"

"Of course I care about you."

"Are you worried about what they might do to me?"

"Yah, I am," she told him.

"Well, that's something I should think about."

She touched his arm, saying: "Yah, you should. But while you're thinking about it, you should take your station at the monitor. I gotta call my daughter now."

"Which daughter?"

"The one who doesn't listen to me."

"Then why are you calling her?"

"There's always hope." She patted his arm, got up from the table, and went over to the phone. While she was punching the numbers, Arne went into the living room to station himself at the monitor. She felt that she had done the right thing by making him realize that he was in danger because he was someone she cared about. And she believed that after all he had been through in Vietnam he could handle it.

"Hello, mom," Patty said.

"Hi, honey. Have you had a chance to talk with Carmine?"

"Yeah. And I have to admit, he doesn't think you're crazy, I guess because he grew up in the Bronx. But he came up with something better than going to Argentina."

"He did? What?"

"His brother has a house on the Jersey Shore. We were going there anyway after my course, but we can go there earlier."

"Well, I don't know. I'm afraid that they could find you there."

"The house isn't in his brother's name, so they couldn't track us there. And even if they did, they wouldn't mess with anyone staying in that house."

"They wouldn't? Why not?"

"It's in the name of someone they wouldn't mess with," Patty said as if that was enough.

Assuming that the person in question was a highly respected mobster, Lena said: "Okay. I'll take your word for it. But I want you to go tomorrow morning."

"We will. We're already packed."

"Thank you, honey. I could be overreacting to this situation, but I want to feel sure that they can't harm you or the kids."

"I understand. And Carmine understands."

When the call ended, she asked God to shower blessings on her daughter's husband, whom she now appreciated more than ever.

Around three in the morning she was awakened by a barking dog, who turned out to be Brady. She jumped out of bed and went into the living room, where she found Arne dozing at the monitor. She shook him, and he snapped out of it, saying: "What?"

"Brady's barking," she told him.

"Yah, I hear him. But I don't see anything on the monitor."

"There's no one in the compound?"

"No." He quickly checked the other views. "There's no one anywhere on your property."

"Then why is Brady barking?"

"I don't know. I guess he heard a dog barking somewhere in the valley."

"I think we should go out and look around."

"Okay," he said reluctantly.

She went and put some clothes on, and they went out, with Arne carrying the rifle. They went into the compound, where Brady was still barking.

"What's the matter?" she asked him. She peered into the doe shed, and the animals seemed all right, except that they were jittery.

"Maybe he saw a coyote," Arne said.

"Yah, that's his job, to scare away coyotes."

They headed toward the buck shed, which was on a rise from which they could look down the valley, and they saw a large ball of fire in the distance.

"Oh, my God," she said, realizing that it was Otto's shack and praying that he had gotten out alive. "I'll go and call the sheriff."

"You don't have to," Arne told her. "I see the flashing lights of his cruiser."

It was coming from the highway, and it was heading toward the ball of fire. Of course there were no fire engines since there was no water available for putting out fires.

"Come on," she said, turning from the buck shed and heading out of the compound. "We have to go there and see what happened."

"It looks like they've moved on to people," Arne said, going with her and carrying his rifle as if he no longer had any use for it. Whoever they were, they had expanded the war beyond the confines of her farm.

NINE

THOUGH HIS JOB and his family kept him busy, Devon still found time to write poetry, and every year his poems were published in journals. When he finished a poem, he would read it to Lena, with the two of them sitting on the sofa with their feet up and their legs intertwined. She would close her eyes and let herself be moved by his voice, as she had from the moment she had first heard him read poetry. His poems fell into several categories that included his feelings for her and their children, his interest in ordinary people, his struggle for faith, and his opposition to injustice. Of course, she was biased, but she believed that Devon was one of the great poets of the century, and shortly after Patty's ninth birthday, her opinion was supported by an editor at a major publisher who contacted him and offered to do a book of his collected poems. The editor, whose name was Frances, had been reading his poetry in journals for years, and had finally gotten support for the project. There was even an advance, though not a large one, to cover the time he would spend in selecting poems for the collection.

Lena helped him select poems. In their first approach he would read a poem to her and ask for her decision, yes or no, but since she always said yes, they tried another approach. He would read her two poems and ask her which she liked better. That was easier for her, and it helped him to weed out the poems he wasn't sure about. By early June they had selected about two hundred poems, which he mailed to Frances in a large brown envelope. Frances evidently liked them all since she didn't eliminate any of them. A month later she sent him a design for the book, which he approved, and from then on things were in a rush since Frances wanted the book to be out in time for Christmas.

The launch was scheduled for early November, with Devon expected to do readings at several bookstores in New York. For the week that they would be away, he got colleagues to cover his classes, and Lena arranged for the girls to stay at her parents' house. Siobhan found a reasonable hotel for them in the theater district, and on a crisp Saturday morning they flew from La Crosse to Chicago and then to New York. They were in their hotel room by the early afternoon, and as soon as they had unpacked, they went out to have the lunch that Devon had talked about—a hotdog with a cup of juice from Papaya King, which they ate while walking around Times Square. Though she had seen it in photographs and in movies, Lena wasn't prepared for the gritty reality of Times Square, and she couldn't ignore the looks that Devon attracted from the hookers. Glancing at him, she realized that he was completely oblivious of them.

That evening they met Siobhan for dinner at a small French restaurant in the West Village. She hadn't seen her friend since the baptism of Brenda, about six years ago. Siobhan had agreed to sponsor Brenda, as she had done for Patty, and she had been a conscientious godmother, always remembering their birthdays and sending them presents for Christmas.

Siobhan was waiting for them at the bar of the restaurant, and after a long, loving hug they both stepped back and looked at each other and insisted that the other hadn't changed, though they were now six years older. Followed by Devon, they went to the table that Siobhan had reserved, and sipping wine, they talked about the book launch. Siobhan had left her job at the publishing company, having found that she could make a living as a writer, but she was still very much involved in the industry, interviewing authors and writing reviews, and she had arranged a meeting for Devon with the poetry editor of *The New Yorker*.

"Thank you," Devon told her. "That was my dream—to see my poems in *The New Yorker*."

"Well, it's not a done deal," Siobhan said, "but she likes your work."

Inevitably, while eating dinner they did some reminiscing about the time when as students they had plotted to meet their professor at the Kool Kat. Though it was one of the many things that Lena had revealed to her husband over the years, he pretended to be shocked by the idea that his two best students would plot against him.

"Against you?" Siobhan said. "Admit it, professor. It's the best thing that happened to you."

"It is," Devon said seriously. "Lena made my life, and I'll always be thankful."

On Sunday they managed to get tickets for the matinee of "A Taste of Honey," which was closing the next day. The only plays that Lena had seen were by the drama group at St. Mary's, so she was thrilled by the performance, and she told Devon she wanted to see another play while they were in New York. To give her the experience of a Broadway musical, he got tickets for a revival of "My Fair Lady," the Wednesday matinee since their evenings were taken.

On Monday they met with Frances at the publisher's office. Frances was an energetic woman in her mid-fifties, and she handed Devon a schedule of the readings and signings which began that evening and ended on Thursday evening. They were all at bookstores except for a reading at the book club of a Catholic church in the West Village. Frances explained that the members of the club had received advance copies of Devon's book two weeks ago, so they should be prepared to discuss his poems.

After dealing with all the business matters, Frances led them out of the building and up Third Avenue to an old Irish pub. At a table in the back of a dimly lit room, they learned that Frances had grown up in the Bronx and gotten her degree at Fordham, with a major in English, and that led to a discussion of Catholic poets, which began with Gerard Manley Hopkins.

"Hopkins is one of my models," Devon said, "though I don't write like him."

"No, you don't," Frances agreed. "You have your own voice. But you deal with similar subject matter."

"I guess I do, but I don't have his perspective as a priest."

"The women at our church," Lena interjected, "who hear him read at the Sunday mass, think he would have made a good priest."

"He has the voice for it," Frances said.

"Well, that's all I have for it," Devon said, smiling.

"They'll like you at the book club," Frances said. "In fact, there's a woman in the club who knows you."

"Really?" Lena said, wondering if it was another woman from Devon's past.

He made a gesture that avowed his innocence.

"I believe she was a student of yours."

"Do you remember her name?"

"It's an Irish name."

"Is it Siobhan?"

"Yeah, that's it."

Lena connected the name of the church from the list of events with the church that Siobhan attended in the West Village, and she was glad. "Was Siobhan the one who arranged the book club discussion?"

"I believe she was."

"She's a friend of mine. We were both students of Professor McLean."

"Did you go to St. Mary's?"

"No, we went to St. Theresa. Back then they only had boys at St. Mary's, but we were allowed to take his course in Romantic Poetry."

"They wanted me to have some better students," Devon explained.

"So *were* they better students?" Frances asked.

"They were the best." He reached across the table and squeezed Lena's hand. "And this one helped me select poems for the book."

"You did a good job. You included all the poems I liked, and there were poems I never saw before."

"They didn't all get published before."

"Well, they're published now," Frances said, raising her glass of Guinness. "Let's drink to their success."

The readings and signings at the bookstores went well. The stores were scattered around the city from the Upper East Side to

Murray Hill to Greenwich Village. There was even one in Brooklyn, which gratified Devon since it was his hometown.

The last event was the book club discussion on Thursday evening, and it was the high point. It was held in the basement of a church on Sixth Avenue, and about thirty people attended, all of them women except for one man, in folding chairs that were arranged in a circle. Siobhan was there as discussion leader since she had picked the book, and she introduced Devon as her former professor at St. Theresa College in Winona, Minnesota. She also introduced Lena as her fellow student and friend. And then she asked the members of the book club to introduce themselves, going around the circle. Their ages ranged from twenties to seventies, and they worked in a variety of occupations. What they had in common was a love of books.

Siobhan then asked Devon to present the vision that guided his poetry, which Devon did in a few words. He then asked members to identify a poem that they liked and to explain what they thought it was about. Since almost all of them raised their hands, he had to assign them numbers so they could follow an order. And seeing how he worked with them, Lena understood why he was such a good teacher. He enabled the members to explain what they thought, to develop their ideas, and to exchange ideas with each other. He made the discussion a learning experience. And when it ended, two hours later, Lena realized that she had learned things about his poems that hadn't ever occurred to her.

Before they could leave, the members crowded around him to get him to sign their copies of the book, and Lena couldn't help noticing how the women adored him, which reinforced her feeling that she had done well in marrying him.

Siobhan led them to a bar around the corner, where they hung out for the rest of the evening, assessing the events and decompressing. Devon had come away from his meeting with the poetry editor at *The New Yorker* with an invitation to submit his next new poem, and Frances was hoping for a review in the book section of the *New York Times*. They agreed that he couldn't have done better.

The next day they did tourist things, which included a visit to the Empire State Building and a ferry ride around the Statue of Liberty, and on Saturday morning Devon's brother Gregory picked them up in his car and drove them to Brooklyn, where before continuing out on Long Island they did a tour of the old neighborhood without getting out of the car.

"You lived here?" Lena asked, appalled by the urban decay.

"It wasn't like this when we lived here," Gregory said. "The families who used to live here moved away."

"Our parents didn't move away," Devon said.

Their parents had died within a year of each other, about five years ago. She had wanted to go with Devon to their funerals, but he had insisted that she stay with their children, pointing out that with nine children, spouses, and grandchildren, his parents would be honored by at least forty family members.

"That was our house," Gregory said, slowing the car in front of a dilapidated brownstone.

"It looks smaller than it did then," Devon said, peering through the car window.

"It was big enough for nine children."

"It had only one bathroom."

"That was a problem when the girls became teenagers."

"I used to pee out of the window of our room because I couldn't wait for them to finish whatever they were doing."

"We both did that."

"You didn't," Lena said, laughing.

"The alternative was to pee in our pants. But the lady next door told our parents about it."

"She was a harpy. What was her name?"

"Miss O'Toole. She hated living next to all those children."

"Well, I have to admit," Gregory said, "we weren't very nice to that lady."

They left the neighborhood and got onto the expressway.

Lena was struck by all the traffic, which gave her a bad impression of Long Island, but when they left the expressway and got onto local roads, she began to see its attractions, which were mainly based on the water that surrounded it. They followed a road along the shore until they reached Bellport, where the next oldest brother, Mike, lived. It was a small town, with a marina and a main street of local stores.

They stopped in front of a large old shingled house on the edge of town. As Gregory explained, the house used to be a place that rented rooms to summer visitors, and Mike had rehabbed it, turning it into a single-family home. They were having the family reunion there because the house was big enough for all of them.

Lena remembered Mike from the wedding, a friendly guy who had charmed her parents. He gave her a salesman's handshake and welcomed her into his house, which from the living room had a view of the water.

"Is that the ocean?" she asked him.

"No, it's the bay. The ocean is on the other side of Fire Island."

"I've never seen the ocean."

"Would you like to see it?"

"Yeah, I mean if it's no trouble."

"Come on," he said. "You're early, and while we're waiting for the others, I'll take you in my boat to Fire Island."

Mike drove them to the marina, where he had a boat. On the way he told them that during the season you could take a ferry to Fire Island, where the beaches were, but the ferry wasn't running at this time of year.

The boat was open, with an outboard motor, like many of the boats at the marina in Winona. It was tied up near the end of the dock, and you had to step down to get into it. Mike got into the boat first and then reached up to help her on board.

As they crossed the bay, she was exhilarated by the smell of salt, and she closed her eyes to shut out all her other senses.

They left the boat at a dock on the other side of the bay and walked along a path that led to the ocean. When they came in sight of it, Lena was amazed by its immensity. She was excited by the thought that Europe was on the other side of it.

Then she lowered her eyes and gazed at the sand, as white and fine as powdered sugar.

"These are the best beaches in the world," Mike said with pride.

She had a wild urge to stroll to the edge and continue going into the water. But she knew it would be cold now.

As they walked along the beach Lena spotted a beautiful shell, which she picked up.

"That's a scallop shell," Mike told her.

"Like they have at the gas stations," Devon said.

She wiped the shell on her pants and put it into a pocket, planning to keep it as a memento of what might be the only time she saw the ocean.

By the time they returned to Mike's house almost all of them were there: the brothers and the sisters, the spouses, and the children, who were hard to count because they were in constant motion. Since it was unseasonably warm, they could use the spacious backyard, where there were washtubs packed with beer and soda as well as a table covered with snacks. In the back was an enormous build-in grill from which drifted the aroma of cooking meat.

With a can of beer in her hand, Lena went around with Devon to talk with each of his siblings. The women asked her questions, showing an interest in her, and they made her feel that her life wasn't much different than theirs, with children as the focal point and a part-time job to supplement their husband's income. Most of their children were in their teens, and more than one of the mothers told her to enjoy her kids before they got to that stage.

They ate in two shifts at tables that were set up in the dining and living rooms, with the children going first. The food was grilled London broil, potato salad, and green salad with ranch dressing, accompanied by more beer.

After a dessert of strawberry shortcake, the adults lingered at the table, some of them having an Irish coffee and others sipping Jameson. They recounted stories of growing up in Brooklyn, playing in the street and getting into trouble. Since their ages were spread over more than twenty years, they had different experiences as children, but now that the youngest had turned thirty, they recognized what they all had in common—being members of the same family—and the longer they talked, the more they talked about their parents.

The party was concluded by a joyous toast led by Mike, who told Devon they were all so proud of him and wished him success with his book.

A few weeks after they got home a review of his book appeared in the *Times*. It said that Devon had a fresh, authentic voice, and that he had clearly established himself as a major poet. A month later he realized his dream of seeing one of his poems in *The New Yorker*.

As they approached the fire she could feel its heat. It had passed the point where the house had collapsed, and now it was only a pile of wood burning. She looked around, hoping to catch sight of Otto, and finally she saw him leaning against the sheriff's cruiser. He was wearing only boxer shorts and a tee shirt.

"Are you all right?" she asked him.

"Yah, I'm all right. But I lost my house, I lost my clothes, I lost everything."

"Thank God you didn't lose your life. We can build a new house, and we can get you new clothes. Were you asleep when it happened?"

"Yah. I was sound asleep. I was lucky to get out of there."

The sheriff, who had joined them in the meantime, said: "They doused the outer walls with gasoline. You can still smell it."

"Then it was arson," Lena said.

"Yah, it was arson. In fact, it was attempted murder."

"But why would anyone try to kill Otto?" she asked, knowing the answer as soon as the question came out.

"For the same reason they tried to kill Rodney."

If it hadn't already been clear to her, it was now abundantly clear to her that anyone she cared about was in grave danger. And while she was glad that her children and her grandchildren would be out of the way by tomorrow, she was sorry for what they had done to Otto, and she felt responsible.

At that moment the deputy joined them, saying: "There are

some tire tracks at the edge of the road, and they look like they're from a big truck."

"What kind of truck?" the sheriff asked.

"A pickup truck, a big pickup."

"Any foot prints?"

"I didn't see any, but they must be there. I should be able to see them tomorrow."

The sheriff turned to Otto and asked: "Do you know if this house was insured under the owner's policy?"

"I think it was. A guy came around a few years ago and took measurements."

"Then the owner should get some insurance money. It probably won't pay for a new house, but it'll help."

"Where will you live in the meantime?" Lena asked.

"I don't have nowhere else to live."

"Then you can live with me. You can have the guestroom."

"Aw, you don't have to do that for me."

"I'm doing it, so don't give me any bullshit."

The men were surprised, as if a doe had spoken up in buck language.

At that point Arne joined them, holding something in his handkerchief. He said: "I found this cigarette butt at the edge of the road."

"Good work," the sheriff said.

"I missed that," the deputy admitted.

"Take it, and handle it carefully. It might give us some DNA."

They lingered for a while, and then Lena said: "Well, if there's nothing more we can do here, I think we should go home."

"Where are the keys to your car?" the sheriff asked Otto.

"They were in the pockets of my pants."

"Oh, geez. We'll have to get a locksmith out here tomorrow."

"Could you give us a ride?" Lena asked the sheriff so that Otto wouldn't have to walk to her house.

"Yah, sure," the sheriff told her. Then he said to the deputy: "I'll be back. We have to stay here and make sure this fire doesn't spread."

"So now we're also the fire department," Jim said.

"We're whatever is needed."

Arne and Otto got into the back seat, where perpetrators rode, and Lena got into the front seat with the sheriff.

"I feel responsible," she told him, believing they couldn't hear her in the back seat.

"You *are* responsible, but no more than anyone else. So don't be too hard on yourself."

"I feel so helpless. I mean, not being able to protect the people I care about."

"I know the feeling. I have it in my work, and I have it in my family."

"How do you deal with it?"

"I do the best I can in my work, and I do the best I can in my family. That's all I can do. And that's all you can do."

She touched his shoulder, saying: "Thanks."

As they turned into her driveway it occurred to her that they might have used the fire to draw her away so they could have a free hand in killing her animals, and as soon as the sheriff stopped his cruiser she jumped out and rushed to the compound.

But the animals were fine, so she joined Arne and Otto at the door of the house, which she had to unlock to let them in.

The guestroom, which was downstairs, hadn't been used since Brenda's last visit in early May. It had twin beds that were usually pushed together so couples could use them as a double bed. The sheets were clean since Lena always changed them after the departure of a guest, so all she had to do was make sure there was a clean towel in the bathroom.

"You have your own bedroom and your own bathroom," she told Otto.

"This is better than my shack," he said, looking around.

"We'll get the locksmith out here tomorrow. Luckily you don't have to drive to Passau until Monday, so you'll have time to get some clothes."

"My clothes wouldn't fit him," Arne said, surveying Otto.

"Devon's wouldn't either," she said before realizing that last year, prodded by Brenda, she had finally emptied the closets and chests of Devon's clothes. "But I can give you my sweatpants to wear in the meantime. You can't go shopping in your boxer shorts."

"Yah, that would be a spectacle," Otto said.

She left the two guys and went into bathroom, where she found that there were clean towels and toilet paper. The bathroom wasn't used except by guests.

Returning to the guestroom, she told Otto: "You're all set. Now, let's try to get some sleep before we have to get up for the milking."

"Thank you for everything," Otto said, taking one of her hands in both of his.

"I'm glad I could do something for you," she said without going into her feeling that she was responsible for what had happened.

"Do you need me at the monitor?" Arne asked as they went upstairs.

"I need you in bed. To sleep," she added pointedly.

She got about an hour of sleep before she had to get up for the milking. She left Arne in bed, quietly snoring, and she went into the kitchen to make tea. She was overdue for a shower, so she had a quick one while the tea was brewing. And she was dressed, ready to help Tara and Lori get started with the milking.

When they arrived she expected them to comment on the fire since they had passed what was left of Otto's shack on their way to her farm. But they hadn't noticed anything, and they didn't seem to know anything about what was happening, not only in the valley but also in the world at large. She envied them for their innocence, and knowing they would lose it soon enough, she refrained from mentioning what had happened.

Returning to the house, she decided to make breakfast for Arne and Otto. She had flour and eggs and blueberries, with which she could make pancakes. While she was waiting for the guys to get up she found the number of a locksmith in the Passau directory. She knew from experience that at least some locksmiths were on call, so even though it was seven thirty in the morning, she called the number and left a message.

As Otto walked into the kitchen, wearing the sweatpants she had left for him in the bathroom and looking as if he hadn't begun to recover from the horror of the night before, the phone rang. It was the locksmith, who promised to come within an hour.

"Do you drink coffee?" she asked Otto.

"Yah, I do. I mean, if you have it."

"Arne drinks coffee, so I'm going to make it for him anyway. How are the sweatpants?"

"They're fine," he said. "I guess they're the same for men and women."

"I think they are. They both don't have flies."

"I took a shower," he told her, sitting down at the table. "I smelled like smoke."

"I bet you did. You know," she said, "it's a miracle that you got out of there."

"Do you believe in miracles?"

"Yah. I've had some miracles in my life."

"What were they?"

She didn't have to think about it. "Meeting my husband, having my children, finding paradise in this valley—"

"I used to think it was paradise, but now I wonder."

"It still is paradise. We just have to stop them from turning it into a desert."

He was silent for a while, and then he said: "People think I don't understand anything because I don't have an education. But I understand more than they think. For one thing, I understand what you're doing to save this valley."

Touched, she said: "Then you understand why they set fire to your shack."

"Yah, I do. And I'm not going to let them drive me away. If it's all right with that doctor, I'm going to build a new home. I mean, something better than that shack."

"I'll help you," she promised. "In fact, we can hire my daughter

Brenda as construction manager. She does good work."

At that moment Arne appeared, looking as if it was still too early in the morning for him. When he saw Otto sitting at the table he said: "So it really did happen. I was hoping it was only a nightmare."

"It wasn't a nightmare," Lena said. "But the locksmith is on his way, so Otto will be able to use his car and go into Passau and buy some clothes."

"He'll need money."

"Yah, I know. I'll give him money. I owe him for today."

"I probably won't get much work done," Otto warned her.

"Don't worry about it. You've earned a day off."

She made pancakes, which they gobbled up as soon as she could make them. She was always amazed by how much food men could eat. And neither of these two men had bellies.

They had finished the last batch of pancakes when the locksmith arrived. Otto got into the locksmith's van and rode with him to where his car was. Arne followed them, intending to wait until they got Otto's car started and then to go home and check on things.

After cleaning up the kitchen she called her brother in Buenos Aires, and she got him after three rings.

"We've had a change in plans," she told him. "If they did what they said they were going to do, then Brenda's on her way to a cabin in the north woods, and Patty's on her way to a house on the Jersey Shore."

"Well, I can see why a cabin in the north woods would be safe," Tony said after a pause. "But I can't see why a house on the Jersey Shore would be safe."

"According to Patty, it's in the name of someone they wouldn't mess with."

"You mean a mobster?"

"A highly respected mobster."

"*Mierda*. What kind of family did she marry into?"

"I don't know, but I think it's the kind of family we need in this situation."

After a pause her brother said: "Well, I guess it helps to have connections. It certainly helps in this country."

"You have mobsters there?"

"Oh, yeah. I have to screen my contracts to make sure they're not mobsters. When someone wants a roundtrip to Paraguay, I'm always suspicious."

"You mean they could be getting drugs to bring back?"

"They could be getting anything, and if I got caught, I'd lose my license."

"So the government cracks down on drugs?"

"They do if they're not involved in the deal. It's the same everywhere," Tony added as if he knew from experience.

"There's a possibility that I'll need your help after all," Lena said. "Last night they burned down the house of the guy who does maintenance for me."

"They burned down his house?"

"It was only a shack, but it was his home, and he was inside it. Luckily, he got out alive. In fact, he wasn't injured. But he lost everything."

"The poor guy," Tony said.

"So now I'm really worried about the young woman who works for me. I'm afraid she could be next, and I want to get her out of the way."

"She's welcome here. Just let me know if she's coming."

"Okay. And I'll let you know when I hear from Brenda and Patty."

With the help of the locksmith Otto was able to start his car and drive to Passau, where he bought underwear, a pair of jeans, and a work shirt at the local store. He returned in time to spend an hour repairing a fence.

By noon she received emails from Patty and Brenda informing her that they had arrived at their destinations, so she could stop worrying about them. By the evening Arne and Otto had agreed to share the duty of sitting all night at the monitor, and feeling generous after a good siesta and a good dinner, Arne volunteered to sit at the monitor that night.

The next morning Lena went to St. Mary's in Passau for the noon mass, at which she thanked God for saving Otto from the fire and for getting her children and her grandchildren out of the way. And she asked God to protect everyone she cared about.

On Monday morning she was ready for work when Heather pulled into the driveway.

Getting out of her car, which she parked behind the other three cars, Heather asked: "What happened to Otto's shack?"

"They set it on fire," Lena said.

"You mean the guys who shot Rodney and killed Tulia and killed Grady?"

"Those two guys are in custody, so it couldn't have been them. But the people who hired them must have hired some other guys."

"Well, somehow I knew it wasn't an accident. Otto doesn't smoke."

"They didn't even try to make it look like an accident. They wanted to send a message to me."

"What do you mean?"

"They want me to know that unless I change my position on the sand mining, they'll harm the people I care about."

Heather was silent, thinking. "Does that include me?"

"It definitely includes you, so I want to get you out of the way."

"Out of the way? Where?"

She had already prepared her brother for the possibility, so she asked: "Would you like to go to Argentina?"

"Argentina? Is that where they played the World Cup?"

"No, that was Brazil," she said, recognizing the error she made when Tony announced that he was moving there. "Argentina is further south."

"How would I get there?"

"By plane. Unless you want to spend a month on a freighter." She knew how long it took by freighter since she had looked into the possibility.

"But that would cost a lot of money."

"It would only be the airfare. You'd have a free place to stay with my brother."

"Your brother lives in Argentina?"

"I told you that. He lives in Buenos Aires."

"Well, the airfare would still be a lot of money."

"Don't worry about the money. I'd pay for it."

"Why would you pay for it?"

"I owe you a bonus for all the good work you're done for me."

"But what about the goats? How would you do the milking without me?"

"I have Arne and Otto. Between the two of them, they could learn how to do the milking."

Heather looked skeptical. "I like Arne and Otto, but I can't see either of them helping you with the animals."

"What do you mean? Arne had his own dairy farm."

"That's my point. He couldn't handle it."

"Goats are easier than cows."

Heather shook her head as if she didn't like the idea, but she finally asked: "For how long would I have to get out of the way?"

"Until the vote on the mining law."

"That's only about a week from now."

"It's eight days from now."

"Well, let me think about it. We gotta go and milk the goats."

"Okay," Lena said. "But I want you out of here by tomorrow morning. If you don't want to go to Argentina, you can go to a cabin in the north woods and join my daughter there."

"Your daughter Brenda?"

"Yah, you know her."

Heather nodded. "That sounds easier than Argentina."

Lena understood. Though she hadn't done it deliberately, she realized that by starting with Argentina as a possible refuge, she had paved the way for alternatives that were more familiar and closer to home.

Heather stayed after the milking to help with the pasteurization, and then she left for her other job. Back in the house, Lena sent an email to Brenda asking if it would be all right if Heather joined her in the cabin. Brenda had gotten to know Heather during her visits, and they got along fine. Within five minutes Brenda emailed back saying that she would welcome the company. It was kind of lonely in the cabin.

Otto had gone to work at the assisted living facility, and Arne had gone to Passau to buy groceries with a list that she had given him. She couldn't believe it, but Arne had spent seven nights in a row with her, and he was settling down with her. Of course she couldn't predict what he would do after the vote when his services as a guard would no longer be needed, or what he would do when football season started, but caught up in the present situation, she really wasn't looking beyond it.

Around noon the sheriff called and let her know that he had contacted the doctor who owned the land where the shack had stood. The doctor believed that the loss would be covered by his insurance, though the shack hadn't been valued at much. He agreed to contribute his own money along with the insurance to build a shack that someday could be rented to people during the hunting and fishing seasons, but in the meantime he would stand by his pledge to let Otto live there as long as he was able to.

The sheriff also let her know that they had made casts of the tire prints at the edge of the road, and that they were looking for big pickups in the hope of matching the prints. The problem was, there were a lot of big pickups in the area, so they would need luck to find the one that parked on the road by Otto's shack. They had also gotten some DNA from the cigarette butt that Arne had found, and they were running it through the system.

Arne returned in the early afternoon with two bags of groceries and a case of beer. It was Otto's turn at the monitor that night, so Arne could spend the rest of the day with her. Believing that her children and her grandchildren were safely out of the way, and hoping that Heather would be on her way to the north woods tomorrow morning, Lena relaxed and enjoyed being with Arne as she had before they killed Grady.

By the time she got out of bed for the evening milking she had an email from Brenda with directions on how to get to the cabin, which she printed.

She met Heather in the compound, asking: "Did you make a decision?"

"Yah, I did. I decided to go and stay with your daughter."

"That's good. I have the directions," she said, handing them to her. "I want you to leave by tomorrow morning. Okay?"

"Okay. But I feel bad about leaving you here."

"They're not going to kill me. They're only trying to make me change my position."

"But what about the animals? I can't see Arne or Otto helping you with them. Maybe you could get Tara or Lori to help you."

"Yah, maybe I could," Lena said, though she already had misgivings about it.

"You know," Heather said. "I was going to stay here, but when I told my parents about the situation, they said I should go to the cabin in the north woods. And I don't want them to worry about me. They worried about me all the time when I was on drugs."

"I understand. My parents worried about me."

"They did? I can't believe it. When did your parents worry about you?"

"When I was in high school and when I was in college. They didn't stop worrying about me until I got married. And even then my grandmother worried about me. She couldn't understand why I married a guy who was Irish."

Heather laughed. "So are parents all alike?"

"In that sense they are. But in one sense children are all alike."

"In what sense?"

"They do things that make their parents worry."

"Did your children do things that made you worry?"

"Oh, yah. For a while it was like they were competing to see who could do things that would make me worry more."

"That's how it is with me and my brother."

"So which of you does things that make your parents worry more?"

"It used to be me," Heather said. "But now it's my brother. He's not on drugs, but he's not doing anything with his life."

"Well, give him time," Lena said. "I think boys need more time than girls. But I don't know. I only had girls."

They did the milking, cleaned the equipment, and made sure that the does were settled. They parted in the driveway, and Lena stood there for a while, watching the tail-lights of Heather's car until it turned left onto the road.

She found Arne in the kitchen with a pot of water on the stove. Except to cook things on the grill, he had never done anything before to help her with dinner, so she was amazed.

"I was looking for the pasta," he told her, "but I couldn't find it."

"It's here," she said, opening the door of the cabinet where she kept it. "What kind of pasta would you like?"

"The flat and wide kind."

"You mean fettucine." She reached for a box. "What kind of sauce?"

"That green sauce."

"You mean pesto. I have some in the refrigerator. I have to keep it there, or it'll spoil. And I don't add the garlic, the walnuts, or the cheese until I use it."

"Why not add them in advance?"

"The garlic gets rancid, the walnuts get soggy, and the cheese gets stale."

"Where did you learn all that stuff?"

"From experience. I didn't learn it from my Polish mother, though I did learn how to make pierogi and kapusta from her."

"We should have Polish food sometime."

"Okay. Next time I go to Winona I'll get what I need."

Remembering that she needed help with the milking the next morning, she went to the phone and called Tara and asked her if she was available for the next week or so. Tara said she was, and she thought Lori was available too, and she would text her. In any case Tara would be there by six thirty the next morning.

Lena returned to the job of making pesto sauce. She peeled a clove of garlic and used the press to add it to the basic mixture of basil and olive oil. She was grinding walnuts in her mortar and pestle when the phone rang. She waited until she heard the voice of the sheriff, saying: "Lena, I'm on the highway, a half mile east of the junction with your road. I have the ambulance with me, and they're getting Heather out of her car."

TEN

THOUGH SHE HAD been warned by many people, including her mother, about what happened to children when they became teenagers, Lena still wasn't prepared for it.

When Patty reached that stage, she turned from being a quiet, bookish girl into a wild party animal. She bounced from one social activity to the next, with groups of kids that she couldn't even name. By the time she was fourteen she had boyfriends, who lasted at most for a few months. They were usually a year or two older, so they had cars, a major attraction since they provided mobility and independence. She wasn't allowed to go out at night during the week, but on Saturdays she always went out, being picked up by a car in the afternoon and not coming home until her curfew, which as she got older went from ten to eleven to midnight.

One night, when she was sixteen, she didn't get home by her curfew. She got home a half hour late, and she was greeted in the front hall by both her parents. She said she was at a party and lost track of the time, and she promised not to be late again. Though Lena felt they should ground her for at least a week, Devon felt they should accept her promise, so they didn't ground her, and two weeks later she got home at three in the morning.

"Where the hell were you?" Devon asked her, raising his voice.

"I was at a party," Patty said, obviously lying.

"Where was this party?"

"At Susan's house," Patty told them, not making eye contact with either of them.

"What's her phone number?"

"You can't call her now. You'll wake up her parents."

"I don't care if I wake them up," Devon said. "I want her phone number."

Patty closed her eyes and took a long deep breath and sighed. "Okay. I wasn't at a party. I was with Bobby."

"Who's Bobby?" Lena asked her.

"He's my boyfriend."

"Have we ever met him?"

Patty shrugged. "I don't know. I think you might have met him."

"How long have you been going with him?"

"A month or so."

"Where were you?" Devon asked her.

"In his car, driving around."

"You were driving around until three in the morning?"

"Yeah, we went to La Crosse," Patty said as if she was improvising. "We hung out there for a while, and then we headed up the river."

"Where did you hang out in La Crosse?"

"At a bar," Patty said.

The drinking age was only eighteen in Wisconsin, so a lot of the kids from Winona went across the river, and if they were under eighteen they had fake IDs.

"What was the name of this bar?"

"I don't remember. It was just a bar."

There was a silence, and then Lena said: "I don't believe you were driving around. You must have stopped somewhere."

"Are you saying I'm lying?" Patty said rebelliously.

"Yeah, that's what I'm saying," Lena said, locking eyes with her daughter.

"All right. Do you really want to know the truth?"

"We really do," Lena said, speaking for both of them.

"Bobby parked the car, and we had sex," Patty blurted out.

Devon flinched. "What did you say?"

"I said we had sex."

Lena was concerned for Devon, who looked as if he had been stabbed in the heart, but at the same time she struggled to find the right thing to say to her daughter. She finally said: "Okay. So you had sex. But that's no excuse for coming home at three in the morning."

"I fell asleep," Patty said, "and when I woke up it was two thirty."

Remembering how as a child she had done the same thing, Lena understood, but as a parent she couldn't accept it. "That's still no excuse. We were worried sick about you. We thought you might have been killed in an accident."

"I'm sorry," Patty said, for the first time showing contrition.

"You're too young to be having sex," Devon told her.

"I'm not too young," Patty insisted. "All the girls my age are having sex."

"Then you're all too young to be having sex."

"I agree with your father," Lena said. "At your age you don't know what you're doing. And you could get pregnant."

"No, I couldn't. My period just ended."

"So you're using the rhythm method," Devon said drily. "That's the method my parents used, and they had nine children."

Patty had no response to that.

"We're not saying it's wrong for you to have sex," Lena told her. "We're just saying you're too young to handle it."

"I can handle it," Patty said, still defiant.

"Maybe you can, but we don't want you to get into trouble."

"I won't get into trouble."

Lena let that issue rest since she wanted to address the other issue. "When we asked you where you were, you lied to us."

"I didn't want to upset you."

"You were trying to protect us?"

"Yeah, I was. I was also trying to protect myself."

"Well, you don't have to protect yourself from us. We'll never hurt you, and no matter what you do, we'll still love you. And you don't have to protect us. We can take anything from you as long as it's not evil, and we know you won't do anything evil."

With tears forming in her eyes, Patty said: "I'm sorry. I won't ever lie to you again."

When Brenda reached that stage, she turned from being a well-disciplined athlete into a crazy daredevil. She hung out with the boys who did stunts like jumping off a cliff into the river or hitching a ride on the back of a truck. She managed not to get into trouble until she was arrested for hopping freight trains. Along with her companions, she was taken to the police station, where Devon had to go and fetch her.

Unlike her sister, she didn't lie about what she had done, but in her own way she was defiant. She acted like it was the railroad detective's fault for catching her.

"They had no right to arrest me," she said as they stood in the kitchen.

"You were trespassing on railroad property," Devon told her.

"But I wasn't hurting the railroad cars."

"You could have gotten hurt," Lena pointed out.

"I knew what I was doing."

"So you're an old hand at hopping trains," Devon said. "How long have you been doing it?"

"I don't know. I guess since I was twelve."

"You could fall off," Lena told her, "and the train could run over you."

"I've never fallen off."

"There's always a first time."

"Why do you do it?" Devon asked as if he wanted to get to the bottom of it.

"Because it's fun. Have you ever hopped a freight train?"

"No, I haven't."

"I haven't either," Lena said.

"Then you should try it."

"We're not going to try it," Devon said. "It's against the law."

"You never did anything against the law?"

They looked at each other. "Yeah, minor things like speeding, or running a traffic light."

"You mean you never smoked weed?"

"Yeah, but only to try it."

"I didn't like it," Lena said.

"I thought it might give me an unusual poem, as it did for Coleridge."

"Who's Coleridge?"

"A poet who used drugs to enhance his performance."

"Did the weed do anything for you?"

"No. It disabled me, so I never used it again."

"Well, let's get back to hopping trains," Lena said. "It's not only against the law, it's also dangerous."

"I know, but I'm careful."

"No matter how careful you think you are, you don't control the situation. The train could suddenly stop or start."

"If you need an outlet for your energy," Devon said, "you could play more sports."

"I already play softball, and I don't like basketball."

"Is there any other sport you'd like to play?"

"I'd like to play football, but they don't let girls play football."

"Well, we have to find something for you to do," Lena said.

"What about bicycle racing?" Devon said. "Do they do that at the high school?"

"No," Brenda said, shaking her head. "But some guys at the college do it."

"Guys at the college?"

"Yeah, I don't know if it's organized, but I've seen them do it. I even joined them once, but I don't have the right kind of bike."

"We could get you one. Where do they race?"

"On the back roads, up on the ridge."

"That would still be dangerous," Lena said, but remembering her trip to St. Paul with a guy on a motorcycle she didn't strongly oppose the idea.

Devon looked into it, and he found that the college had a club of guys who did bicycle racing. They had informal races among themselves, and a few times a year they participated in races outside of the area.

So they bought the right kind of bike for Brenda, and she joined the club.

As she continued through high school, Lena knew better than to encourage her to socialize with groups of kids, or to go on dates. It was clear that Brenda had no interest in guys other than as teammates or competitors in sports.

As soon as they turned onto the highway in Arne's pickup, Lena saw the flashing lights of the sheriff's cruiser and the ambulance a half mile ahead of them. The sheriff hadn't told her anything about Heather's condition, presumably because at the time he called they still hadn't gotten the victim out of her car. And Lena prayed that Heather was all right, feeling responsible and wishing she had arranged for Heather to go away earlier.

Approaching the scene of the accident, she saw what had to be Heather lying on a stretcher with the sheriff and a paramedic standing by her. Arne stopped his truck behind the sheriff's cruiser, and they got out and walked quickly toward them.

"They got her out alive," the sheriff said.

"Thank God," Lena said before saying a silent full prayer of thanks. She went to the stretcher, where Heather was conscious but still in a daze, and she asked the paramedic: "Can you tell me how she is?"

"She has injuries on her head and on her arm," the young woman said. "When we get her to the hospital we'll find out if she has any internal injuries."

"We don't see any evidence of internal injuries," the young man said. "But you never know."

"Can you give me five minutes to ask her some questions?" the sheriff asked.

"Yah, but no more than five minutes," the young woman said.

By then Lena had spotted Heather's car in the ditch at the right-hand side of the road. It was rolled over like a turtle on its back.

The deputy was kneeling beside it, inspecting something with a flashlight.

"How did it happen?" the sheriff asked Heather.

"When I turned onto the highway," Heather said hoarsely, "a big pickup came out of nowhere and banged into the rear of my car. I tried to outrun it, but I couldn't. It kept banging into me. Then it pulled up alongside me and sideswiped me off the road."

"Did you see the driver?"

"I saw the guy in the passenger seat, but his head was covered by the kind of black hood that terrorists wear."

"What color was the truck?"

"I think it was brown."

"Did you get any numbers off the license plate?"

"No. I didn't think of getting numbers. I was only trying to get away from them."

"Your five minutes are up," the young woman told the sheriff.

"She's all yours," the sheriff told her.

"I'm sorry," Lena said to Heather, gently clearing some strands of hair from her forehead.

"It's not your fault," Heather said. "You warned me to get out of here."

"I should have warned you earlier."

"Don't worry. I'll be all right."

Lena stood by and watched the paramedics carry the stretcher into the ambulance.

At that moment the deputy joined them, saying: "There were signs of paint from another vehicle on the driver's side."

"Could you tell the color?" the sheriff asked him.

"Yah, it was brown."

"Well, that confirms what Heather remembers. So it was a big brown pickup, probably the same one that parked on the road near Otto's shack. And we have some prints from its tires. But we don't even have a single digit of its license number."

"It must have continued down the highway after sideswiping her," the deputy said. "There's no place you can turn off until you get to Arendal."

"Then it either went through Arendal, or it turned off there."

"Let's go there now and see if anyone noticed it."

"What time did Heather leave your place?" the sheriff asked Lena.

"It was just before nine," Lena told him.

"So the incident occurred shortly after nine, and since Arendal is about ten minutes from here, the pickup must have gotten there around quarter after nine."

"They have a speed limit of twenty," Lena pointed out. The limit was posted long before you got into town and long after you got out of town, which made Arendal a famous speed trap.

The sheriff understood. "If they slowed down in Arendal, someone might have had time to notice them, and if they didn't slow down, the local cop might have stopped them."

The sheriff and the deputy left for Arendal while Arne and Lena turned around and headed back to her place. They were silent for a while, and then Arne said: "Well, they got Heather. So who's next?"

"I think you're next," Lena said frankly.

"Yah, that's what I was thinking."

"I told Heather to get out of here, and she was going to stay with my daughter in a cabin in the north woods. She was leaving tomorrow morning."

Arne frowned. "So you want me to go and stay with your daughter in the north woods?"

"Yah, I do. Unless you want to go to Argentina," she added.

"Argentina? I don't even know where that is."

"It's south of Brazil, where they played the World Cup."

"What's the World Cup?"

"It's like the Super Bowl for soccer."

"I can't watch soccer," Arne said. "It's too slow, and they hardly ever score."

"Well, that's where Argentina is—south of Brazil."

"But I don't know anyone who lives there."

"My brother lives there. I'm sure I mentioned it."

"I'm sure you did, but I don't have a good memory. Anyway, I'd rather go to the north woods. I could go fishing there."

"Then you should go there tomorrow morning."

"You trust me to stay in a cabin with your daughter?"

"Yah, I do. My daughter's gay."

"Oh, yah. I'm sure you mentioned that."

When they got to her house they found everything in order. It was almost eleven, and they were exhausted, so they decided to go to bed.

They were just lying down when the phone rang. She rushed into the kitchen and answered it.

"They were stopped in Arendal," the sheriff told her. "They were going over fifty in a twenty zone, so the driver got a ticket. The local cop had no reason to hold them, so he let them go. But we know the truck, we know the driver, we have a bulletin out on them, and we will catch those sons of bitches."

She reported this news to Arne, who decided that maybe it wouldn't be necessary for him to go to the north woods and stay in a cabin with a gay woman.

The next morning Tara and Lori arrived on time to do the milking. They knew what they were doing, and they worked effectively. They were good kids, and whenever she heard someone complain about the kids from the present generation, she used Tara and Lori as examples to defend them. As far as she could see, the only thing wrong with this generation was that they had less opportunity to get decent jobs, and that certainly wasn't their fault. It was the fault of people who didn't care about kids.

As she watched them get started with the milking, it occurred to her that the people who had tried to kill Heather might target Tara and Lori next, and she decided to have them stop coming here until after the vote on the law. If they were here, they would be in danger, so she would have to do the milking without them and without Heather for the next seven days. She didn't know how she was going to do it, but somehow she would find a way.

Back in the house she called Tony to let him know that the young woman she had mentioned in her previous call would not be going to Argentina and staying with him for her safety. She told him what they had done to Heather, but she assured him that they wouldn't hurt her since they needed her vote to allow sand mining in the county.

Around ten she called the hospital to see if Heather could have visitors, and they said yes, so she made a list of groceries and headed for Passau. By then Arne had gotten up and had left to go and check on things at his place.

As she passed the scene of the accident she saw Heather's car, still on its back, and she wondered if it was totaled. If so, then

193

Heather should collect enough insurance to replace it, but if she didn't collect enough, then Lena would help her. Which reminded her to call TIAA to ask about the process for withdrawing funds and about the possible tax consequences. She decided to call them in the afternoon.

She found Heather in a hospital room that could have been the room where Rodney stayed, except that it had a different number. The sight of a plaster cast that ran from the middle of Heather's lower arm to the base of her fingers made Lena feel bad about what had happened, and the sight of bruises on Heather's face made her feel even worse.

"How are you doing?" she asked Heather.

"I'm doing fine," Heather said in an upbeat voice. "They didn't find any internal injuries, so all I had was a slight concussion and a broken wrist."

"It's your right arm."

"Yah. It's the only time I ever wished I was left-handed."

"Well, you have to take it easy for a while."

"I will. Don't worry. I assume that Tara and Lori are helping you with the milking."

"They are, and I was just thinking what good kids they are."

"They really *are* good kids. I should have been as good when I was their age," Heather said as if she was more than a generation removed from them.

"Whatever you did when you were their age, you've more than made up for it."

"I hope so." Heather paused. "Did the sheriff catch the truck that knocked me off the road?"

"No, but the local cop did. He stopped it for speeding through Arendal. So the sheriff has all the information he needs to catch them."

"I hope he does, and I hope they get life in a hell hole."

"They'll get justice," Lena said, making an effort to separate that concept from revenge.

"I understand that they did it to hurt you, and that makes them terrorists, who kill innocent people to hurt their enemies. Not that

I'm innocent, but you know what I mean."

"I know what you mean. And you're right—they're terrorists. They're trying to achieve a political goal by using violence."

"They're like those guys who go to crowded places and start shooting or blow themselves up. And you know what they all have in common?"

Lena waited to hear what it was.

"They're all losers. They're such fucking losers," Heather said with passion, "they make me feel good about myself."

"But you don't need them to feel good about yourself."

"I wasn't saying I do. I was just saying they have that side effect."

"Is the hospital going to release you today?"

"They said they're going to, but I gotta perform an evacuation before they let me go."

"Perform an evacuation? Wow, you're picking up the language. Just remember, you can't feel pain, you can only feel discomfort."

"I know. And luckily the discomfort in my wrist isn't too bad."

"They probably gave you something for it. When that wears off, you'll feel more."

"I can take it," Heather said. "The only thing I couldn't take is if they hurt you."

"They won't hurt me. They still have other people they could hurt."

"Well, take care."

"I will," she said, leaning over to kiss Heather. "And don't worry about the animals. They're in good hands."

When she got home with the groceries the light on the phone was flashing. There were two messages: one from the sheriff and the other from Vern. She called the sheriff first, and in her conversation with him she learned that the big brown pickup was stopped by a cop in Winona, and that the two guys were in custody. The sheriff said it was a good thing they were caught in Winona since he had no more room in his jail. If the paint found on Heather's car and the treads from the tires matched the casts, then the county would have a case against these guys for two attempted murders. Within a few days they would know the results, and in the meantime the guys were in custody, where they could do no further harm. The sheriff ended the call by reminding Lena that the people who had hired these guys and the previous guys had unlimited resources, so that they could keep hiring new people to do their dirty work.

Next she called Vern, who said he had met with Rodney, and he liked him. He had seen the same qualities she had seen in the young man: reliability, trustworthiness, and love of animals, so he had hired Rodney as an intern for the rest of the summer, and if all went well, Rodney would become his assistant. Since he had veteran benefits, he could start taking vet tech courses in the fall.

After those two calls, and after her visit to Heather, she was feeling better about things. She made herself some tea and went out to the deck with the local paper. She had finished reading it, and she was just sitting there, looking into the peaceful woods, when she heard Arne tromping up the stairs. He went into the kitchen, where he stopped for a while, and then he came out to the deck with a bottle of beer. He leaned over and kissed the top of her head, and then he settled into the chair opposite her, sighing as if he had something on his mind.

"When I went home this morning," he told her, "there was a car in my driveway, a black Mercedes that must have cost a bundle. If it had been a pickup, I would have been ready with my rifle, but I didn't think a thug would have a Mercedes."

"Who was he, a banker?"

"He looked like a banker. He wore a suit, a shirt, and a tie. And he had a leather briefcase."

"What was in the briefcase?"

"Money. It was filled with stacks of one-hundred dollar bills."

"And what was the money for?" she asked, guessing.

"It was for me," Arne said as if he still couldn't believe it.

"You mean the guy gave you the money?"

"He offered it to me," Arne said. "He said it was a down payment for my farm."

"How much was the down payment?"

"A hundred thousand dollars."

"And how much did he offer to pay for your farm?"

"A million dollars."

"I assume he doesn't want it for dairy farming."

"He wants it for sand mining. He said there are huge deposits of sand on my property."

"Does he know we're about to pass a law against sand mining in this county?"

"He mentioned it. But he said that if the law wasn't passed, then he'd buy my farm for a million dollars."

She sat back in her chair with her arms folded. "That sounds like a bribe."

"Yah. It feels like one." Arne took a swig of beer and sat there looking untroubled by the situation.

"Now, what about the down payment. Did he give it to you?"

"He offered it to me."

"With no strings attached?"

"Yah. We were in my kitchen, and he pushed his briefcase across the table to me."

"What did you do?"

"I looked at the money, and I imagined what I could do with a million dollars. I could move to Florida and live like a king. I could help my son start his own business." Arne had a son by a woman he had never married and never heard from after she left him with the three-month-old consequence of their having sex. The son was in his early forties now, and he lived in St. Paul, where he kept trying to start his own business. He supported himself by tending bar at a popular hangout on Selby Avenue, where Lena had met him on the only trip she had taken with Arne. He was a charming young man, who obviously loved his father but also just as obviously wished his father could do more for him.

"So did you take the money?"

"What the fuck do you think I am?" he asked her indignantly.

"Well, if I'd been in your position, I would have considered taking it."

"I did consider taking it. You bet I did."

"But you didn't take it."

"No. I didn't. If I'd taken it, I would have been like Judas."

"Judas?" It was the first time she had heard him make a Biblical reference.

"Yah, Judas. The guy who betrayed Jesus Christ."

"I know who he was. I was just surprised to hear you compare yourself with him."

"Don't you get it? The guy was offering me money to betray you!"

"Yah, I get it," Lena said, realizing with a pang how much she had underestimated Arne. "I don't know what to say, except that I admire you for not taking it."

"Well, don't go overboard," Arne said. "I knew that if I did take it, then I'd have to convince you to vote against the law. But I knew I could never convince you to change your position. And that would leave me in deep shit."

"You mean they would have felt you betrayed *them.*"

"Yah. Imagine what they would have done to Judas if he'd taken the money and not delivered Jesus to them."

She saw that he hadn't refused to take the money because of his loyalty to her but because of his fear of what they would do to him when he failed to deliver. And somehow she was more deeply touched by this explanation than by the other. He wasn't a hero, but neither was she. They were only human. "So where does that leave you?"

"I don't know. I guess it leaves me wondering if I should go and stay with your daughter in the north woods."

"I think that's a good idea. If trying to bribe you didn't work, they'll try something else."

"So tell me how to get there."

"I printed directions for Heather. I'll print them for you."

She went and printed the directions, and then she called Brenda to tell her there had been a change in plans. Brenda had met Arne, so he wasn't a stranger, and though he wasn't exactly her type, she was at the point where she would have welcomed anyone for company.

It was a six-hour drive to the cabin, and if Arne left now, he could get there while it was still light. He might also get of the county before the enemy had time to bring in re-enforcements. So after a long kiss in the driveway, he headed home, where he could pack what he would need for the next seven days.

After he was gone she went into the house and upstairs to her bedroom, where she stood before the image of Our Lady of Częstochowa and prayed for the safety of Arne, who she understood was going to the cabin not only to avoid being killed but also to spare her the feelings she would have if he was killed because of her. Instead of showing how macho he was, he was showing consideration for her.

A half hour later the phone rang, and it was the sheriff.

ELEVEN

PATTY REGAINED CONTROL of her life in her senior year of high school, she got good grades, and she did well on the SATs, so she had a choice of going to St. Mary's with free tuition because her father worked there or going to St. John's because her father had gone there. She decided to go to St. John's, which had offered her an ample scholarship, and her being in New York gave her parents another reason to go there on visits.

One of the high points of their visits was attending her graduation ceremony and seeing her awarded Summa cum Laude and Phi Beta Kappa. A party for her was given by Mike, who during her years at St. John's had driven her from the campus to his house at Bellport for Easter and other occasions. Based on her performance as an undergraduate she was admitted to a doctoral program at St. John's with a graduate assistantship that covered her tuition. To pay the rent for an apartment that she shared with another student in the program she worked as a waitress at a restaurant in Queens.

She completed the program, including her dissertation on Gerard Manley Hopkins, in less than four years, and she took a tenure-track position in the English Department at St. Catherine College in Yonkers. Lena had never heard of Yonkers, and though Devon had grown up in New York, he had never been to Yonkers, so they visited Patty when she was moving there from Queens, and they helped her get settled in an apartment within walking distance of the college. She led them on a tour of the campus, which overlooked the Hudson River with a view of the Palisades on the other side. They were pleased that after going to Catholic schools and a Catholic university, Patty would be teaching at a Catholic college.

During her first year at St. Catherine she began calling them on Sunday evenings to keep in touch, and from these conversations they learned that she loved teaching and that she was very happy at the college. The following year, from a phone conversation, they learned that she had a boyfriend whose name was Carmine. She didn't tell them much about Carmine except that he was a really nice guy.

That summer, after teaching a course that ended in early August, she brought Carmine on a visit to meet her family. By then they were spending whole summers in Eden Valley, where they had replaced the original fishing shack with a house that could accommodate their family, so they picked up Patty and her boyfriend at the airport in La Crosse and drove them back to the valley. Lena's first impression of Carmine was that he was an attractive young man, with good manners, but he didn't talk much. She eventually learned that he only had a high school education, and that he worked in a body shop owned by his brother, so she imagined that he felt overwhelmed by Devon.

Devon didn't talk down to him and even showed an interest in his job, despite having no interest in cars, but they quickly ran out of things to talk about. Instead of holding him captive in the house, the next morning Devon took him trout fishing in the stream that ran through the valley, and from that experience they began to bond.

Having learned from her daughter that Carmine knew how to cook, Lena took him into the kitchen that evening, and together they made dinner. Carmine dredged the trout with flour and dipped it in egg wash and lightly fried it and dressed it with lemon sauce. To accompany the trout, he made a pasta with a fresh tomato sauce, and Lena quickly sautéed zucchini from her garden. While eating the dinner, and drinking two bottles of chianti, they continued the process of taking Carmine into their family.

That night in bed Lena and Devon discussed the relationship between Patty and Carmine. Their main concern was the huge difference in education between them.

"I don't see what they have in common," Devon said.

"Maybe that's the attraction," Lena said. "They're so different."

"Yeah, I know. But I can't imagine what they talk about."

"They talk about everyday things."

"I guess they do. But still—" He didn't have to complete the sentence.

"I can see the physical attraction," Lena said. "I mean, he's a really cute guy."

"I know he is. But that could wear off."

"It didn't wear off for us."

"Yeah. But we have other things going for us."

She found his hand and squeezed it. "We're blessed. But you know, at first my parents were skeptical about our relationship."

"They were?" he said, teasing her.

"They thought you were too old for me."

"It wasn't your parents, it was your grandmother."

"Good old Babcia. She was always skeptical."

"For sure she didn't believe our story about Myers-Briggs."

Lena laughed, remembering it, and then she asked: "Do you think it's possible for parents to understand their children?"

"I don't know. I mean, we're living in such different times. You know, my students could be my children."

"Do you have trouble understanding them?"

"Yeah, but not any more trouble than I have understanding my own children."

"Well, at least I couldn't have been your child."

"That's why I can understand you."

"You think you can."

"Yeah, I do." He moved over so that he could kiss her.

The following spring Patty and Carmine were married at St. Stan's, with Brenda as the maid of honor and his brother who owned the body shop as the best man. His parents were there, and some of Lena's cousins were there. But her mother and her father were no longer around, nor were any of her uncles or aunts, so it was a much smaller wedding than hers and Devon's. But the bride and groom looked very happy, and that was the important thing.

Instead of going free to St. Mary's, their second daughter went to the public university in Minneapolis. She wanted to get out

Winona, and Lena didn't blame her, remembering how she had once wanted to get out of Winona. Though they had two children in college, it helped that Patty had her scholarship and that Brenda's tuition was relatively low, so they managed to get through the year financially.

Brenda had never been much of a student, and she didn't like college, so after a year she didn't return. But she stayed in Minneapolis, where she lived near the campus in an apartment that she shared with three other girls. On her visits to see her daughter, Lena always found different girls in the apartment, coming and going like people through a turnstile, with Brenda being the only constant. Brenda was supporting herself with a job as a bartender at a popular hangout in Dinkytown, so even though she wasn't a student, she was still connected with the university.

After several years of working at this job Brenda enrolled at a community college in a program for construction management. She had always liked building things, beginning with her Lego Toys, and ending with a treehouse in the backyard, so she was following a natural vocation. With her certificate from the community college she got a job with a construction company, where she learned how to apply what she had learned in the program, and a year later she brought her partner to Eden Valley to meet her family.

They had long known that Brenda was gay, and they were just hoping that she would develop a stable relationship with someone. So they were delighted to meet Jane, a tall blond girl who had worked for several years as a carpenter with a company in St. Paul and was ready to start a business with Brenda renovating houses. Their market would be the Crocus Hill neighborhood of St. Paul, where people with money were buying the old houses and renovating the interiors, especially the kitchens and bathrooms. Brenda would provide overall management for the projects, and Jane would lead the teams of workers at the sites. They would have their office on St. Clair Avenue, where the rents were lower than on Grand Avenue, and they would form a corporation to shield them from liability.

"So what are you waiting for?" Devon asked.

"We need your blessing," Brenda said.

"You don't need our money?"

"We have our own money," Jane said. "We've been saving it."

"Well, you have our blessing," Lena said, getting up from her chair and going over to hug Brenda. She then went to Jane and hugged her. They were two of the most satisfying hugs that she had given anyone.

The business went well. The two women didn't become rich, but they built a reputation for doing high quality work, and they had a waiting list of projects. They debated whether or not to expand, but they decided that it wasn't worth the hassle just to make more money, so they maintained their size and selected their clients.

They bought a house on Lincoln Avenue, right in the middle of their market, and they renovated it. The house had more living space than they needed, but they used two bedrooms for their offices and saved rent. They used the downstairs as a showplace.

They would have liked to get married, but the law didn't permit it, so they lived together as if they were married, attending Sunday mass at St. Luke's like other families.

The sheriff was at Arne's place, and after assuring her that Arne was all right, he asked her to drive over there immediately. It was four thirty, so she figured that she had time to drive over there and get back in time for the milking, which somehow she would have to do with only Brady to help her.

It took her about fifteen minutes to get to Arne's place. She hadn't been there for a while, and for some reason it looked more forlorn than she remembered—maybe because he wouldn't get a million dollars for it.

The sheriff's cruiser was in his driveway, and so was Arne's pickup. The windshield of the pickup was shattered, and there were bullet holes in the side. It made her wonder if the sheriff had told her the truth about Arne being all right.

Holding her breath, she went into the house, which was the

usual mess. She went into the kitchen, where she saw Arne sitting with the sheriff.

"What the hell happened?"

"They tried to kill Arne," the sheriff said. "But they obviously missed."

"If you were in the pickup," she asked Arne, "how the hell did you survive?"

"I wasn't in the pickup," Arne said. "For some reason they thought I was, and they opened fire. They blasted the shit out of my poor truck."

"If you weren't in the pickup, how could they have thought you were in it?"

"They were in the woods," the sheriff said, "and I figure they must have seen a reflection off the windshield, maybe a bird, and they were just itching to fire."

"They didn't come and look in the pickup to see if they got you?"

"No, they didn't," Arne said. "They must have assumed they got me."

"You gotta remember," the sheriff said. "By now we're dealing with the third string."

It was only then that Lena unwound and went to Arne and hugged him, saying: "Thank God they didn't get you."

"Thank the bird or whatever it was," Arne told her.

"They're going to figure out that they didn't get him," the sheriff said, "so we have to get him up to that cabin in the north woods."

"I can't take my truck."

"I could drive you there," Lena offered.

"I have a better idea," the sheriff said.

At that moment the paramedics who had been at the scene of Heather's accident came into the kitchen with a stretcher. They must have just pulled up in their van.

The sheriff gave them instructions, and seeing what his plan was, Lena went into the living room and got two cushions from the sofa, which she laid onto the stretcher. Arne brought a pillow, and the young woman arranged the cushions and the pillow and then drew a blanket over them, so it looked like there was a dead body on the stretcher.

The paramedics carried the stretcher out to the driveway, where in plain sight of whoever might be in the woods watching, they slid the stretcher into the van and closed the doors behind it. Within a few minutes they drove away.

After waiting a while the sheriff pulled his cruiser to the side door, and Arne slipped into the back seat, where he lay down out of sight. The deputy, who had gone into the woods to flush out whoever might still be there, joined them now and got into the passenger seat of the sheriff's cruiser. And off they went, following the ambulance at a safe distance.

Lena waited a while longer, and then she followed, knowing that the ambulance would take its load to the county morgue, and the sheriff would drive to Winona, where he had to go anyway to interview the guys who had sideswiped Heather. When they got to Winona, Arne would rent a car and drive up to the cabin.

She got home in time to do the milking. She was trying to get Brady to understand what she wanted him to do when Otto marched into the compound.

"You look like you could use some help," he said.

"I could," she said. "I told the girls not to come here for a week."

"You mean until after the vote."

"Yah. I don't want them to be in danger."

"Well, I'm in danger anyway, so I might as well help you with the milking."

"Okay," she said appreciatively. "I'll go inside, and I'll open the door, and you get twelve does to go up the ramp."

"Twelve?"

"Yah. That's how many milking stations I have. So I can't handle more than twelve."

With Otto helping her, the milking went smoothly, and she decided to ask him to help her until after the vote. As he had said, he was in danger anyway because he was living in her house, and he was evidently willing to take the risk. He probably felt safer staying in Eden Valley than he would feel flying to Argentina.

Returning to the house, she thought about Arne, who should be on his way to the north woods. She had gotten used to having him with her at night, and she wished he was with her now, but she knew he had to get away, and she believed the sheriff's plan would fool the killers. At the same time, she knew they would keep trying to make her change her position on the sand mining, and she wondered what they would do next.

When she went into the kitchen she saw the light on the phone flashing. It was a message from the sheriff, saying: "I'm calling to let you know we got to Winona, and Arne's on his way north in a rented car. So he should be fine."

Relieved, she opened the refrigerator and got out the leftover chicken from the night before and put it into the toaster oven. After one of her visits, Brenda had bought her a microwave, but Lena wouldn't use it, believing it would damage her brain, so it was in the basement along with other gadgets that she would never use. She had thought of having a garage sale to get rid of them, but she hadn't done it because she didn't want to be responsible for damaging other people's brains.

She ate dinner alone at the table, and then she checked her email. There was a message from Brenda saying that Arne had arrived at the cabin. Lena thanked God, and headed for bed with the feeling that everyone she cared about was safe. For the first time since the night of the last board meeting, she had a deep, untroubled sleep.

When she awoke the next morning she noticed that Arne wasn't there in bed with her, and then she remembered that he was in the cabin with Brenda. With a smile, she wondered how the two of them were getting along.

She was having tea when the phone rang. It was Heather, who said: "I can't make it this morning. They haven't let me out of the hospital yet."

"That's okay. Otto will help me."

"Otto?"

207

"Yah. He's very good with the animals.

"What about Tara and Lori?"

"I told them not to come here until after the vote."

"You did? Why?"

"I don't want them to be in danger."

Evidently ignoring how she might be in a similar situation, Heather said; "Well, they should let me out today, so I can be there tomorrow morning."

"No, I don't want you to come here until after the vote."

There was a pause. "You think I'd be in danger?"

"Yah. And I don't want you to be in danger."

There was another pause. "Okay. I guess you have Otto and Arne to help you."

"I don't have Arne." She told Heather what had happened to him, and how he had gone to the north woods to stay with Brenda.

"I can't imagine him and your daughter sharing a cabin."

"Well, Brenda said she was getting lonely."

"She won't be lonely with him there."

"He knows she's gay."

"I didn't mean sex. I meant he'll want to do things that he likes to do."

"He likes fishing, so maybe they'll go fishing together."

"Can you imagine them fishing together?"

It *was* kind of funny. "Or watching football together?"

"Football doesn't start until July. And they don't get football in that cabin, do they?"

"Brenda says she gets everything."

"Does that include porn?"

"He doesn't watch porn. He only watches football."

"Then maybe they'll watch movies."

"He doesn't watch movies."

"What does he watch besides football?"

"That's a good question. I don't think he watches anything besides football." She sipped some tea. "He likes things live. I mean, if he could go to a live football game, he wouldn't watch it on television."

"I guess that's why he likes the Legion. It's live."

"Have you ever been there?"

"I went there once. Some guys dared me to go there, so I went there, but I didn't feel welcome there. I felt like I was intruding on something personal."

"Like drinking beer?"

"It's a male thing, but unless they get drunk, it's harmless."

"I've never seen Arne drunk," Lena said. "I've seen him tipsy, but not drunk."

"Norwegians can hold their liquor."

She knew that Heather was half Norwegian and half German, and that she was speaking from experience. "Would you go back to the Legion?"

"No. The guys there are too old for me."

"Where would you go to find guys?"

"I don't know. I guess I'm not looking in the right places."

"Well, you never know where you'll meet someone."

Heather, who had known Devon since she was in her teens, unexpectedly asked: "Where did you meet your husband?"

"In a college classroom."

"That wouldn't work. The students are too young for me."

"He wasn't a student. He was the professor."

"You're kidding. I knew he was older, but not that much older."

"He was ten years older than me."

"Then I should look for someone ten years older than me, so I can have a marriage as good as yours."

"Our marriage wasn't perfect, but it was good. We never stopped loving each other."

"Do you love Arne?"

"I like him, and I care about him. And he's the opposite of Devon, which could be what I need at this stage of my life."

"Well, you probably won't know how you feel about him until after the vote."

"I probably won't," Lena said, impressed by the girl's perception.

In the early afternoon she drove over to Jordan's farm to see how he was doing. She found him in the barn spreading fresh straw on the floor. She pitched in, and when they were done they went into his house, where he offered her an herb tea. She accepted the offer, just to keep him company while he drank his tea. Unlike most of the men in the county, he didn't drink alcohol. It wasn't for religious reasons. It was for health reasons.

Sitting at the kitchen table, she asked: "How are Anna and the kids?"

"They're fine," Jordan said. "They miss the farm, and they want to come home."

"In a week they will come home."

"Yah. If all goes well."

She gave him an update, telling him what had happened to Heather and Arne, and how the sheriff now had four guys in custody, who were being questioned intensively about who had hired them.

"It's the mining company," Jordan said, "or the people who own it."

"But if those guys don't talk, then nothing will happen to those people. They'll keep using money to get their way."

"What I don't understand is why those people don't realize that their strategy isn't working."

"What strategy?" Lena asked, just to make sure they were talking about the same thing.

"The strategy of using terrorism to make you change your position."

"Well, it hasn't worked so far."

"Is there any chance that it would work?"

"I don't think there is, though I could be missing something."

"So if this strategy isn't working, then why don't they use a different strategy?"

"A different strategy? Like what?"

"Like using terrorism to make *me* change my position."

"I guess they could try that," Lena said, hoping they wouldn't, "but they must believe they have a better chance with me."

"You mean because you're a woman?"

"Yah. A lone defenseless woman," she said flippantly. "They believe I'm the weak link in the chain, so they keep trying to break me."

Jordan nodded. "That sounds like their mentality. You'd think with all their money they'd be more sophisticated."

"You'd think they'd hire better people. But it must be hard to find good people who are willing to kill."

"You mean it *should* be hard."

"Yah, that's what I mean."

On the way home she reflected on their conversation. She had come away with the feeling that Jordan expected those people to try a different strategy, and she had tried to allay his concerns. She knew he wasn't worried about himself but about his children, whom they could find if they really wanted to. She had made up her explanation on the spot as to why they hadn't targeted him, and he seemed to have accepted it. And now, unable to think of a better explanation, she stood by it. They believed she was the weak link.

When she got home there was a message from the sheriff asking her to call him. Getting him after two rings, she asked: "What's happening?"

"We've made some progress," the sheriff told her. "One of the guys we're holding in Winona said they were hired by a local guy."

"You're kidding. I thought it was the mining company."

"Well, the local guy could be representing the mining company. In any case, we have a description, and it sounds like a member of your board."

"What?" It could only be Lester, who she suspected was a lobbyist for the mining company. "You mean Lester?"

"Yah. We're going to put him in a lineup and see if this guy picks him out. If he does, then we'll have a key link in the chain."

"When are you going to put him in a lineup?"

"As soon as we can find him," the sheriff said. "He's not answering his phone, and he's not at his house. I hope he hasn't fled."

"Why would he flee?"

"He might feel we're closing in on them. We caught the guys who tried to kill Arne."

"That's great. How did you catch them?"

"They were hanging out at a bar in town. There was something that made the bartender suspicious, so he called us, and we caught them there. They had a rifle in the trunk of their car, which is probably what they used to shoot at Arne's pickup. We'll find out soon."

"So you have six guys in custody."

"Yah. And we don't have room for them, so we'll have to send these two guys to Winona. That's the advantage of living near a big city," the sheriff added wryly.

"Do you have a bulletin out on Lester?"

"It went out just before I called you. Don't worry. We'll get him."

After ending the call, Lena sat down at the kitchen table, still in shock from what the sheriff had told her about Lester. She had never liked him, but the worst she had thought of him was that he was a lobbyist for the mining company. She had never imagined that he was involved in the strategy of using terrorism to make her change her position.

In her mind she constructed a scenario in which the sheriff caught him, made him confess that the mining company had paid him to implement their strategy, and then got the company to identify the people behind it.

She knew it was only a scenario, but she hoped it would become a reality.

She was about to go and meet Otto in the compound to do the evening milking when the phone rang. It was Patty, crying: "They took them, they took them."

Stabbed by fear, she said: "What are you talking about?"

"They kidnapped Julia and Anthony."

"What? How could that have happened?"

"They went to get ice cream," Patty said, choking on sobs, "and on their way home they were grabbed by two guys who took them away in a van."

"It happened in broad daylight?"

"Yeah. Right after dinner."

With rising anger, Lena said: "I thought the house was in the name of someone they wouldn't mess with."

"I only made that up," Patty admitted.

"You made that up? Why the hell did you make it up?"

"So you wouldn't worry."

"*You lied to me so I wouldn't worry?*" Lena said as if she had never done such a thing with her own parents.

"Well, if you didn't have a stereotype about Italians," Patty told her, striking back, "you wouldn't have believed it."

"So it's my fault they got kidnapped?"

"No. I'm not saying that, I'm only saying—"

"You're only saying you didn't believe me when I told you that you were in danger."

"All right. I didn't believe you. I thought it was your Polish paranoia."

She didn't point out that her daughter, who was half Polish, had a stereotype about Poles. She only said: "You should have listened to me and gone to Argentina."

"I know I should have," Patty said, suddenly docile.

Lena took a long deep breath and calmed down, reminding herself that it didn't matter who was right in this situation. All that mattered was the safety of the kids. "I assume the police are trying to find them."

"The police and also the FBI, which we contacted through Carmine's brother's connections."

"I don't want to hear about Carmine's brother's connections. I want the name of the FBI agent who's in charge of the case, and I want his phone number."

"Hold on," Patty said. A moment later Carmine got on the line and gave Lena the agent's name and phone number. She thanked him and asked him to put Patty back on the line.

"Now, listen," she told Patty. "We're going to get your kids back safely. Whatever it takes, we're going to get them back safely."

"I hope so," Patty sobbed.

"Have faith," she told her daughter. "And pray to Our Lady of Częstochowa."

TWELVE

THE PLAN WAS for Devon to retire after turning sixty-five, and for them to sell their house in Winona and live full-time in the valley, where they would operate a goat farm. Lena had fallen in love with goats after seeing a pair of baby goats at the county fair in Passau several years earlier, and she had done a lot of research on raising goats and making cheese. It took him a while, but Devon eventually got on board and became a committed partner in the project.

First they had to sell their house in Winona so they would know how much they could invest in the project. Luckily, there was strong demand for residential housing at the time, and they sold the house in less time and for more money than they had expected.

Next they had to move to the valley, which forced them to part with things they wouldn't have room for but didn't need anyway. It was both a wrenching and liberating experience, and they were glad when the empty moving van finally lumbered out of the driveway.

When they were settled in the valley they began the process of making decisions for the project. The first decision was what type of goat to raise. The baby goats at the county fair were Nubians, with their floppy ears and Roman noses, and it turned out that they were especially good for milk and cheese. So they decided to raise Nubian goats.

They then had to decide how big a herd of goats to maintain. They had two hundred acres of land, about a quarter of which was wooded, leaving about one hundred and fifty acres for the pastures and the compound. They traveled to another valley to inspect a goat farm, and they learned a lot from the young couple who had built the farm and made a successful business of it. Their advice on housing, fencing, and feeding proved to be invaluable. Since that farm had a herd of fifty goats on two hundred acres, they concluded that a herd of fifty would be the right number, give or take a few goats.

Next they had to decide on the design and deployment of the buildings. They needed a doe shed, a birthing shed, a buck shed, and a dairy barn, which would contain the milking room, the processing room, and the storage room. Since Brenda and her partner had a lot of experience in designing and building projects, they hired them as contractors and paid them what they would have earned on other projects.

Next they had to construct the fencing. The young couple in the other valley had stressed the importance of fencing since goats were adept at climbing over fences, knocking them down, and creating escape holes in them. The couple recommended solidly founded chain-link fences that were five feet high, with outside corner braces so that goats couldn't climb up them and tight latches on the gates so that goats couldn't wiggle them open with their lips.

They divided the non-wooded land into four pastures, three for the does and one for the bucks since they learned from the young couple that the pastures should be rotated to avoid overgrazing and fouling. One of the pastures for the does and the pasture for the bucks included some woods so that they could browse on shrubs and young trees.

Next they had to buy equipment for milking, pasteurizing, and making cheese. Again they followed the advice of the young couple and they bought the same items, which they had installed in the dairy barn.

Then they had to buy a dog who could serve not only as a herd dog but also as a watch dog since there were coyotes in the woods who would love to dine on tender kids. The dairy farmer down the road advised them to buy an English shepherd and gave them the name of a kennel that specialized in English shepherds, so they drove over to the kennel and bought a puppy, whom they named Grady.

Finally, they were ready to buy the goats. They got advice from several sources, including the young couple and the 4H club, and they traveled to Wisconsin to meet the breeder and see his animals before making this decision. And they were standing in the driveway when the first truckload of goats arrived. It was a joyous occasion.

By the end of their first week as goat farmers they realized that they had a lot to learn about feeding, milking, and caring for goats. In the weeks that followed they relied on the knowledge and experience of the local vet and the local 4H kids, including the owner of those baby goats at the county fair. They had ups and downs and periods of anxiety, especially at the time of their first kidding. But they agreed that as challenging as it was to raise goats, it was nowhere near as challenging as raising human kids.

It was in the spring, when everything was going smoothly, that Devon learned he had lung cancer. Of course he had smoked his whole life, so they shouldn't have been surprised, but in those days everyone smoked, and they didn't know anyone else who had lung cancer. When he came home from Mayo that day and gave her the news, she refused to believe it, and when she finally did believe it, she confronted God, asking: "Why Devon? Why have you done this thing to him? Why have you punished him this way?"

As she learned more about his condition from visits to the doctor, she changed tactics and begged God to cure him. She went every day to St. Mary's in Passau and lit candles for him. She went to St. Stan's for Sunday mass and prayed to Our Lady of Częstochowa. She stood before the image of Our Lady in their bedroom and prayed to her every morning, every evening, and many times during the day.

Devon was courageous, and even toward the end he hardly ever revealed how much pain he was in. But she could tell how much he was suffering, so by then she was praying: "Lord, please take away his pain."

And that prayer was answered.

As soon as the call from Patty ended, she called the sheriff and told him what had happened. She gave him the name and number of the FBI agent, and asked him to call her back as soon as he learned anything.

Then she went to the compound, where Otto was waiting for her. It was almost seven now, and the udders of the does were bursting.

"I'm sorry," she told him. "I just got a call from my daughter Patty. They took her kids."

"You mean they kidnapped them?" he said, looking shocked.

"Yah. They kidnapped them."

"I thought your grandchildren were in a safe place."

"They were supposed to be in a safe place. But my daughter lied to me."

"She lied to you? Why did she lie to you?"

"So I wouldn't worry. I lied to my own parents for the same reason," Lena explained, "so I understand why she lied to me. But I'm still pissed at her. I mean, she didn't believe me when I told her that she was in danger."

"Kids never believe their parents when they tell them that they're in danger."

"Then what's the use in having parents?"

"I don't know," Otto said, shaking his head. "I guess so they can tell their children that they're in danger, even if they don't believe them."

"Yah, I guess. Let's go and milk those poor does."

It was hard to keep her mind on the milking. All she could think about was Julia and Anthony being held by people who would have no qualms about killing them. She knew exactly what they would do. They would call her and tell her if she didn't change her position on the mining law, they would kill her grandchildren. And she would be in the predicament of having to choose between her family and the future of the earth.

When they had finished the milking and the cleanup, she remained in the compound long enough to make sure that the does were settled for the night, and then she went into the house. There was no flashing light on the phone, and not having the patience to wait for the sheriff to call her, she called him. "Did you talk with the agent?"

"Yah, I did. I was just about to call you and give you an update."

She waited for the update.

"He has information on the van, and he's trying to track it. He's covering five states, so he can pick up their trail no matter which direction they go."

"Do you think they'll contact me?"

"I think they will," the sheriff said. "We have a man from the FBI who has equipment to track their call. He just arrived from Minneapolis. He has a van, and Jim will lead him to your place. They're on their way now."

"What if they call before he gets here?"

"Don't answer the phone. They'll call back."

"Okay," she said. "I know what they'll ask me to do. They'll ask me to change my position on the mining law. So what should I tell them?"

"Tell them you'll do whatever they want. But they have to guarantee the safety of your grandchildren."

"How would they do that?"

"By releasing your grandchildren before the vote."

"You mean I should ask them to trust me?"

"They're asking you to trust them."

"I know, but they're in a stronger position than I am."

"Well, I don't really believe they'll release your children before the vote. But it wouldn't hurt to ask them."

She had an idea. "What if we delayed the vote?"

"It would buy us time. And you might have to delay the vote anyway if one of your board members doesn't show up."

"We only need four members for a quorum. You haven't found Lester?"

"We haven't found him yet. But we have the information on his car, so we're going to find him sooner or later."

"You know," she said after thinking about it, "if Lester doesn't show up for the meeting, then my vote against the law wouldn't be enough to nullify it. We'd have a tie, and we'd have to start the process over again."

"And that would buy us even more time."

"We wouldn't need more time. If I voted against the law, they'd have to release my grandchildren."

"You mean you'd trust them to keep their word?"

She thought about it. "I'd have to trust them, wouldn't I?"

"You would if we don't find them. But if we find them and rescue your grandchildren, you won't have to vote against the law."

"I prefer that solution," she said as lightly as possible.

About ten minutes later the man from the FBI arrived, and while he was setting up his equipment in the living area, using the jack that was located there, she heated a pizza in the oven. When it was ready she called Otto and invited the FBI man to join them, but he said he had already eaten.

She offered Otto a bottle of beer, which she shared with him. She listened while he told her that his landlord had engaged a local contractor to clean up the remains of the shack and build a new one. The contractor expected to finish the project by the middle of August, and Otto wondered if he could stay with her until then. She told him he could stay with her as long as it took to build a new shack. Then, having heard the latest developments on his side, she gave him the latest developments on her side.

"This kind of thing never happened here before," he said, shaking his head mournfully. "It was always peaceful here in this valley before they discovered the frickin sand."

"It was," she agreed. "It was paradise."

After they finished the pizza she cleaned up and went into the living area to see how the FBI man was doing. He had finished setting up the equipment and was sitting at the monitor, looking at the views from the cameras. He told her he would sit there and wait as long as necessary for the phone call. And when it came, she should drag out the conversation as long as possible to give him time.

She left him and went into the bedroom and said a prayer to Our Lady of Częstochowa, and then she sat down on her side of the bed and reached for the book that was always on the table, though at times it got buried under other books. It was the complete collection of Devon's poems that was published a year after his death. The publisher did a beautiful job and put her favorite picture of Devon on the back cover, along with quotes from favorable reviews. For many years she read one of his poems every night before going to sleep, but she stopped doing that when Arne started spending the night with her. Now, resolving to resume the practice, she leafed through the pages and found a poem she especially liked. It was about love, and it was written before their wedding, almost forty-five years ago. She read it slowly, respectfully, and she was moved by it the way she had been moved the first time she read it, lying in bed at Devon's apartment. When she got to the end of the poem she closed her eyes and recited: "Yes I said yes I will Yes."

She was jolted by the phone ringing.

She walked quickly from the bedroom to the kitchen, passing the FBI man along the way and giving him a thumbs-up sign, which he acknowledged.

"Hello?" she said tenuously.

"Is this Lena McLean?" a voice said. It was electronically distorted to make it unrecognizable, and it didn't sound human.

"Yah, this is Lena. How can I help you?"

"We have your grandchildren," the voice told her. "If you want to see them again, you'll do what we want."

"Okay," she gulped. "What do you want?"

"We want you to vote against the mining law."

To give the FBI man time, she said: "I'm not sure what law you mean."

"You know what law I mean."

"You mean the law that our board will vote on this Tuesday?"

"Yeah, that's the law."

"So you want me to vote against it?"

"Yeah. And if you don't," the voice warned her, "you'll never see your grandchildren again."

"If I do what you want," she said after a long pause, "how do I know you'll release them?"

"I give you my word."

"And I'm supposed to trust the word of a kidnapper?"

221

"You have no choice. You have no bargaining power with us, so do what we say."

"Okay," she said obligingly. "I'll vote against the mining law next Tuesday."

"You're a smart girl," the voice said. "Now, don't fuck with us, and we won't fuck with you."

The phone hung up at the other end. She held her end open until the FBI man came into the kitchen and told her she could hang up.

"Did I give you enough time?" she asked him.

"Oh, yah," the FBI man told her. "I know where that call came from, and I already passed the information to our people in New Jersey."

Since he didn't expect them to call again, he started uninstalling the equipment, and while he was doing that she called Patty to give her an update. She related her conversation with the anonymous voice, and told her that the FBI man had successfully traced the phone call.

"So the police know where they have my kids?"

"They know where the call came from, and that should help them find your kids."

"But if they don't find them before the vote, you're going to do what they want, right?"

"I'm going to do whatever is necessary to get your kids back alive and well."

"It's a no brainer," Patty said. "But you sound like you have doubts."

"I don't have doubts about what I'm going to do. I have doubts about what *they're* going to do. So it would be better if we rescue your kids before the vote."

"You don't mean—" Patty broke down before she could say it.

"Don't worry. The police are going to find them and rescue them. Just keep hoping, and keep praying, and everything's going to be all right."

A few minutes after the call ended, the FBI man let her know he was leaving. She followed him down the stairs and locked the door behind him, and then she went back upstairs and into her bedroom, where she said another prayer to Our Lady of Częstochowa.

The next day passed without any developments, so she had nothing to report to Patty, who called three times. She didn't sleep much that night, and by the next morning she had reached the point where she had even more doubts about what the kidnappers were going to do. She figured that they would have a lot to lose by releasing hostages who could identify them and testify against them, so they would be inclined to eliminate the risk of that happening.

It was Saturday now, with only three days left before the vote, and during the morning she tried to keep busy by finding things for Otto to repair, including a leaky connection to the water tank, a loose latch on the gate to the compound, and a hole in the fence that contained the bucks. She left him working on the hole in the fence and returned to the house to see if there were any messages.

There was one from the sheriff, who said: "We caught Lester. We're taking him to Winona now, so we can put him in a lineup."

She thanked God, and figuring it would be at least an hour before the sheriff had anything further to report, she did the laundry and cleaned the house. She made a list of things she could get at the co-op in Passau, and she also made a list of things she could only get at the supermarket in La Crosse. Since a round trip to the latter took more than two hours, including time for shopping, she wouldn't be able to go there until after the vote.

Around noon the sheriff called.

"I have good news," he told her. "The guy who shot up Arne's pickup identified Lester as the guy who hired him. When we confronted him with that evidence, he broke down and confessed. He admitted that he hired all those guys, beginning with the guys who killed your dog and your doe, and ending with the guys who shot up Arne's pickup. And he said he was hired by the mining company to do their dirty work."

"What about the kidnapping?" Lena asked impatiently.

"At first he denied having anything to do with that, but after we found records on his cell phone of calls to the number that the kidnappers called you from, he admitted that too. So we offered him a deal."

"What kind of deal?"

"If he calls the kidnappers and gets them to release your grandchildren, we'll see that he gets a reduced sentence."

"Did he accept that deal?"

"Yah, he did. And he already tried to reach them."

"But he hasn't reached them yet?"

"No. They might have heard that he's in our custody."

"Who would they have heard it from?"

"The people who hired him."

"Did he tell you who they are?"

"He gave us some names."

Understanding the chain of command, Lena said: "If the kidnappers won't take orders from him, then they have to get orders from those people."

"Yah, they do. So we're going after them."

"Where are they?"

"They're in Texas. We gave the information to the FBI agent in New Jersey, and he's in touch with the FBI in Texas."

"You know," she said, "I'm afraid that unless we get the kids released before the vote, we won't ever see them again."

"I'm with you there," the sheriff said. "So we're going to get the kids released before the vote, whatever it takes."

She called Patty and told her that the guy who had ordered the kidnapping was now in custody. He was cooperating with the police, and at the same time the FBI were working on the people who had hired him, so the only way out for the kidnappers would be to release the kids.

Sunday passed without any further news from the sheriff, and she refrained from calling him to get an update since she knew he would call her if there was anything to report. She went to mass at St. Mary's in Passau, and in the afternoon she went out to the far pasture where the does were peacefully grazing, and she walked among them, making sure that they were all right: Lucinda, Flavia, Jovana, Vesta, Nereida, Aurora, Marcella, Delecia, and all the others, with their Roman names and their Roman noses. She knew them all, and they knew her.

The next morning the sheriff called and reported that the FBI had met with one of the people named by Lester, and that after a long discussion the guy agreed to make a phone call that might get the hostages released. Of course he insisted that he had nothing to do with the kidnapping but only had connections that might be helpful.

Lena thanked God, but she understood that she would have to wait and see if the phone call was effective. She called Patty and reported the news.

The board meeting was scheduled for seven the next evening. A half hour before the meeting she was still waiting to hear from the sheriff, and she called him, hoping to hear some good news at the last minute. But he still had nothing to report, except that according to the FBI the guy who only had connections made a phone call to the kidnappers.

The meeting was delayed by about ten minutes while the lawyer who advised the board confirmed that with four members they would have a quorum. The town hall was packed, and when Jordan asked for comments on the proposed law, a few people spoke against it. But then the people in favor of the law began to speak, one after another, and it became clear that a large majority of people at the meeting supported the law.

When the time came for the vote, Jordan asked the board members to declare their positions, beginning with Neil, who voted in favor of the law. Next was Gary, who voted against it. And then without any explanation, Jordan skipped her and declared his own position on the law and voted in favor of it.

With two votes in favor of the law and one vote against it, Lena knew the decision was hers, and before voting she addressed the meeting, saying: "There are people from outside our community who want to make money from mining the sand that lies below the surface of our valleys. When they're done with the mining, they leave deserts behind them that are good for nothing. Just to make money, they're willing to destroy the earth that God gave us. And knowing that I was against the mining, they hired guys from outside our community to make me change my position. They killed my dog, they killed my favorite doe, they tried to kill my handyman, they tried to kill my helper, they tried to kill my boyfriend, and finally they kidnapped my grandchildren. They did all these things to make me change my position. And they're still holding my grandchildren, whom they've threatened to kill if I don't vote against this law."

There were murmurs of people expressing shock.

"Since I have faith in God," she told them, "and since I have faith in our law enforcement officers, I believe that no matter how I vote, my grandchildren will be released. So I'm casting my vote in favor of the law."

A large majority of the people cheered.

Emotionally drained, she bowed her head, knowing she had done the right thing and praying that her grandchildren would be released.

With the meeting adjourned, she faced the people, including the guy who had threatened her at the last meeting. He made an ugly face at her, but then he slunk away.

At that moment Jordan touched her arm, saying: "Thank you."

She turned to him and said: "It's not over yet."

"I know, but I share your faith, and I share your hope for the future."

Driving home, she felt that a stage of her life had ended. She had run for the board on the mining issue, and now that this issue had been resolved, she no longer saw a reason for being on the board. She would serve out her term and not run for re-election. She would devote her time and energy to her animals.

When she got home she saw the light on the phone flashing. It was a message from the sheriff, who said: "I have good news. Please call me."

She called him right way.

"Your grandchildren are safe," he told her. "They were released about an hour ago."

She thanked God silently, and then she thanked the sheriff out loud.

"Don't thank me. I only did my job."

"You did more than your job."

"Well, I do the best I can. How did the meeting go?"

"It went well. We passed our law."

"So you must have voted for it."

"Yah, I did. I did the right thing."

"That took a lot of faith."

"Whatever it took," she said, "I feel drained."

"I know the feeling," the sheriff said. "I'm heading home now, and when I get there I'm going to crash. I'm going to sleep until noon if they let me."

"Where are you now?"

"I'm on the road back from Winona, where I made sure those guys were in jail."

"They belong in jail. So the guy in Texas did have connections."

"Yah, he did. I think he was involved in everything they did to you, and I hope that Lester will give us more on him."

"Yah, I hope so. If we don't stop him, he'll do the same thing to other communities."

"Well, at least we stopped him here."

A few minutes later she called Patty, not to give her the good news since her kids were probably home by now, but to make sure that they were all right.

"They're fine," Patty said. "They've had a traumatic experience, but they'll recover. We've all had traumatic experiences."

"Yah, we have," Lena agreed.

"Well, how was your meeting?"

"It was fine. We passed the law."

"How did you vote?"

"I voted for it."

"Did you know before you voted that the kids had been released?"

"Oh, yah," she lied. "So I was able to vote my conscience."

"I'm glad. That made it easier for you."

She waited for Patty to say something more.

"I'm sorry I got you into that predicament," Patty told her. "I should have listened to you. And next time I will."

"I hope there won't be a next time."

"Yah. Now, when are you going to come and visit us?"

"I don't know. I have a lot of loose ends. But maybe in August, if I can get things organized by then."

"Okay. I love you."

"I love you too."

When they ended the call she began to think about the loose ends. She had to let Brenda and Arne know they could leave the cabin in the north woods, and she had to let Heather and Otto and Tara and Lori know they were no longer in danger. She also had to let Siobhan know how the story had ended. And then there were the goats and Brady, who hadn't gotten enough of her attention lately.

Before addressing the loose ends, she went into her bedroom and gave thanks to Our Lady of Częstochowa for protecting the people she cared about. She also thanked her for saving the valley from destruction.

BOOK CLUB GUIDE TO

Eden Valley

Tom Milton

Introduction

Lena McLean, who raises goats and produces cheeses in a beautiful valley in southeastern Minnesota, has her life disrupted by the discovery in the region of rich deposits of the sand used for oil fracking. This frac sand is found nowhere else in such abundance, so mining companies are willing to pay a lot of money for the land of struggling dairy farmers, who see a onetime opportunity to unload their unprofitable farms and retire to Florida. But mining frac sand would leave the land as barren as a desert, with no future value, so the community is divided between people who want to make a quick fortune and people who want to preserve the environment. Lena gets elected to the county board on her position against the mining, and she becomes the target of a large global organization that wants to exploit the sand deposits. To achieve its objective of getting her to change her position, the organization pursues a strategy of terrorism, committing acts of violence against her animals, her workers, her friends, and her family to reinforce the message that the only way she can protect them is to vote against a proposed law that would ban frac sand mining in the county.

Twenty-seven years earlier, Lena and her husband Devon discovered the valley on a day trip from Winona, where they lived with their two teenage daughters. To them the valley looked like paradise, and seeing a parcel of land for sale, they promptly bought it. They took vacations in the valley with their daughters in a fishing shack that was built by a previous owner, and then they replaced the fishing shack with a house where they could eventually live. When Devon retired from his job as a professor at St. Mary's University, they sold their house in Winona and moved full time to the house in the valley. After seeing two adorable baby goats at the country fair, Lena decided that they should raise goats and make cheese that they could sell to food stores and restaurants in the Twin Cities, so with the help of their younger daughter Brenda, who with her partner had a business in St. Paul remodeling houses, they built a dairy barn and sheds and fences, they acquired a herd of Nubian goats, and they bought an English shepherd. They had run the goat farm only a year when Devon died of lung cancer, so Lena is alone now, with help from a young woman who recovered from opioid addiction, a handy man who lives in a fishing shack on the adjacent property, a recently retired school custodian who lives on his family's no longer active dairy farm in the next valley, and a sheriff who was a friend of her husband.

At a town meeting to discuss the proposed law against frac-sand mining, Lena receives her first threat from a man in the crowd who tells her that if she doesn't change her position on the proposed law, she will be sorry. When she gets home that night she finds the body of her shepherd lying in the driveway, executed. She calls the sheriff, who begins an investigation that expands as opponents of the law escalate their efforts to make her change her position. She soon realizes that they don't want to kill her, at least not yet, but instead they want to terrorize her by threatening her animals, her workers, her friends, and her family. As the situation becomes worse she finds strength in her religious faith, which is grounded in the Polish community in which she was raised. From her teens into her twenties, she only wanted to escape from that community with its strict rules and narrow expectations, but after breaking away from it to marry a man from outside who was ten years older she came to appreciate its legacy, and she struggled to endow her wayward daughters with an equally strong moral foundation.

She met Devon in the fall of her senior year of college when she took his course in the Romantic poets. He had recently arrived from New York with a reputation as a promising poet. With his urban sophistication, he was the opposite of the type of man whom her mother expected her to marry, beginning with the fact that he was Irish and not Polish. When she heard him reading poetry in the class, she immediately fell in love with him, but she never dreamed that he might reciprocate her feeling. When he did, she hid their relationship from her parents who she didn't expect to approve of him. When they finally learned about it, she was relieved that they were willing to consider Devon as a suitable husband. And until they had their first child, they lived with her parents in the big house that her great-grandfather built during the boom years of the lumber industry in Winona.

Now, with the vote on the law coming up, Lena works with her colleagues on the country board to hold together their coalition, and she works with the sheriff to pursue an investigation of the crimes being committed against her. On his advice she has surveillance cameras installed to protect her animals, but they don't prevent the assassins from killing her favorite doe, so she hires a bodyguard, a young veteran from the war in Iraq who is trying to find a role for himself in civilian life. When he is wounded, she gets the retired school custodian to replace him. Meanwhile, the sheriff has apprehended the two men who wounded her first bodyguard, and he is trying to find out who hired them. She believes it's a global organization with interests in oil fracking and related industries, with unlimited resources to keep hiring assassins.

A Conversation with Tom Milton

In this novel you address another major issue, and with the current political conflict about climate change, your story is timely. It's a local component of the global issue of when and how to replace fossil fuels with environmentally friendly sources of energy. But how in the world did you find out about frac sand mining?

My sister lives in a region in southeastern Minnesota that's rich in deposits of a type of sand that's essential for oil fracking. There aren't many places in our country with such deposits of frac sand, so the mining companies are attracted to the region. She showed me a place near the Mississippi where the sand was mined, and it was like a desert, devoid of life and unfit for any future purpose. She also gave me newspaper articles about a proposed law that would ban the mining of frac sand in her county.

Is the character of Lena based on your sister?

Only in the sense that she lives in that region and has taken a position against the mining. But she's not on the county board, she doesn't raise goats, and she's not Polish.

If she doesn't raise goats, how do you know so much about them?

I buy goat cheese at my local farmers market from the parents of a woman who with her husband raises goats in upstate New York. They showed me pictures of the goats and the farm, and they told me about its operations. In fact, Lena's favorite goat is based on a goat that they told me about.

How did you develop the Polish background for Lena?

My sister took me to Winona and showed me a basilica built by the Polish community about a hundred and fifty years ago. It's an impressive church, like you find in Europe, and it made me curious about the people who built it. I did some research, and I learned that the original Polish settlers in Winona were from a group called Kashubians, who were driven from their homeland near the Baltic by the Prussians. Of course their experience of being displaced from their homeland helped to form their identity.

I guess it explains where Lena got her toughness in the face of adversity.

It does, and it explains where she got her religious faith. During the years when their country disappeared from the map, their religious faith held the Poles together as a people. They were a people without a country, but they had a religion.

Like many young people who grow up in a tight ethnic community, Lena wants to escape from it, and she takes risks to explore alternatives. In that sense, she's like Eva in A Shower of Roses, *who can't wait to escape from the Polish community in St. Paul.*

From what I've seen, the desire to escape is common with young people in any such community. They need to get out and reach a certain stage in their lives before they appreciate the legacy of their community.

Did you grow up in an ethnic community?

In a way, yes. But I was aware of communities around me that were tighter than mine, as I learned from dating girls from those communities.

When she met the man whom she later married, did Lena see him as a way out of her community?

Yes. I mean, he was Irish, not Polish, and he was from New York, which opened another world for her.

Let's talk about Devon. When he appeared on the scene, I didn't know what to expect from him.

I didn't either. I don't know what to expect from most of my characters. In that sense, they're like children. You don't know what to expect from them.

I guess that makes things more interesting for authors—and for parents. But there were stages when Lena and Devon were worried about both their children.

They were worried, but they didn't clamp down on them. I tried to show letting their children develop on their own but at the same time keeping them out of serious trouble.

I noticed that they instilled in their children the value of telling the truth, yet they also appreciate the value of a protective lie. You developed that tension especially in the relationship between Lena and her older daughter Patty.

Lena has a harder time with Patty, who in many ways takes after Devon and reminds her of him. Lena needs to realize that she has limited control over Patty, which has implications for the climactic scene of the novel.

What about her relationship with Siobhan?

Siobhan is a kind of alter ego. Siobhan realizes Lena's dream of escaping from her community and living in New York.

Does Lena have regrets about not going to New York with her friend?

I think at times she does, but most of the time she accepts her decision to stay in Winona and live her life there. Among other reasons, there's the need for someone to stay in Winona and take care of the family, and her only sibling, her brother Tony, is living in Buenos Aires with his wife and family, so he's not around when things happen to their family.

You lived in Buenos Aires, so you know how far away it is.

It's as far away now as it was then. The only difference is that phone calls are easier now.

Going back to the plot, I can see it's about terrorism, which I would define as the use of violence to achieve a political objective.

You're right, it's about terrorism. In this story a large global organization uses violence to achieve a local political objective. And the question is how do you respond to terrorism? Do you fight back? Do you defend yourself? Do you compromise your principles to disarm the threat? Or do you stick to your principles and resist violence with nonviolence.

At different times Lena is tempted by all those possible responses.

For me the main area of interest is how she finally does respond, and what it takes for her to respond that way.

You know, when I think about it, you've dealt with terrorism in your other novels, beginning with No Way to Peace *and including* The Admiral's Daughter, All the Flowers, Infamy, *and even* Sara's Laughter, *in which a crazy modern-day prophet tries to bomb an abortion center. Why are you so interested in terrorism?*

We have terrorism everywhere, and that includes our present political discourse, which is rife with the kind of threats that lead to violence. Terrorism is the universal mode of action in our time. In previous times it was practiced by people called terrorists, or anarchists, but now it's practiced by everyone. If you don't like something, you buy an automatic weapon and you make your point by killing people instead of having discourse with them.

How do you stop that kind of thing?

It would help if you didn't make automatic weapons so easy to get, but that wouldn't stop people from driving vans into crowds. You can only stop them by enabling them to make their point in nonviolent ways.

What does it take to resist violence with nonviolence?

I think it takes an unwavering commitment to nonviolence. And it takes faith.

Discussion questions

1. Discuss how this story can be viewed as an exposition on terrorism, or the use of violence to achieve a political objective.

2. What different ways of responding to violence does Lena consider?

3. Why does Lena resist having a bodyguard? How does she feel when Rodney succeeds in wounding one of the assassins?

4. Explain why Lena is so deeply committed to saving the valley from frac sand mining.

5. How do the actions of the people who are trying to get her to change her position on the mining law reveal an understanding of Lena?

6. Why did Lena impulsively decide to buy land in Eden Valley?

7. What does Lena's escapade with Carlo tell us about her?

8. What role does Siobhan play in the plot and in Lena's development?

9. What do think would have happened to Lena if she had gone with Siobhan to New York?

10. When Devon first appeared on the scene, what did you expect from him? Did his behavior conform with your expectations?

11. To what extent does marrying Devon enable Lena to escape from her community?

12. How would you describe Lena and Devon as parents?

13. Which of her two daughters does Lena have more challenges with? What are these challenges?

14. Discuss the use of protective lies between Lena and her children.

15. How would you describe Lena's relationships with Heather and Kenny?

16. How does her relationship with Arne evolve during the story?

17. How important is her relationship with Earl, the sheriff?

18. Why is Lena sometimes influenced more by Vern, the veterinarian, than by Earl?

19. Discuss the roles of Jordan and the other county board members (Neil, Gary, and Lester).

20. Describe how despite her effort to escape from the Polish community in which she was raised, Lena retains some important legacies from that community.